My Mother Road

Phyllis York

To Taggert, the soul I never knew I needed.

If you ever plan to motor west,

Travel my way, take the highway that is best.

Get your kicks on route sixty-six.

It winds from Chicago to la,

More than two thousand miles all the way.

Get your kicks on route sixty-six.

Now you go through Saint Louis

Joplin, Missouri,

And Oklahoma City is mighty pretty.

You see Amarillo,

Gallup, New Mexico,

Flagstaff, Arizona.

Don't forget Winona,

Kingman, Barstow, San Bernandino.

Won't you get hip to this timely tip

When you make that California trip

Get your kicks on route sixty-six.

Won't you get hip to this timely tip

When you make that California trip

Get your kicks on route sixty-six.

Get your kicks on route sixty-six.

Get your kicks on route sixty-six.

Lyrics: Bobby Troup

My Mother Road

Phyllis York

Chapter 1

Annette Sterling Banks opened the trunk at the front of the Beetle and slung in her canvas bag. She never could get used to the idea that there was no engine there. It was in the back, a tiny thing as far as engines go, but big enough, she hoped, to get her where she needed to go.

If it isn't, I'll walk, she thought. *Well, maybe hitchhike.*

She ached to be away, heading down the open road, leaving behind all the grief and numbness of the past few months, but she paused at the side of the car for a last look at the farmstead in which she had grown up.

The house was small and immaculately kept, its neat white painted wooden shingles contrasting nicely with the dark gray shutters bracketing every window. Mom's thriving flower beds lined the front and sides of the large railed country porch. Across a small mowed yard sat the chicken house and coop. None of the dozen or so hens there were slightly interested in her leaving; there were too many fascinating things to peck in the dirt. Behind the house a couple hundred feet was the red barn, its galvanized roof gleaming in the morning sun. Dad had let the cows out before taking Mom to church, and the animals were languidly munching on the lush midsummer grass in the meadow. None paid her any attention.

In the distance behind the barn rose the Ozark hills, their morning mist a glowing halo that seemed to shrink as the sun warmed the day.

It was peaceful and lovely here, but she had little use for peace or beauty these days. She opened the door and got in the little car, tossing her large brown purse and her husband's book in the passenger seat.

Nettie pressed the clutch and turned the key, and Ophelia started as if she, too, were eager to be away. Nettie shifted into reverse and backed into the yard, then engaged first gear and headed down the long gravel and dirt driveway.

"I'll be back, Mattie," she promised, and she thought she was telling the truth.

***

More than sixteen years passed.

***

"Lord, our Father, hear our prayer. Please, take care of Mrs. Beulah Newman as she recovers from hip surgery, and be with Jonah Wilkey and his family as he returns home from another deployment overseas."

Matilda Banks was definitely not squirming in the hard pew despite the numbness of her tailbone. She sat uncomfortably beside her grandmother, whose head was bowed and eyes were closed — as Tildy's should be.

Grandma was a murmurer. "Yes," Grandma murmured quietly, or "Oh Lord," as Brother Bowman's exhaustive prayer droned on, requesting blessings on everyone the man had ever even heard of, it seemed.

Grandma, clad in her simple blue and white church dress, prim with her pocketbook in her lap under her Bible, occasionally raised a white-gloved hand when the prayer touched a subject for blessings she felt strongly about.

"Father, please bless our great president and guide him to Your will and wisdom in his decisions, and please keep our law enforcement officers safe as they keep us safe from those who would ..."

Matilda could find no pattern in the prayer, as usual. Brother Bowman would bounce back and forth from asking blessings for local folks to praying for the sick on the other side of the world. Amazingly, he had never repeated himself that she could remember.

The prayer was the last obstacle to overcome before freedom. Matilda liked church, though she was pretty bored most of the time. She always dreaded coming and couldn't wait for it to end, but afterward she always felt good. It didn't make any sense.

First you had the short opening message from Brother Bowman, which was kind of a rehash of the church newsletter stuff about attendance and offerings numbers, as well as exhortations to support whatever charitable effort the church was focused on at the time. Then everybody sang a couple hymns, which Matilda liked. Then the age groups broke apart for Sunday School, which to Tildy seemed like a dumbed down version of a sermon now that she had graduated out of the kids' class — mostly play with a religious theme — and was in Young People. Tildy found the Young People — some as old as 21 — amazingly boring.

After Sunday School, everybody returned to the pews for a couple more hymns. Brother Lanahan almost always requested "When We All Get to Heaven," and that always got the place really rockin', which kind of annoyed Grandma, who didn't think people should be be enjoying themselves so much in the Lord's house.

Around that time the latecomers showed up for the sermon, ignoring the looks of disapproval from their early bird peers. Once Tildy had asked Grandma if they could go in late sometimes too. The meltdown had been spectacular.

"And the sinners, oh Lord," Brother Bowman intoned. "Please help those who are slaves to the sins of fornication and adultery, drug use and alcohol. Those whose hearts have been ..."

Whoah, he's on fire today, Matilda thought. *Is he going to name every sin?*

It was safe for her to look around. Grandma would not have opened her eyes before "Amen" if there were elephants

6

stampeding among the parishioners. Tildy knew from years of experience who else in the congregation would be looking around too. The good people who kept their eyes closed had no clue that a quarter of their fellow churchgoers — not all of them kids — were sneakily peeping.

Landover Baptist Church was small by Landover, Missouri, standards. The twelve pews on each side of the main aisle might hold as many as two hundred on Easter Sunday, all stuffed elbow to elbow, but most services drew less than a third of that. Grandma and Matilda sat three rows deep on the left side facing the altar. As always, Grandma sat on the aisle seat as if guarding against an escape attempt by her wayward granddaughter.

Tildy leaned forward and looked past Grandma to the pew on the other side of the aisle. About half the time her friend Brandon would be there with his family, making funny faces and imitating Brother Bowman so that she had to stifle giggles. The family hadn't made it to Sunday School today, but Tildy had hoped they might get there for the sermon. No luck. The pew was empty.

Behind it, however, she saw the Widow Kershaw and two of her daughters, both grown now. Mrs. Kershaw, her hair subdued in a steel gray bun at the back of her head, was staring straight at Matilda, her eyes blazing with righteous judgment.

Matilda stifled a gasp and leaned back, bowing her head and closing her eyes. *She had her eyes open too,* she thought grumpily, but she knew that wouldn't matter to Grandma if Mrs. Kershaw ratted her out.

Brother Bowman seemed to be winding down. Matilda offered a small prayer of thanks, and then almost laughed out loud at the irony. All the lonely animals in the dog pounds had been blessed, and the pastor had even snuck in a wish for the St. Louis Cardinals to have a blessed season. He would get talked about for that, Tildy was sure.

"Father, we also ask that you keep the Sterling and Banks families close to your heart as Matilda turns seventeen this week. Amen!"

Brother Bowman, red-faced and perspiring from his marathon prayer effort, directed a huge smile at Tildy where she sat with her grandma. She wanted to crawl under the straight-backed wooden pew as a chorus of "Amen!" rose around her.

After the service, several people hugged Tildy and wished her a happy birthday as they left the church. Her grandmother elbowed her when she wasn't standing up straight or shaking each hand that was extended to her. Tildy avoided rolling her eyes because she knew from years of experience that it made a sound only her grandma could hear.

The Widow Kershaw gave Tildy a hard look as she brushed by on her way out of the church, but she didn't stop to speak to Grandma, so Tildy didn't care. She wondered if Mrs. Kershaw didn't want it known she was looking around during the prayer too.

Grandma let Tildy drive home after joking that the Lord probably wouldn't kill them in a fiery crash on His day. Tildy smiled all the way. She loved to drive. It felt good to be in control and trusted, and she was careful to obey every rule of the road and keep her speed comfortable for her grandmother, which meant well below the posted limit.

Granddad was sitting on the sagging front porch, smoking, as they pulled up. He got rid of the evidence before they exited the Buick, expertly flicking the cherry off the end of his cigarette into the yard and smoothly putting the butt in the back pocket of his tattered jeans with his thumb as he leaned forward in the wicker chair. He would forget it was there, Tildy knew, and Grandma would find and remove it and probably several others before throwing the jeans in the washer.

"Happy birthday, Mattie. I'm ready for your birthday lunch. Are you?" He pulled his walker close so he could stand.

The stroke he'd had years before dragged the left side of him downward. He often said that he felt he looked like a melting candle when he saw himself in the mirror. Matilda just saw her fiercest friend. She grinned and nodded as she linked her hand in his and went into the house.

It smelled of chicken and dumplings. It was Tildy's favorite meal, and Grandma had left it simmering in the crockpot all morning. "You can't make chicken and dumplings without letting them set," she had said as she always did.

Grandma was a great believer in letting food set so the flavors could mix together, whether it was chili, stew or the occasional casserole. Matilda didn't know if this was a standard cooking technique, but she knew just about everything Grandma made was amazing. Whenever Tildy cooked for the family, she tried to do everything the exact same way.

Tildy took the wicker basket from the cabinet under the sink and went out to the chicken house to get the eggs. The hens hadn't really started laying in earnest yet — it was too early in the spring — but there would be a few.

The roof of the structure sagged a little, and it had been decades since its last paint job. She ducked a little as she went through the doorway despite that the frame was a couple inches above her head when she was standing straight. Tildy was careful not to touch the dusty walls in her church clothes as she used the big steel dipper to scoop a little feed out of the bin.

This wasn't strictly kosher. The chickens got fed in the morning and a little in the evening to encourage them inside to roost for the night. Grandpa was always grumbling that the MFA feed cost the earth and it shouldn't be wasted, but Tildy was the one who had to get pecked while collecting the eggs if she didn't distract the crazy creatures.

Tildy flicked the dipper, flinging the feed through the chicken-wire window that gave access to the nests. The stupid birds squawked like they had never seen such a thing and rushed to beat each other to every morsel, pecking madly at the floor of the coop.

"You guys are so competitive," she told them, lifting the window high enough to hook it to the wire that was nailed to a rafter. "Where's the love, man?"

The ladies ignored her, scrabbling against each other for feed. There were only three eggs. There had been two this morning. Matilda probably hadn't needed the basket, but you always brought the basket.

"Hey, thanks for pooping in the nests again," she said. "Makes this whole experience so much more fun."

The chickens didn't care.

Tildy heard the poorly muffled rumble of Caroline's truck coming up the driveway. She closed the window, dropped the dipper back into the feed bin and closed its lid, then went out to greet her aunt.

Caroline was kicking off her dusty boots at the back door. "Happy birthday, kiddo," she said. She smiled. "Hard to believe you're seventeen. I remember you when you were only this big." Caroline held her hand at a level about an inch below Tildy's current height.

Tildy laughed. "Wow, you can remember last year? Who says you're going senile!"

"Let 'em say it to my face," Caroline challenged with mock rage. Then her expression softened and she looked confused. "Wait a minute. What were we talking about?"

They were laughing as they went through the creaking screen door into the warm kitchen.

Tildy put the eggs in the fridge and returned the basket to the cabinet, then washed her hands at the double sink.

Grandma already had the dumplings in a bowl on the dining room table next to another bowl full of mushy canned peas. Those were definitely not Tildy's favorite, no matter how much margarine they were soaked in, but dumplings had to be accompanied by peas for some reason, and you had to take the good with the bad.

Granddad shuffled in and sat down in his place at the head of the table, pushing his walker out of the way so Caroline could take her seat on his right. Caroline dished his food onto his plate and situated his spoon in his hand for him without comment. He could have done it himself; his right side was not nearly as impaired as his left, but Caroline had been taking care of him since the days he could barely move at all, and he never argued when her ministrations were a little excessive.

"This looks great, Mom." Caroline pulled a hunk of bread off the loaf in the center of the table and put it on her father's plate beside the dumplings before grabbing some bread for herself. "Do you want to have cake or presents first, Matilda Jean?"

"Definitely presents," Tildy said, popping a dumpling into her mouth. It tasted as good as it smelled, and that was saying something. Letting them set in the slow cooker had definitely done the trick.

When everyone had finished eating, Grandma cleared the table, Caroline and Tildy washed the dishes, and Granddad mumbled something about taking a look at that loose porch step and sneaked outside for a Camel.

Everyone gathered back at the table when chores and minor crimes were done, and Matilda took a minute to snap a photo of her family gathered at the table. The Polaroid camera had been a present last year, and she never got tired of shooting it, but the film cost eight dollars so she now only used it for special occasions. The device whirred and spat out the square picture, which Tildy carefully laid on the table face up so it could develop. She would put it in her album later.

Tildy tore through the wrapping paper on her presents. The first two gifts were wrapped in red poinsettia paper left over from Christmas. The first was the George Orwell novel *1984*.

"Thanks Grandma." Tildy smiled even though what she had asked for was the Van Halen album, *1984*.

The second gift was also from her grandma. It was a pair of sparkly pink jelly shoes that were all the rage among the middle schoolers. It was harder to smile that time, but she did so without looking toward her beloved Converses on the mat by the back door.

Aunt Caroline slapped a ten dollar bill on the table. "I hope it's the right color and that it fits." Tildy laughed, just as much at her grandma's pained expression as at her aunt's joke.

The last gift was from Granddad. It was rolled up in the Kmart shopping bag he'd gotten it in. It was the cassette tape of *1984*. "Yes!" She threw her arms around him and squeezed him tight. She followed up by hugging her grandma and Caroline too.

"Thank you guys so much for everything. You are my favorite people in the whole wide world."

Matilda took another photo of the cake her grandma had made her. Spice cake with white frosting, topped by twelve tiny candles. A dozen came in the box, and Grandma wasn't going to waste another 69 cents until Tildy was a lot closer to 24, she said. Tildy grinned. The same candles were reused from Granddad's birthday two months ago, and he hadn't been as close as she was to 24 for a lot of years.

After the festivities, Tildy gathered up her new belongings to take them to her room. In years past she would spend the evenings of her birthday with her dad's parents, but this year had been hard on them. Grandpa Wyatt was recovering from bypass surgery, and Granny Margaret was just too exhausted for company. They had dropped off a large stuffed turtle for a birthday present late last week. Tildy suspected she was always going to be a toddler to them, but she didn't really mind.

Matilda dropped everything but the cassette tape on her bed. She clicked open the plastic cassette case, careful not to break the hinge, and popped the transparent gray cassette into her tape player. No stereo boombox for her, not yet. The combination radio/cassette player didn't do the music justice, but the futuristic techno sound that flowed out of the tinny speaker still gave her goosebumps.

A knock on her bedroom door made her jump. "Hey, can I come in?" Caroline asked after she already had stepped into the room.

Tildy turned down the music just as Eddie Van Halen opened up on his guitar, Frankenstein.

Caroline was pushing the gifts to the end of the bed to make space. She put an old cigar box there and sat down beside it, resting her hand on the closed cover.

Matilda flopped down on the opposite side of the box with her knees on the floor and her elbows on the bed. "What's up?"

Caroline reached out and turned the volume knob on the top of the tape player all the way down. "These are letters that your mom sent me when she left. I've kept them over the years, and I think you are old enough to have them now."

Tildy's heart felt like it skipped a beat. She looked at the box, then back at her aunt. "Cool. Thanks." She reached across the bed to her little table and turned the music back up.

"This is important, Matilda. This may be the only connection you have to Annette. These are her words and thoughts."

Which you never thought about giving me until now? Tildy thought. She felt a little angry at her aunt, but she opened the box, and was surprised that the yellowed contents made her stomach knot up.

"If you have any questions about anything I'll be around," Caroline said. She rustled Matilda's hair and left the room, closing the door behind her.

Matilda climbed onto the bed and sat with her back against the headboard. She placed the little box in her lap and opened the first envelope. The letter wafted the caramel scent of tobacco and old paper into her face. Her stomach knotted again.

August 11, 1967

    Sis,

    I'm writing to you from the side of the road between Amarillo and some town that I forget the name of - Cow Bend or Horse Face or something like that. I expect to stop there tomorrow and see if I can talk a mechanic into looking at Ophelia's undercarriage, which is making a strange noise now that drowns out the radio. (I'm sure it would be easier to convince the mechanic if I had any available cash, but I'm fresh out. I might be stopping to look for work for a week or two.)

    I can only imagine how worried you and Mom are, and it's probably a good thing there is no address where you can write me back just yet. I can only tell you that I am fine and I will come back, but I don't know when. I can't explain it very well, but I feel like I would be betraying Mark's memory if I didn't at least try to follow the route we mapped out together, the one I told you about.

    I had a hot dog at a gas station for lunch today, and I have an egg salad sandwich that I am saving for dinner. I would kill for a Dr. Pepper to wash it down with, but you can't have everything. I'm not in danger of starving is what I am trying to tell you.

    It is so flat here you can kind of see how the horizon is curved, and it's starting to look more and more like the desert. I swear I saw a tumbleweed of all things earlier! I expect tomorrow I'll run into Wiley Coyote toting an ACME box across the plains, chasing the Road Runner. I'll try not to fall off any of the cliffs going after him. Ha ha.

    I was thinking about it as I was driving this morning and I want to try to explain a little more about why I'm taking the trip. It's for Mark, I mean, I mostly hope it's for Mark, but some of it is for me, and believe it or not, I think and pray that some of it will be good for Mattie someday. I don't think I am a very good mother right now (and I know you and Mom don't either) but I want to be, and I don't know if I can do that as I am right now.

A few weeks ago I was home with the little devil by myself and I realized I was almost out of cigarettes. I didn't want to get dressed up just for a quick trip to the gas station, so I just threw on a scarf and a jacket, got Mattie nestled on the passenger side floor of Ophelia on a blanket, and went to get some Marlboros.

Of course I was halfway to Knight's when I realized I needed about a dozen other things from the store that I hadn't been able to get before because Mark's check hadn't come. I thought about going home and changing, but I figured a quick trip to Connor's would be okay. It was the middle of the day, and it wasn't likely I was going to run into anyone I knew.

Wouldn't you know it, I was almost done at the drugstore when who should I run into but Irene Kershaw, Mrs. Snoot herself, from church. She pretended she didn't see me for a minute, which was fine with me, but then after I ducked down the soft drink aisle I came around the corner at the end and there she was, right next to the comic book rack.

It was kind of funny because she was holding one up by the corner and my first thought was, is she going to buy a comic book? Maybe she's a secret Batman fan. But she was looking at it like she looks at everything, you know, like nothing is good enough, and everything everybody else has ever done has been wrong and sinful to boot.

We were face to face though, and she couldn't pretend she didn't see me. She was still making that same disapproving face when she looked at me and Mattie, who was in the cart and kind of sniffling because she was getting over that cold, remember? "Is that you, Annette Sterling? I hardly recognized you," she said. I figured it would be hard to tell my Sunday School teacher for ten years that I was somebody else, so I just smiled and said hello.

I was so embarrassed because I knew I looked like a five-car pileup, and I knew as soon as she left the store she was going to start gossiping all over Landover about how I was going downhill and my mother must be so ashamed.

Like Dad always says though, when there's nothing you can do, do nothing, so I just stood there and got ready to take my lumps. I know you won't believe this, but I was really nice. I asked after Charlotte and Ben and how Mr. Kershaw was recovering from that thing at the stave mill (which I don't really think is what happened, but I don't think anyone will ever know for sure). But Mrs. Snoot was determined to be vicious. After all the pleasantries were over, I was getting ready to turn my cart around and escape, and then she said, "It must be so hard, being a single mother. We will pray for you."

She said it like she wasn't going to pray for my well-being, but for my wayward soul, like in her mind there was no difference between me as a war widow and some girl who had gotten in trouble. What's worse and I can't even believe I'm telling you this is that instead of telling her off or asking her how she was able to buy that almost new Corvair with her husband laid up just two months after being named church treasurer, instead of defending myself, I just busted out crying.

That's how that whole damn town sees me, like some girl who did something wrong and now is stuck with a child and no husband. I don't know what to do about it, but I'm thinking about it a lot on this trip, and I hope I come up with some answers.

The funny thing was that when I started crying in the store Mattie did too, and between us we were bawling so loud that Mrs. Snoot scooted away as fast as she could. So I guess I won? Ha ha.

Well, I know this is getting hard to read because my hand is cramping up and this stupid pen is running out of ink as you can probably tell by the scribbling in the margin, so I will end this. I hope you will give Mom and Dad and Mattie a hug for me, and I will write again soon and let you know how Ophelia's doctor visit went.

Love, Nettie

Chapter 2

Tears flooded Tildy's cheeks, soaking the collar of her white church blouse. She got up, unbuttoned the shirt, wiped her face, and tossed the blouse onto her closet floor. Matilda put on her gray marching band t-shirt and returned her attention to the box on her bed and the letter laying next to it.

"Did the police ever find out what happened to her mother?"

Matilda was five when she heard that question for the first time. It had never occurred to her that the police -- or anyone, for that matter -- were looking for her mother. Mama was just a picture hanging in the hallway. In a fake wood-grain plastic frame that was bracketed by matching sconces, it served as a shrine to the mother she couldn't remember. There had been other pictures of her mother around the house, but the older Tildy got, the more of them disappeared into a drawer or album.

Annette was barely mentioned in her grandparents' small farmhouse, at least not in front of Matilda. The opposite was true when she visited her father's parents. Their walls were covered in pictures of her father, Mark, and the flag from his coffin sat in a glass case on the coffee table. Beside it was a picture of him in his Army uniform. He'd died in Vietnam a few weeks before Matilda was born. Mark's parents told Tildy confidently that her daddy, Mark, would have adored her.

Once Matilda started school, kids asked about her parents, and she would just shrug. The only thing she knew about them for sure was that her father died fighting communism so she could be safe, and that her mom was never the same after that.

"Your mama ran off with the milkman," Lester Owens said as the school bus rumbled down a gravel road. Lester wasn't popular with the kids his own age at the junior high. He also was unpopular with the little kids because he bullied them.

"My dad said she hopped on the first guy to come 'round after her old man got killed," the boy said, smirking.

At six years old, Tildy had no idea what he meant, but she was crying when her aunt met the bus at the end of her grandparents' driveway.

"What's a matter?" Caroline said before Tildy made it off the bus steps.

"Lester said Mama hopped on a milkman!" Tildy's large eyes were full of tears.

Caroline's face went to stone in an expression Tildy knew meant somebody was in big trouble. "Wait here," Caroline commanded.

Her aunt climbed onto the bus. Tildy jumped as Caroline's voice boomed. "Lester Dale Owens!"

Matilda barely heard the feeble "Yes ma'am?" She felt a little guilty tattling because she knew how it felt to be the subject of her aunt's wrath. But she didn't think gap-toothed Lester was smirking now.

"I swear to God, I'll beat the fire out of you if you ever say another thing about my sister. That's a promise."

"My dad said it," Tildy heard. "I was just..."

"Listen to me, if your daddy has something to say about a member of my family, he can sober up and drive over here. I'll beat his ass too." Aunt Caroline turned to the bus driver. "Sorry, Jackie."

"No need to be sorry, Caroline. That boy's got a mouth on him. See you in church Sunday."

As the bus pulled away, Caroline grabbed Tildy's hand as they walked together toward the house.

"Sissy, your mama loved you very much. She still does. One day, she'll come home and tell us what kept her away for so long. You'll see."

Tildy kept her aunt's promise in a secret place in her heart. It stayed throughout her childhood despite being unfulfilled as the years passed. One day Mom would come home, and she would love Tildy, and they would go places together and walk hand-in-hand and read stories together and go to Silver Dollar City every week. Well, maybe not *every* week.

But her mother's return kept not happening.

Tildy knew she couldn't possibly remember her mother's voice. She had been an infant when Annette left. But the words in the letter had been spoken in her mind by someone with a clear and melodic way of speaking, both no-nonsense and full of fun at the same time.

Nettie.

That letter made her feel closer to her mom than she ever had. Caroline had said she and her sister used to sing at church together. Tildy felt like she was a little closer to understanding what that must have sounded like.

She called me Mattie. So did Granddad, but no one else ever had. Tildy had kind of named herself as she was learning to talk because Matilda was too hard to say.

She realized she was still standing by her closet and staring at the letter and the box. She wanted to read all the letters at once and she also wanted Caroline to change her mind and come back and get them. The letters *hurt.*

When there's nothing you can do, do nothing. Granddad still said that sometimes. He never meant that she should literally do nothing, though. He meant that if you really have to go through something you don't want to go through, just get through it. Like living with a stroke.

Tildy picked up the dumb stuffed turtle, Samson, and sat back down on the bed, hugging the stupid thing.

All the letters and postcards had postmarks, so Tildy organized them by date. The first letter was dated August 11,

1967, and the last was dated November 30, 1967. Her stomach was in a full-fledged tizzy now. After setting up the envelopes and postcards she took a photo of the tableau. It was the last picture in her cartridge.

She began removing the contents of an envelope, reading and rereading it, putting it away, and moving to the next. She studied the pictures on the postcards. There were pictures of Oklahoma tornadoes, Texas longhorns, New Mexican pottery, and the Arizona Painted Desert.

There were also doodles and scribbles in the margins. She could picture her mom stopping in the middle of her writing, thinking about what she wanted to say next for a long time. Annette was no artist, but the repeated drawings of Snoopy were recognizable and made Tildy smile.

Her mother had been sprinkling her father's ashes along Route 66 because they had planned to drive the Mother Road on their honeymoon, but they never got the chance. Mark had been drafted within days of graduating high school. They had rushed to marry after his basic training and before he shipped out.

All their dreams had been destroyed because of the Vietnam War.

Tildy had sometimes wondered if her mom had run off because she didn't want to be responsible for raising a child on her own.

She opened the last letter, and found a Polaroid of two women with long hair. The picture hadn't aged well. It was faded and discolored. The women were wearing t-shirts that someone had painted NO WAR on, and they were holding their hands up in dual peace signs. One of the women had straight blond hair, and the other woman had dark brown curls that went everywhere.

Tildy ran her hand into her own curly brunette hair and closed her eyes. Could she remember touching her mother's face?

This woman in the picture felt so much more familiar to her than the happy posed pictures her family had let her see.

The last letter had been dated November 30, 1967. Tildy wanted more. She needed more. She felt like she was just starting to know this person. A rumbling outside her window pulled her back to the present. It had been a cool 47 degrees when they'd left for church, but the temperature had dropped throughout the morning. Now thunder was rumbling closer to their farm.

"Matilda, come help me get the clothes off the line before the rain starts," her grandma yelled down the hall.

Tildy put the letters back into the cigar box and closed it. She was surprised to see the glowing red numbers on her bedside alarm clock said it was after four. She'd been in here for hours and felt wrung out.

A thick gray swell of clouds was rolling ever nearer as they pulled the clothespins off the towels and put them into the pin bag. Other kids in the area had dryers. This was, after all, 1984. But her grandma didn't see any sense in spending money on something that a little time and patience would do for free. And she was a clothespin hoarder. If she heard one snap because Matilda was rushing, she'd bristle up.

"Careful, Tildy. I don't got time or money to go replacing every clothespin you break."

"You could take some of the money that I get each month and buy yourself a dryer."

"And then you would have nice dry clothes not to go to college in. Don't get smart. Just be careful," Grandma said.

Tildy had received a check each month after her dad died. She didn't know exactly how much it was, but it helped buy her school clothes and put a little food on the table. Much of it went into the college fund her grandparents had started for her. She'd much rather have a car because she wasn't even sure that she wanted to go to college. Everyone just brushed it off when she'd tell them she wanted a 1969 Chevy Camaro instead.

"That's no car for a girl," they said.

Aunt Caroline had gone away to college, and she assured Matilda that she'd love it. She'd quit and moved back home to help raise Tildy and take care of Granddad after Annette left.

"Give me those towels." Her grandma took the bundle out of her arms. "Where you at today, girl?"

"Nowhere. Sorry Grandma." Tildy picked up the blue plastic basket and carried it to the house. The smells of impending rain and clean laundry made her feel warm and safe.

"Grandma, do we have any of the things that my mom left behind?"

There was silence for a while, as her grandma pushed the back door open. "I don't know where any of it is. You'll have to ask Granddad. Why?"

"I think I am ready to get to know her. Am I like her at all?" Matilda set the basket on the kitchen table and began carefully folding the towels.

"You are taller than she was. You got your daddy's height." Grandma picked up the towels as Matilda laid them down and refolded them correctly. She pulled the basket towards her. "You can't fold for beans. She couldn't either. My towels always looked like they had been mauled by possums."

Tildy smiled. "Possums will maul anything," she quipped, and Grandma barked a laugh.

"You know what I mean, rotten child."

"Anything else? About Mom, not the possums."

"You have her smile," Granddad said, stumping down the hallway with the aid of his walker. "That, 'I'm up to something' smile. Usually meant she'd need a whooping."

Grandma snorted. "You never whipped nobody."

"I could whoop you," he said, chuckling.

"You'd have to catch me first, and I'd just hide your walker." Grandma finished the towels and put everything back in the basket to deliver to the linen closet.

"Granddad, do you know where the things my mother left behind were put?"

He looked to his wife before answering. "They're in the garage. Is there something you are looking for?"

"No, I just want to see her things."

Rain started splattering against the windows. "I'll put the bucket under the leak," Tildy volunteered. She pulled an old copper pot out from beneath the sink and positioned it over the rust stain on the linoleum. Within minutes there was a steady tink tink tink sound coming from the pot.

"I'll get up there once it warms up and fix the flashing," Granddad said, as he had each time it had rained for as long as Tildy could remember. "Come on, and I'll show you where the stuff is."

Tildy followed him out the door. The garage smelled of wood and cigarette smoke. Granddad lit one up and sat in his chair next to the wood furnace. He pointed to an old, weathered box on a shelf that sagged from the weight of broken tools and unidentifiable pieces of long departed lawn mowers.

"Can I get one of those?" she asked.

"*You* are gonna get *me* whooped," he said, handing her the cigarette he'd just lit and lighting another.

In truth Grandma was aware that Tildy smoked, but as long as neither of them talked about it, it could be ignored. Grandma probably knew there was little she could do or say to stop her, Tildy thought, and a few cigarettes were nothing next to the trouble that some kids got into. Caroline had told Tildy that the family matron had discussed it with her once, saying "At least she's not smoking the weeds."

Tildy took a long drag off the cigarette and got busy moving things off the big box, an Army foot locker that had belonged to Granddad when he fought in Korea.

She grunted when she tried to move some old green ammunition boxes that were full of nails and screws now. Next were old radios Granddad planned to rebuild and a wooden box full of Coke bottles he was going to return to the gas station that had closed more than a decade ago.

"You ever think that you have too much stuff?" She gestured to the piles of junk that lined the walls of the garage.

"Nope. Bring it over here." He pushed his walker to the side to make space.

Tildy held her cigarette between her lips and dragged the heavy box to where her Granddad sat. She was trying to be careful, but it still thumped to the cracked cement floor.

"It's got a lock on it. Get my key bucket." One of the most maddening things her granddad did was to put padlocks on everything. If it had a hasp it got a padlock. If it didn't have a hasp, he'd attach a hasp. As far as Tildy knew, no one had ever broken in to steal his old carburetors and broken hacksaws, but like he always said, "There might come a day."

Tildy grabbed the rusty old Maxwell House can that sat beside the door and handed it to him.

"That's a Master lock, so it'll be a..." He trailed off as he dug through the keys.

Someone started to raise the garage door. Tildy handed her cigarette to her grandfather, giving him two. The door stopped moving when it was about halfway up and a soggy Caroline ducked under it, then dragged it back down from the inside.

"She's going to kill you both if she catches you," Caroline said as Tildy exhaled a lungful of smoke. Her aunt shook the rain from her hair and took the second cigarette from her father. Caroline pulled up a milk crate for herself and Tildy beside him. "What are we unearthing today?"

"Some of your sister's things. Tildy wants to see them." Granddad tried a few keys before tossing them back in the can.

Caroline looked at Matilda. "You sure you're ready for this?"

She shrugged. "Yeah. Sure."

"Bingo!" The long ash fell off his cigarette. He wiped the ash and dust off the top of the foot locker and opened it up.

Matilda took his and Caroline's cigarettes right out of their mouths, opened the cast iron door of the furnace and threw them inside. She didn't want the ashes falling onto her mother's things.

The first things Matilda saw were newspapers. Granddad moved them to the side and pulled out a yearbook that read *1965 Landover High School.*

"Her junior and my senior yearbook. I had wondered what ever happened to it," Caroline said. She flipped it open and turned to a page that had a photo of Mark in front of a Volkswagen Beetle. "Ophelia," she said in a whisper.

"He loved that car," Granddad said.

"Annette loved it too. That's what she took off in." Caroline handed the book to Matilda as Granddad began pulling other things out of the locker.

"It's probably the car our Mattie was made in. But it's so little they must have been gymnasts," Granddad said, cackling. Caroline shot him a frosty look and he dove back into the box's contents to escape. Tildy stifled a giggle, but she felt a little uncomfortable.

"Here's some books, and a clarinet." Granddad set a small stack of books on Caroline's knee, then raised the instrument to his lips and puffed into it. A sick whistling was the only sound.

"Sounds better than it used to when Annette played," Caroline said.

"Busted reed or something. These things have reeds?" Granddad asked. Tildy nodded, smiling.

The next thing he pulled out were some photos and albums. After a few minutes nobody was speaking. Granddad would pull something out, sigh over it, hand it to Caroline, and she would hand it to Matilda. Matilda would look at each item, hoping that it would lead her one step closer to knowing her mother, and then set it to the side.

The bottom of the foot locker was filled with record albums. "Your mama loved her music. She and Caroline would always be fighting over who was going to get to use the record player," Granddad said.

"Annette always won. It didn't matter what we were fighting over. Mom always took her side."

"She was the baby, Caroline. It was nothing more than that," he said.

"Can I I take this stuff to my room? I promise to be very careful with it, and I'll put it back after I have a chance to look through it."

"Go on. It's all going to be yours someday anyway." Granddad pulled his walker as close to him as possible, stood, and left the garage by the side door.

"It's not like him to let go of his treasures," Tildy said.

"His biggest treasure was your mama, and he still hasn't let her go." Caroline pulled a cigarette out of her dad's pack. "You want some help taking this into your room?"

"No. I think I can get it." Tildy felt possessive about her mom and her mom's things for the first time.

Tildy struggled getting the foot locker into the house, however. It had slid easily enough through the mud from the garage and even up the porch steps and to the back door, but there she was met by her grandmother.

"You plan on dragging that muddy thing across my floor?"

"Of course not," Tildy lied. *Not now, anyway.* There was an old braided rug on the floor of the hall closet. Tildy wrestled the foot locker onto it, then grabbed the end of the tattered rug and dragged the box the rest of the way to her room.

After Tildy pulled it to the end of her bed, she closed and locked her door. This felt like something that needed to be done in private. She took an old shirt out of her dresser and wiped all of the years of dust and the recent mud off the box. The shirt was black with muck, so she tossed it into the trashcan in the corner. *Two points.*

This time when she opened the box she took out each item one at a time, making a list that included the cigar box and its contents she had received earlier from Caroline.

There were the letters and postcards Annette had written to Aunt Caroline. The newspapers were local. One of them had an article about Dad's death, another had his obituary, and another was Matilda's birth announcement. The other newspapers held no significance for Matilda that she could discern.

She searched every page of the yearbook for pictures of her parents. They were homecoming candidates. Her father towered over her much shorter mother. Mark was wearing a pale colored suit, and her mom had a frilly floor length dress with poofy sleeves. They were looking at each other like there wasn't a camera within a hundred miles. Matilda wished the photo wasn't in black and white.

The clarinet was nearly identical to the one Matilda played in marching band. It needed to be cleaned up, but it could easily be played again. She wondered why no one had ever suggested she use it when she had started to play. Her own instrument had cost so much.

Matilda scooped the three books into her arms and sat back on her bed. She spread the books beside her. *Hamlet* and *Catcher in the Rye* were still on the reading list for AP Lit. The third book was *The Great American Road Trip*. It was a travel book with maps, photos, and illustrations of sights and attractions along Route 66.

A photo of her mom and dad standing by a much younger and nerdy looking Brother Bowman at the pulpit looked up at her from the foot locker. It must have been their wedding day. Her dad wore the same pale suit, but her mother wore a simple ankle-length dress. Other pictures were from their prom and other school functions.

Her mother's baptismal Bible and a pair of bronzed baby shoes were stuck together with a sticky substance. Matilda tried to separate them, but feared she'd tear the Bible cover. Grandma would know how to safely clean and separate the items.

Her mother's jewelry box was pink, and when Tildy wound it up a tiny ballerina spun as music played *Singing in the Rain*. Matilda didn't know the lyrics to the song, but she hummed along with it while sorting through its contents. Her father's class ring had a blue birthstone and a baseball engraving. It was wrapped in tissue and secured inside a Bandaid tin. A pair of pearl earrings, a class of 1967 pin, and a blackened alligator clip were beneath another stack of letters. These letters were from her father while he was in the Army.

January 18, 1967

Baby,

I ship out tomorrow for Vietnam. They haven't told me where I'll be stationed, but I'll write you as soon as I know anything. It breaks my heart that you still haven't gotten over the morning sickness. If I were there I'd hold your hair when you threw up just like the night we tried Casey Jemes' moonshine when we sneaked out of our cabins at church camp.

You being so sick is the only thing that saved us when your dad pulled up. He was going to kill me that night. I know you say that he would never have actually pulled the trigger, but you couldn't see his eyes while you were puking.

If he'd have shown up a half hour sooner we'd have both been dead. You spread out on my Boy Scout sleeping bag wearing nothing but the moonlight. That is the image I keep in my head. It's the only thing that carries me through some days. You are the only thing that will carry me through this damn enlistment.

As soon as my enlistment is over we are taking that honeymoon. We'll bring the baby or ask Caroline or one of our our moms to watch him or HER (I still think it's going to be a girl.) After I've reacquainted myself with every freckle on your body I'm going to take over Dad's engine shop. I know we haven't talked about it in a long time, but it seems like the most sensible way to take care of our family and help my parents out.

They are going to call lights out in a minute, so I guess I'll close. I love you Annette. Please tell our baby that I love him or HER too.

Love, Mark

Matilda wasn't breathing when she let the letter fall into her lap. A painful lump beat at the back of her throat. Her parents were so in love. Her dad had been right about Granddad. He definitely would have shot him. She folded the letter up carefully putting it back in its envelope.

Matilda looked through the record albums but left them in the foot locker. There were the New Christy Minstrels, Sonny and Cher, Simon and Garfunkel, and several others.

Tildy thought that there had to be more that remained of her mom than would fit in a three foot box. She touched each item and hoped it would light a fire of remembrance somewhere inside her.

The letters her dad had written to her mother were more intimate than those her mother had sent to her Aunt Caroline, but she decided to read another one.

September 2, 1967

Babe,

I haven't seen this much mud in all my life. Everything is wet and stinks like rot. Manny, the guy that freaked out the first night we landed, was killed yesterday. He wasn't ten feet from me when he got shot in the head. I can't stop seeing it in my head. His eye came out of its socket, and he was just dead. Big Jim shot the Vietcong that got Manny. That's how it works over here. You just have to hope that at the end of the day the scales favor our side.

I miss you so much. I keep your letters dry in my pack, and they smell of you. I picture your hair spread out around you while we were swimming in the Gasconade. Camping with you on our wedding night is the happiest memory that I own. When I'm scared or sad I picture you wrapped in that old wool blanket watching me fail at lighting a campfire.

The guys are saying that there's talking that LBJ might get us home by Christmas. The truth is that it's not likely, but I hope it happens soon. I pray every night that you and our baby are safe and sound. I hope I'm home before you have it, but I guess that's not likely. Please, tell everyone including you and our baby I love them and will see them soon.

Love, Mark

Chapter 3

"He never got to meet me," Matilda said across her lunch in the school cafeteria on Monday. Her sandwich was chicken salad on wheat bread, the chicken saved out from the batch that had gone into yesterday's dumplings. She also had a boiled egg, an apple and some carrot wedges. Other kids got potato chips in their brown sacks, but their lunches weren't packed by Grandma.

The cafeteria was maybe half full, with most of the occupied tables near the front where the food lines went and the trays were returned. Large windows along the east wall let in the sun, which felt good on Tildy's back.

Across from her sat Missy and Brandon, who had been her best friends as long as she could remember. Half the trouble Tildy got into came from listening to Missy, who would dare just about anything and could charm her way out of most repercussions.

"That's so sad," Missy said, but she was only half paying attention to her. Her attention was drifting to a table near the windows. "Do you think Nick and Tatum are doing it?"

"What? No. He's a goon, and she's saving herself for Michael J. Fox." Matilda threw her brown paper sack towards the trash can, but Brandon karate-chopped it out of the air almost as soon as it left her hand.

"Brandon, er... Cameron, pick that up this instant." The lunch monitor snapped her fingers toward him. Brandon leapt to obey. You did not want to get on the lunch lady's bad side.

"You're so lucky to have an identical twin," Missy said when he returned. "You can always blame it on Cam when you get in trouble."

"Only our mom can tell us apart," he said, straightening the collar on his knockoff Polo shirt.

"Your mom and every other woman on this planet." Missy motioned towards Cam's table. He was holding hands with his girlfriend while simultaneously playing footsie under the table with the girl across from him.

"He's a slut." Brandon dipped a fish stick into his mashed potatoes. "I'm a one-woman-man."

"More like a no-woman-man," Missy laughed.

"I never heard you complain," he said, then yelped as Missy kicked him under the table.

Matilda pretended not to notice, as she'd been doing since the two had messed around at the beginning of junior year. They had been at the drive-in watching *Jaws 3D*, and she'd dozed off in the backseat. She woke up a few minutes later to the two of them making out hot and heavy. No amount of forcing herself to go back to sleep worked. She just slid down in the seat, and put her fingers in her ears. Ever since then she had avoided going to the movies, or anywhere else, alone with them.

"I've read my mom's letters five times, at least." She swirled a water puddle on the lunch table with her index finger. "She just doesn't seem like she planned to not come back."

"Maybe she killed herself." Brandon yelped as Missy kicked him again.

"Jesus Christ, Brandon. You can't just say that." Missy covered her face with her hand. "I'm sorry, Tildy."

"It's okay, guys. I considered that too, but the last letter she sent sounded more hopeful than any of the others. There must be a reason she hasn't come back. She mentions a few names in the letters. I think I'm going to go to the library after school and search the Yellow Pages."

"Want company?" Brandon asked, slurping the juice from his peaches off his spoon.

She just shook her head. "Nah, I probably won't find much, and then I've gotta head straight home." Tildy picked up her bookbag from the chair beside hers and stood up. "I'm heading to the senior's smoking bathroom. I'll see you in class."

"If Wickman catches you in there again, she's going to ream you out," Missy said. She had been trying to get Tildy to quit smoking since they were in eighth grade.

Matilda shrugged. With less than six weeks left of junior year, she wouldn't have to sneak much longer.

She had been over five foot eight since she was fifteen. The only people that questioned whether she was old enough to use the smoking bathroom were Miss Wickman and Coach Fergus. Wickman had gone to school with her grandparents, and Fergus seemed to hang around restrooms instead of teaching his kids to throw passes and block touchdowns, or whatever it was they were supposed to do.

The coast was clear today, and she was able to make it all the way through her cigarette without anybody coming in. She straightened her sweater before stepping out of the bathroom -- straight into Miss Wickman.

"Follow me, Miss Banks," the crone said, rheumy eyes flashing in victory.

Matilda rolled her own eyes as Wickman took her purse and led her to the office.

As soon as they were inside the office, Wickman dumped the contents of Matilda's purse on the counter in front of the school receptionist, Mrs. Copeland. Wickman took the pack of Belair 100s and the various lighters and demanded to speak to the principal.

"Jesus," Tildy said, grabbing her tampons and the rest of her belongings and stuffing them back into her blue denim purse. "I've got rights, you know, like protection from search and seizure."

"This school has rules not rights, Miss Banks." Miss Wickman didn't even turn to look at her.

Missy and Brandon waved to Matilda from outside the office. Brandon made an OK sign with his thumb and forefinger. Tildy smiled and shook her head in annoyance.

"What's the problem, Miss Wickman?" Mr. Adams came out of his office wiping crumbs off his plaid tie.

"Miss Matilda Banks thinks she doesn't have to follow the rules." She waved the pack of Belairs at him.

He sighed. "Come on, Tildy."

She followed him into his office, and Wickman huffed off to go ruin someone else's day.

"You know you can't smoke inside the school until you're a senior. Do it before or after school. Is your grandma home?" He slid her his phone to dial the house.

"Probably." Matilda leaned back in her chair to accept her fate. Now she was in for it.

"Mrs. Sterling?" Principal Adams said into the phone. "Matilda was caught smoking again. Can you come pick her up today?" He hung up the phone. "She'll be here in half an hour. You can wait on the bench by the front door."

"Can I get my smokes back if I promise not to use them at school?"

He handed her the rumpled blue pack back, and she headed outside to sit by the curb.

It was a very warm March day. Matilda slid her round sunglasses on and lit a cigarette. After a few minutes, she was relieved to see that it was Caroline picking her up in her old truck.

"You are so damn lucky that your grandma was at the VFW when Adams called."

"Wickman caught me coming out of the senior's."

"Ugh. I do not miss old Witchman. She hates everyone."

Matilda agreed, climbing into the passenger's side and slamming the truck door. It wouldn't latch unless you slammed it.

She guessed in a way it was admirable that old Witchman didn't play favorites. "I don't know why she doesn't just retire," she said as Caroline rocketed out of the school parking lot onto High Street. "She's got to be ninety or so."

"Maybe sixty," Caroline said. "She hasn't even been torturing kids for half a century yet. I think she just looks older."

Tildy had a new thought. "Did she know my mom?"

Caroline chuckled. "Oh yeah. Your mom was her mortal enemy."

Matilda turned the radio down. "Why?" It felt weird to be speaking about her mother again so soon after getting the letters.

"Your mother was smart as a whip. She could have skipped school twice a week and still made straight A's. Well, old Witchman sent a letter home to tell your grandma that she believed that Annette had cheated on an Econ test. Annette took a red pen and corrected all the spelling and grammar errors in the letter before giving it back to her." Caroline laughed as she drove. This was the most honest laughter that Tildy had heard from her aunt in a long time.

"So, Mom wasn't a perfect angel all the time?" Matilda watched Caroline.

Her aunt frowned. "Your mama was one of the best people I've ever known, but she wasn't an angel. None of us are, Smokey the Bear."

"I want to know more about her, but I don't know where to start."

"Look in the mirror, Sis." The words were so quiet that Matilda pretended she hadn't heard them.

"Can we run by the library on the way home? I need to do some quick research."

Caroline nodded, and drove towards the library while turning up Johnny Cash on the radio. He seemed to be walking the line because of a girl.

Matilda waited at the neat circulation desk for the librarian. "Do you have phone books from Tucumcari, New Mexico, or Holbrook, Arizona?"

The women resembled a pterodactyl. Her dark eyes were set too close together atop a nose that was long and thin enough to be a Ginsu knife. "What?" the woman squawked. "What? No. We only have major metropolitan areas in the reference section. Call the operator. This isn't Bell Telephone."

"I'm sorry that your ancestors died in the Ice Age," Matilda said as sweetly as she could as she headed to the pay phone outside.

"What did you say?" the pterodactyl squawked behind her as the door closed.

Tildy picked up the phone and dialed zero.

"Operator. How may I help you?" a metallic voice said.

She flipped open her notebook. "I need information for Tucumcari, New Mexico."

"Hold one moment." An instrumental version of the Fifth Dimension song *Up Up and Away* played in the background. Tildy liked it. *Would you like to fly in my beautiful, my beautiful balLOON?*

"Tucumcari information. How may I help you?" This woman had a much nicer voice than the first operator she'd spoken to.

"Yes, I'm looking for a Larry Noble." Matilda checked her notes to make sure she was asking for the right person.

"Sorry, I have no Larry Noble, spelling N-O-B-L-E. I have a James Noble and a B. Noble. Would you like those numbers?"

She felt deflated. "Yes, please." She jotted the numbers down. "Can you look for someone in Holbrook, Arizona?"

"No, ma'am, but I can transfer you. Please hold." There was just buzzing this time instead of hold music.

"Holbrook, Arizona. How may I help you?" This operator was a man. That weirded Matilda out. She considered herself a feminist though, so she guessed she supported this man's career decision.

"Operator, hello?"

"Sorry sir."

"It's ma'am."

Damn it. "Sorry, ma'am. I am needing the number for the Church of the Blue Oracle."

"Hold please." A pause. "There is no such number."

"How about Father Paul?"

"Last name?"

"I don't know."

"I can't look up numbers without a last name. Anything else?

"Crystal Stardream?"

"Please spell the last name?"

"S-T-A-R-D-R-E-A-M."

"No such listing. Anything else?"

"No sir. I mean no ma'am." The line went dead before she finished speaking. *I'm just scoring points with everyone today*, she thought. Her so-called research was at a dead end. Matilda stuffed her notebook back into her bookbag and left.

An electric co-op truck was parked beside her aunt's pickup. Caroline had been seeing Willard Moody for years, but nobody talked about it where Tildy could hear. Moody and his wife were still technically married, but they had lived on opposite sides of town for at least a year. There were suggestions by the rumor mill that Aunt Caroline was the reason for the couple's split, but it seemed like everyone in town was always ready to believe the worst of her aunt. Caroline was opinionated and blunt, plus she didn't go to church and was known to have purchased beer.

Caroline was sitting in Willard's truck wearing his cowboy hat. He was pretending to try to steal it back.

"Hey kid," Willard said when he saw Matilda.

"What's going on, Willard?" She tossed her purse into Caroline's truck. "How's the electric business treating ya?"

"Can't complain. How's smoking in the girls' room treating you?"

"All I gots is complaints," Tildy said, theatrically scuffing the toe of her shoe on the pavement.

"One more year, and then you're a free bird. You can take off, and travel the world. Ow! What was that for? You pinched the crap out of me," he said to Caroline.

"She's going to college," Caroline said firmly, tossing his hat at him.

"Sorry I got you in trouble, Willard," Tildy said, trying not to show her amusement.

"All I gots is trouble, kid." Willard was smiling as he backed his truck out of the cramped parking lot.

"Get in. I need a Dr. Pepper," Caroline said. She climbed into the aging — she liked to say vintage — Silverado and tore out of the parking lot.

Matilda held the door frame to keep from sliding across the seat.

"Did I ever tell you about the day your mom and dad got married?" Caroline asked.

"No," Tildy said, not taking her eyes off the car they were tailgating.

"Mark got his draft notice the week he graduated. Grandma blamed that for the impromptu wedding, but in truth your mama had designs on that boy ever since they were in elementary school."

"How old were they when they became a couple?" Matilda asked, pumping an imaginary brake pedal as they rolled through a stop sign. Caroline rarely let her drive.

Caroline laughed again. "Your mama told me in third grade that she was going to marry Mark Banks. Of course, I, being a mature fourth grader, just laughed at her.

"Man, I've always envied the fact that she just knew. They didn't play the field, or ride out a bad relationship waiting on a good one. She just knew they would be together forever."

Matilda knew that Caroline was talking more about her own string of unstable relationships than Annette's brief idyllic one.

"She called my dorm to say she was getting married. She and Mark drove to Springfield to pick me up, because I wasn't allowed to have a car on campus. She didn't tell me that they hadn't told either set of their parents. As a third wheel, it was an awkward-ass conversation to sit through twice. I kept saying, 'Yeah, but what're you gonna do?' In the end both sets of your grandparents attended the wedding."

"I'm glad everyone was there. Was that the last time you were all together?"

"I had midterms, so I didn't get to attend Mark's graduation from basic training." Caroline held the steering wheel with her elbow, and lit a cigarette. "The next time we were all together was at Mark's funeral." She picked a piece of tobacco off her lip as she pulled into the drive-in, but didn't say anything else.

The local drive-in only had a few good items on their menu. Caroline ordered a Dr. Pepper and got Tildy a chocolate shake and an order of fries.

"You ever gonna marry that boy?" Matilda asked.

"Nope." Caroline swirled the ice in her soda and watched as Matilda dipped a fry in her shake. "That is disgusting. Don't you spill a drop of that in my truck."

"This is the food of the gods." Tildy licked the chocolate shake off her fingers.

"Maybe one of those fat Asian gods." Caroline strained her neck to look through the restaurant windows to see who was cooking.

"She in there?" Matilda asked, straining her neck to see as well.

"I don't think she works on Mondays, but I'm afraid to order food, because she might spit in it."

"It's been years. She can't still be angry that you and her husband are lovers."

"Don't say lovers. It sounds gross. He's gonna get a divorce when he gets a few more bills paid off." Willard had said that for years. Since before he bought his Trans Am, as a matter of fact.

"Is it true that she's pregnant?"

"Yeah, but it's not his. He thinks it belongs to Roland Tate that works at Tire Town." There was no way that Caroline believed a single word she was saying now. "He's gonna help her out until the kid is born, or until Tate mans up."

"Is he staying with her again?" Matilda dribbled milkshake down her shirt and cussed, but Caroline ignored it.

"Not yet, but he's paying most of her bills, so he's going to. Probably this weekend. He's gonna sleep in the living room."

"I'm sorry, Aunt Caroline."

"Everything is gonna work out." She sipped her soda, and stared into the distance."We almost had a kid last year. He was terrified. Said he wasn't ready to be a father. I had to drive to Kansas City by myself to take care of it. Someday, I'll be ready to have a baby, and I'll have a man that is ready too."

Matilda was stunned. She and Caroline always had been pretty open with each other, but this was unlike anything they'd ever talked about. Tildy wondered if her aunt was starting to see her as more of a grownup.

"I'm sorry that you had to go alone. I wish you'd have let me go with you."

"It wasn't as bad as I heard it would be." Caroline started the truck and cranked the radio. It wasn't even music; it was a mattress liquidation commercial.

The ride home was silent other than the blaring country music station. Kenny Rogers and Dolly Parton were singing about being islands in the stream, again. Tildy was so sick of that song she wanted to flood them both.

Caroline drove with her wrist, holding her drink. Her left hand picked at the frayed fabric by the door handle. She pulled up to the front of the house but didn't shut the truck off.

"I'll be at my place if you need me." She drove off as soon as Matilda got out.

Caroline's place was an old Airstream that sat at one end of her parents' property. It wasn't much, but you could see the Niangua River from it when all the leaves were gone in the winter. The place was close enough that she could eat her meals with the family, and far enough away that her parents wouldn't be in her business.

Matilda opened the front door and the scent of pine cleaner and something amazing cooking in the slow cooker filled her senses. These would always be the smells she thought of when she thought of home.

With her grandparents at their VFW meeting, she decided to take advantage of the empty house and use the record console. She sorted through her mother's albums and picked one; Bob Dylan's *Highway 61 Revisited.*

She dusted the album before putting it on the turntable the way she'd seen Granddad do before. The album slid down on the spindle. Tildy didn't remember if she had to move the arm, or if it would move when she slid the power lever on. After a few seconds she got the album playing, and turned it up as loud as possible without the sound distorting.

Beneath the albums was a manila folder that had been mailed to her grandparents from the Landover Funeral Home. She hadn't found it before, because she hadn't removed all the albums from the bottom of the locker.

Inside the folder was her father's draft notice, death notice, some military paperwork, and a program from his funeral. At the very bottom was a tiny envelope tied with red string. Tildy read the letter.

Charley and Lauren,

I am sending you the items that were left at the funeral home to help arrange Mark's service. With Annette's delicate condition right now I didn't want to trouble her with them.

The cremation is complete, and you can pick up his ashes whenever is convenient for you. I've included his wedding band with these documents. Your whole family is in our thoughts and prayers as you deal with this difficult situation.

Michael and Janet Sherwood
Sherwood Funeral Home

She gathered a few of her mother's items, and carried them from her room to the dining table. She opened the old Band Aid box and unwrapped the tissue that held her father's class ring. She put the ring on her thumb and slid his wedding band onto her middle finger. It hung loosely.

She fluttered through her mother's books. Inside the copy of *Hamlet* was an inscription.

Annette,
This above all: To thine own self be true.
Love, Mark and Ophelia

She'd never thought of her father as an intellectual. Tildy had never really known what to think about him or her mother.

42

The copy of *Catcher in the Rye* didn't have an inscription, but it did have some cigarette rolling papers as bookmarks. They didn't seem to be marking anything of importance. Maybe they were just hidden, so Grandma wouldn't know Annette smoked.

The Great American Road Trip was a spiral bound travel guide. On its inside cover, in red ink, was a drawing of a handful of hearts and "Mark's copy." On the bottom of the page was what she assumed was a conversation between her parents.

When we get married this is our honeymoon. You, me, and Ophelia finding the heart of America. Circle everywhere you want to go, and give it back to me next period. I'll do the same thing in my copy.

Nobody has proposed yet.

Hint Hint

I can't wait to explore the world with you.

Will you marry me.

Of course I will, because I love you.

I love you too.

Her parents were so in love. It was nice to know that they didn't get married because they had to. That had been hinted to her by more than one person through the years. Matilda flipped through the book and found tons of notes written in the margins. There were circles around cities, and lines through some destinations.

When Matilda found the entries for Adrian, Texas, she became embarrassed reading the things her parents were going to do beneath the stars while camped out near the "MidPoint of Route 66." The whole book read like one of her grandma's Harlequin romances.

Unfortunately for her parents, they were a Shakespearean romance instead, she thought. Star-crossed lovers torn apart by circumstances outside their control.

She wondered if the other copy, her mom's, was just as steamy. Tildy wondered for a moment where it could be before she realized her mom had obviously taken it with her on her trip.

While Bob Dylan sang "Desolation Row," Matilda walked around on the front porch smoking a menthol. She watched as the cherry ate away at the white paper when she inhaled the mentholated death. That's what Missy called Matilda's favorite brand. She wouldn't listen to reason that menthols were obviously healthier because they were, you know, minty.

Tildy picked at the peeling paint on her grandma's brick red shutters. There were so many projects around this house that needed done. Before her mother had left, Granddad had been a foreman at the bluejeans factory. He made good union money, and they had a brand new car.

Caroline had one too many beers a few years back, and told Matilda that they'd spent every penny they had saved trying to find Annette. "Took out a mortgage on this place just in time for Dad to have a stroke. Your mom could be a selfish bitch when she wanted to."

This had been a slap in Matilda's face at fourteen years old, but now she understood it more. Everyone in this family seemed to be stuck in the summer of 1967 in some way or another, and she'd never realized it until now.

A crunching in the distance meant someone had pulled onto the dirt drive. She stubbed her cigarette out, and dropped it down into the creepy cherub planter that Grandma kept on the porch. She didn't usually let more than a few pile up in there before throwing them into the furnace, but now this angel was about half full of mentholated death.

Matilda took all of her mother's things to her room, closed the console, and arranged one of Grandma's six million doilies on top of it. She went out to help her grandparents unload all of their items from their weekly VFW meeting.

There were a dozen small flags that would have to be rolled up and put away, the remains of the weekend's pull tabs that would have to be burned, and all the used BINGO cards that would have to be counted and burned as well.

Her grandfather wore his VFW uniform proudly. It was always neat and pressed. Grandma only had a vest, but it was covered in pins, ribbons, and patches. Granddad had even met JFK during his presidential campaign because the candidate chose to speak to the local Veterans of Foreign Wars chapter. Granddad might never admit to voting for a liberal president, but Kennedy was the only president whose portrait hung in this house.

"Are there any cookies left over?" Matilda asked, putting the flags away.

"In the tupperware. Just a couple, so you don't lose your appetite before dinner," Grandma said as she helped Granddad remove his hat and tie. "Were you in the victrola?"

"The record player? Yes. I was listening to mom's records. I was careful."

"You know I don't like that hippie music," her grandfather said as he dropped into his recliner. VFW always wore him out, and he got a little grumpy when he was tired.

"Hippies are like vampires. They only exist in the movies," Matilda said, shoving half an oatmeal cookie in her mouth and wondering if the VFW would ever achieve chocolate chip technology.

"Don't be an ass," Granddad said. "Turn on channel three so I can watch the news."

Grandma may have had an addiction to doilies, but Granddad needed his weather more than a junkie needed his crack. Matilda turned on the television and slunk to her room as the weatherman, Tom Dye, explained the week's forecast. She put the Bob Dylan album back in the box and layed on her bed to read through some more of *The Great American Road Trip*.

Many people experience the Mother Road in the comfort of a cross-country bus. With bus stops in nearly every city on Route 66, it's a fun and affordable option for many.

Matilda reread the line a few times before drifting off. She dreamed about her parents. They were in her Lit class, and they were writing notes inside a book. Annette would write something, and slide it across the table. Mark would read what she wrote, and then write a reply. They did this for a long time before Miss Wickman took the book. When Wickman threw the book in the trash can, her parents disappeared.

Matilda started crying and pulling everything out of the trash. "I'll never find her without that book," she kept saying until she woke herself up.

In a panic, she checked to make sure that the book was still on her bedside table. It was.

"Am I late for school?" she said as she walked into the kitchen.

"No, you're not," her grandma said, pulling some repurposed butter bowls out of the fridge.

"What?" Matilda looked around. It was already getting light outside.

"It's almost dinner time. This is still Monday." Her grandma felt her forehead. "You all right?"

"I guess I dozed off, thought it was Tuesday morning."

"That's from listening to that hippie music," Granddad said as he came to the table for dinner. "It messes with your brain. Just keep listening to your heaven metal."

She thought about correcting him, but if assuming her music was churchy meant he'd keep getting her cassettes, then she'd keep her mouth shut.

"I want a microwave oven for Christmas, Charles." Her grandma set dinner on the table.

"They cause cancer," he said, slathering margarine on a piece of white bread. "Ralph Nader said ..."

"I don't care who said what. If you want to smoke cancer sticks then I am going to have a cancer oven. Discussion over." She dropped a slotted spoon in the green beans and headed out the back door as Granddad's jaw dropped onto the floor.

"I think she won that one," Tildy said, trying not to laugh.

Her grandparents didn't argue often, but when they did Matilda made herself scarce. She scooped some mashed potatoes onto her buttered bread and walked toward the front door.

"I'm gonna walk down and let Caroline know dinner's ready."

"Buncha rats deserting a sinking ship here," Granddad grumbled to himself before the screen door slammed shut behind Tildy.

It was a good ten minute walk to Aunt Caroline's. The property was a little over a hundred acres. Tildy walked down the worn dirt path that bisected the property, making sure to close the three cattle gates she had to open. Her grandparents helped pay their bills by renting pasture land to local farmers. The whole place had been a thriving farm at one time.

The spring birds were beginning to build their nests in the cedars that ran along the creek edge. It was too early in the season to have to worry about copperheads, but she knew how to handle herself around snakes, both literal and figurative. Her granddad told her a hoe to the neck would serve to take out many a man or beast.

She didn't carry a hoe today, but she had carried a hatchet, a golf club, a tennis racket and a shotgun in the past. She'd never had to use any of them, but she'd whacked the snot out of some gopher holes with a golf club after she'd watched *Caddyshack*.

"I really can take care of myself," Matilda said to any animals that were eavesdropping. Maybe it wasn't so weird that her mother had taken off across the country alone. She was only a few months older when she left than Tildy was

now, and Tildy thought she herself would be fine driving across the country.

She could see Willard's truck parked by the silver trailer her aunt lived in. He was revving the motor up, and she could hear them yelling at each other. Matilda considered turning around and heading back to the house. Instead she pulled a dead branch off a toppled maple and kept walking closer.

"She's not a whore. At least we were married when she put out!" was the last thing he yelled before he peeled out and tore down the old river road.

Caroline was still throwing things at his truck even though it was already too far gone.

Matilda sprinted towards her aunt. When Caroline saw her she pulled her robe closed and went back up the little stairs to the camper. Tildy followed.

Caroline's face was red, and her robe sleeve was soaked in snot and tears. She stood in the trailer doorway for a minute. Tildy knew she was getting herself under control.

"You okay?" Matilda asked.

"I'm fine. Never hint to a man that you know their secrets," she said, and moved to begin gathering items Willard had left behind or given her over the years.

Tildy would have helped, but she had no idea which things her aunt might want to keep and which to throw out. Instead, she stood in the doorway awkwardly and watched her aunt.

Caroline was still a pretty woman. Lines of worry and grief seemed to be etched more deeply on her face every year, but even now, when she laughed, she could be a heartbreaker if she wanted, Tildy thought. Matilda didn't understand why Caroline had stayed so long in a relationship that was bad for her. *Why can't she see she's way too good for that Willard bum?* But if she were going to be honest, Tildy had to admit she liked Willard too.

All of the items Caroline collected were dumped into the burn barrel in Caroline's front yard. Caroline poured charcoal lighter fluid over the mound of shirts, records and tapes, decorative knick-knacks, and letters.

She lit two cigarettes, handed one to Matilda, and threw the still burning wooden match into the barrel. It took a few seconds for the fuel to catch, but it was beautiful when it did.

"Want to clean your trailer while we have a nice blaze going, Firestarter?" Tildy joked, just to break the silence.

Caroline snorted. "Don't make me beat you."

The women leaned against each other until the fire died down. Caroline went into the house and grabbed herself a beer and Matilda an RC Cola and brought them back outside.

"I think it's over this time," she said, cracking the beer.

Matilda didn't say anything, because she knew Caroline had been fighting this battle for a long time.

"Him and her been living together a while, I guess." She poked the fire in the barrel with a short stick of rebar that had been laying where her porch was supposed to go a few years back. "Their baby's due anytime. Says he thinks it's a boy. He just knows. I hate that son of a bitch."

Caroline gulped the rest of the Coors and threw the empty can into the fire, then wiped her tears on her sleeve. "I shouldn't have come back to this godforsaken town. There is nothing here but dead ends."

Matilda squeezed Caroline's hand. "I'm glad you're here."

"You're the only reason I am." Caroline took her robe off and threw it into the fire too. With just her Glen Campbell t-shirt on, she went back into the trailer. "I'm not gonna be up for dinner tonight. Run home, and let your grandma know before she gets worried." Caroline pulled the aluminum door of her home closed.

Matilda didn't want her aunt to be alone, but she also didn't want to walk home in the pitch black.

Why is everything so fucked up?

She felt like Caroline had given up her future because of her. But it wasn't her fault. She had just been a baby. If anyone was responsible, it was her mom.

Her mother was the missing piece of this machine, and without her nothing worked quite right. "I should go to where she mailed the last letter, and find her," she said aloud.

Then she shook her head. "Don't be stupid, Matilda. You'll get yourself killed." Matilda could hear each member of her family and friends saying it.

As she was closing the second cattle gate behind her, Tildy saw beside the path in the dimming light the stump that had been there since before she was born. How many times as a little girl had she sat on it to wait for Caroline to come along to dinner? She didn't know what kind of tree it had been -- maybe cedar. From the top, it looked like there as a faded orange heart sunk deep in the center of the wood.

Now she sat down to think.

Nothing has worked without Mom. Everything went to crap when she didn't come back.

Tildy didn't know what Caroline had been studying at college. Tildy had never asked. Her aunt might be a doctor or architect or stock market guy now if she hadn't had to quit. Because of Annette.

And Grandma, who might share a laugh now and then but she was mostly angry and so easily hurt. Tildy couldn't believe she had always been that way. For the first time, Tildy considered that her grandmother was grieving and always would be grieving. It wasn't like Annette had died and left them sad but also able to carry on. None of them had carried on. Tildy found herself hurting, crying on the stump of a tree that had died before she was born.

Granddad, whose strength and pride were wiped out because of his stroke. Matilda was fuzzy on the details, but it seemed like on the rare occasions anyone had ever talked about it, his illness was linked with the period during which his younger daughter disappeared.

Hot tears coursed down Tildy's cheeks. How different might all their lives have been if Annette had only come back?

Tildy had never felt like an orphan because she always had been surrounded by the people who loved her, but she felt alone now. *It's not just Mom being gone. It's having to take care of me for all these years.*

Her mother should know the hell she had put this family through. She should be held accountable. *People's lives have been turned upside down because of her selfishness.* The voice that spoke that thought in her mind sounded like Caroline's, but it also sounded right.

After a while Tildy wiped her tears on the sleeve of her jean jacket and stood up. The sky was overcast, and there were no stars or moon to guide her, but she could see a dim light in the direction of her grandparents' house. *Grandma turned the porch light on,* she thought. New tears threatened, but Tildy staved them off by walking toward the light.

By the time she made it back to the house she'd decided to go find her mother and make her answer for what she'd done.

That night while everyone was sleeping she packed her school bag with peanut butter, crackers, and Vienna sausages. She emptied the items out of her marching band bag, and filled it with a few days worth of clothes and toiletries. Matilda sneaked into the garage and got one of her granddad's canteens. It took a lot of washing, and she still wasn't thrilled about the way it smelled, but it would work.

The last few things she gathered were the letters her mother had sent Caroline, *The Great American Road Trip,* and all the money from the VFW Bingo day.

She started the letter several times. They needed to know she would be coming back.

Grandma, Granddad, and Caroline,

I've gone to find my mom, but I'll be home very soon. Don't worry about me. You've raised me to be a strong woman! I took $247.25 from the Bingo money. Please, replace it from my college fund.

We deserve answers for what she's done to this family. When I come home I'll have those answers.

Somebody, please, let Missy and Brandon know that I am all right.

I love you all very much.

Tildy

She folded the letter, placed it on her dresser, and tried to sleep. The alarm rang while she was already pacing her room. There was no way she'd slept more than a half hour the night before.

Her supplies were in the bags she would have taken to school today anyway. Nobody would notice if they seemed to be bulkier than usual. Tildy got dressed, ran a brush through her hopeless curls, and picked up her things. She opened her door and stopped to look back. It might be awhile before she slept in her bed again.

The dumb turtle looked back at her cheerfully. "Hold the fort, Samson," she told him solemnly, then had to laugh. *Maybe I'm being a little dramatic. Excuse me, but I have never run away before.*

"Grandma, don't forget I have marching band tonight, so I'll be home late," Tildy said as she wolfed down her egg and buttered toast sandwich. Grandma was a great believer in a complete breakfast while Tildy would have been content with a quick bowl of Wheaties, but they had evolved this compromise over the course of years.

"I'm going to have Aunt Caroline drop me off this morning on her way to work." She hugged her grandma tight. "Give Granddad a hug for me when he gets up."

It was almost 6:20, and her aunt would be driving up the path any time. She felt the clunk of the last cattle gate in her stomach. Caroline nodded when she saw her.

"Band," Tildy said, putting her things into the bed of the truck.

"Hey, sorry about …" Caroline began.

Matilda put her hands up. "There's no need for you to be sorry. I love you."

"I love you too, brat." Caroline didn't speak much on the ride to school. "There's nobody here yet. You want me to wait with you?"

"They'll be here anytime. I don't want you to be late." Tildy gathered her things and waved as her aunt pulled away. When the truck was no longer visible on High Street, she walked the quarter mile to the bus stop.

"Can I get one Discover America pass?" she asked the old man that was restocking a display of chewing tobacco.

"You eighteen?" he asked without looking at her.

"Obviously," she lied.

He stopped what he was doing, and went to ring up her ticket. "That's $55.63 after Uncle Sam takes his cut, and this ticket will let you ride any of our buses for thirty days."

She grabbed some beef jerky and a Dr. Pepper. "These too."

"Let's call it $57." He shoved her items into a small paper sack. The man watched her count all $57 in ones.

"Waitress," she said, and he nodded. "When's the first bus going west due in?"

"Oh, anytime now." He went back to stocking things.

Matilda went outside, tore open the jerky, and waited for the bus. She had time to finish her snack before the silver bus pulled into the station.

The only person getting off the bus was Jonah Wilkey, the local hero. He was dressed in his service greens. Tildy was surprised there wasn't a band and a crowd to welcome him.

"Hi, Jonah! Welcome back," she said. "They told us at church you were coming home."

"Tildy! Hi," he said, looking uncomfortable.

Jonah was probably pushing forty. He had been defending Laclede County against Communists for longer than Tildy had been alive. She had met him a few times as she was growing up when he was on leave and attending church with his folks. He always seemed a little embarrassed by all the attention he got as one of the town's heroes.

"Thank you for your service," Tildy said to him as she waited for the bus driver to come take her ticket. She was surprised when he rolled his eyes.

"You're welcome, Tildy, but please don't let on I'm back if you talk to anybody," he said. "I was worried they would send a committee if I said when my bus got in."

"Oh, they would have," Tildy said. She was smiling at his discomfort. "Probably a band and some jugglers."

Jonah laughed. "Maybe not that, but I am hoping I can keep this kind of low key."

"I won't say anything," Tildy said. "I'm probably the safest person you could have run into. I'm getting on the bus."

"Safe travels," he said, and hoisted his huge green duffel bag over his shoulder, giving her a little wave as he walked into the bus station.

The driver was standing by the open compartment beneath the bus cabin. "Where you heading to today, Miss?" He was adjusting his cap over his salt and pepper hair and looking at her like he wondered what a kid would be doing on her own. He probably had daughters around her age.

"I'm going west. Trying to stick close to Route 66."

"Well, first stop's Springfield, Missouri, birthplace of Route 66." He took her large band bag and put it in the compartment beneath the bus. "Keep your valuables close by," he advised.

She followed him back onto the bus. "Do I just sit anywhere?"

"Yeah, we don't got assigned seats." He laughed as if he had made a joke and climbed into the driver seat.

The bus was a little over half full. Matilda pulled her purse close and sat a few seats back across from a dark haired lady and a small boy.

She closed her eyes, and said a small prayer before the bus pulled away from the station.

Chapter 4

Matilda watched the town where she'd spent her entire life disappear into the distance. It was only fifty miles to the Springfield hub where she would make her first transfer.

She'd been shopping in Springfield a few times through the years and knew it was a large city, the largest she'd ever seen.

The bus stopped in a few small towns to pick up or drop off riders. The ride would usually have taken Aunt Caroline a little over an hour at the national speed limit of 55 miles per hour. On the bus it took almost three hours because of all the stops. Tildy didn't really mind. She spent the time looking through *The Great American Road Trip* again. She almost had the touristy stuff memorized, but she didn't get tired of rereading the notes from her parents back and forth in the margins.

It was better to hide in the book than to have to interact with her fellow passengers. As they got closer to Springfield, the number of riders grew at each stop until almost everyone was sharing a seat with a stranger. Tildy found herself pressed against the window wall with a young man sitting next to her. He had gotten on in Marshfield and plopped himself next to her without asking or even excusing himself for the intrusion. Instead, he turned on a small radio he held and broadcast a local talk station to everyone within earshot. Apparently she was supposed to be concerned about whether the U.S. should keep Marines in Beirut, according to the radio people.

Eventually the bus took the exit for downtown Springfield. A few minutes later it pulled into the station. Tildy was already nervous. There were over twenty buses parked in the area with many different destinations on their placards. It seemed like it would be very easy to get on the wrong bus and end up God knows where.

When the bus driver said that everyone had to debus, she got scared. What if someone took her bag beneath the bus? What if she got on the wrong bus? What if she had to pee? Because she really had to pee.

"Your first time?" the lady across the aisle from her asked.

'Is it that obvious?" Tildy laughed.

"We're old hats. Just stick close to us." The lady stood, picking up her little boy. "I'm Molly. This is Christopher. We're heading to Tulsa. Where are you headed?" The woman stepped into the aisle and blocked traffic until Matilda got out of her seat.

"My name's Matilda." She stayed beside Molly and helped carry her suitcase.

After retrieving Tildy's bag from the luggage compartment under the bus, the three of them trooped together through the throng and into the station. Molly explained that her and Christopher's luggage would be transferred to the new bus by the staff since they had Tulsa tickets.

"This is the departure and arrival board," Molly said, nodding toward it. "Tulsa is bus 89. Which city do you need?"

Matilda was overwhelmed by the number of people bustling past her. You got crowds like this at the county fair in Landover, and maybe at KMart on the last weekend before school started. *I'm going to have to get used to more people,* she thought. She felt like she was in everyone's way and wished for a quiet corner somewhere where she could breathe.

"I'm going to Tulsa too, I guess. Where is the restroom?" she asked.

"We have a half hour until our bus loads. You can use the bathrooms right past the ticketing counter." Molly pointed Matilda in the right direction.

When Matilda came back to where she had left Molly her bag was still there on the bench but her new friend was gone.

"Matilda!" A woman's voice called out for her, but it was too crowded to see where it was coming from. A loud whistle cut through the cacophony, and then she saw Molly waving to her.

"Holy mackerel. I thought I lost you," Tildy said.

"Sorry, Christopher woke up, and needed to use the restroom. Come on, let's go wait out by the bus."

When they were outside the door Matilda lit a cigarette. "Is it always this crowded in big city stations?"

"Big city?" Molly barked a laugh. "Wait 'til you see Tulsa. And Tulsa is nothing next to St. Louis. Still, I guess it might be a little busier here than usual for a Tuesday. It'll make it harder to get good seats on the bus."

Tildy felt her cheeks heating. Molly's tone was a little patronizing, and normally Tildy would have gotten her back up, as Grandma would say. But she was keenly aware she was a fish out of water. Little Christopher had more experience in this wide world than she did.

Everything was different here, from the style of the streetlights to the smells of weird foods coming from nearby restaurants.

Mostly, however, it was the people. In Laclede County, it would be rude to pass by even a stranger without at least a nod or a hello, but here, if people did that, they wouldn't have time to do anything else. And it seemed they had a lot to do. Everyone was in a rush, from the ticket clerks to the drivers and janitorial workers to the bus customers. Even the people who were just waiting for their next bus seemed like they yearned to wait faster.

The ones who did glance her way made her uncomfortable. She wasn't an idiot; Aunt Caroline had told her that even the best of men were only worth half as much as they thought, and most hid the beasts they could be under a very thin layer of civility and decency. Still, Tildy had rarely experienced them being so obvious about it. More than one set of masculine eyes darted away as soon as she looked at them, and there were some that just stared back. And smiled.

If she hadn't run away, tonight she would be home waiting for prime time television with Caroline beside her on the couch and Granddad in his armchair. Grandma would go to her room, saying she was going to read the Bible but probably looking through *McCall's* instead. She just got the women's magazine for the recipes, but Tildy couldn't remember her grandma ever trying one out.

Tildy suddenly missed her family so much she felt tears threatening in the back of her eyes. They didn't even know she was gone yet.

She didn't want to cry in front of Molly. She coughed into her hand and asked about Christopher. "How old is he?"

"I am four. Smoking is gross," the dark headed boy pronounced, putting his hands on his hips in judgment.

"Christopher! Be nice." Molly looked amused and a little embarrassed, and Tildy realized Christopher was spoiled rotten. "Sorry," Molly said.

"Oh. It's cool. He's right. It is gross, but I've been doing it too long to quit now." Matilda had trouble making small talk. In truth, she had trouble talking to small children. Other than in church, she'd never been around many little kids. "Are you guys visiting friends in Tulsa?"

"We live in Tulsa. We were visiting my parents in St. Louis. We go a few times a year." Molly was straightening Christopher's hair. "What are you doing in Tulsa?"

"I'm trying to find my mom who has been gone since 1967." Matilda felt self conscious admitting that it took her over sixteen years to begin the search. "I didn't realize she needed finding until this week," she amended.

Molly nodded in a *I'm sure you're crazy* way. "I don't know what I'd have done without my mother."

"Well, I have my grandparents and my aunt. I wasn't alone," Tildy said.

"You didn't have a dad either?" Christopher said, and it looked like he was going to cry.

"He died in Vietnam when I was a baby," Tildy said. Hearing herself sum up her own story in a few short words made her realize how truly sad it was. Molly seemed to agree.

"Can I hug you?" Molly asked.

"I guess." Tildy accepted the hug, a little uncomfortable.

Christopher broke the mood by developing a game. He would walk along the painted lines in the bus lot like they were tightropes, waving his arms in panic when he began to lose his balance and step off a stripe. He challenged Tildy, so she joined him. After a few minutes of that it got too easy, so they tried walking the stripes with their eyes closed. Although Christopher cheated often, squeezing open an eye to get himself back on track, Tildy excelled. He didn't have the experience of years of marching band behind him.

"Bus 89 to Tulsa boarding now." The bus driver put their bags beneath the bus and checked their tickets before they boarded.

"Always sit near the front if possible. Men are less likely to mess with you up here," Molly said as she sat down behind the driver seat.

"Good to know." Matilda sat across the aisle from her and the boy.

"Also, make yourself as big as possible, and people are less likely to sit beside you."

Matilda scooted to the middle of the seat and tried to look larger as the other passengers boarded.

She settled into the routine of the bus. They stopped every hour or so, and sometimes they'd change drivers or switch buses or just take a ten minute break for the smokers. The seat arms in the buses had little ashtrays built in, but a NO SMOKING sign was mounted under the windshield next to the driver.

"I've never been out of Missouri before. This is exciting," Tildy said when they crossed into Oklahoma. Molly nodded from the other seat. It was hard to carry on a conversation over the engine and road noise. Tildy didn't really mind. The terrain outside her window was already changing from her familiar Ozark hills to the flat plains.

Route 66 originally ran through the edge of Kansas, but Interstate 44 bypassed Kansas altogether. She recited to herself the quote from *The Great American Road Trip*. Too bad. It would have been cool to be able to say she'd been to Kansas too. Missy had been to Dodge City where she had an uncle on the police force. Tildy always pictured it with the dirt streets and saloon from *Gunsmoke*, but she knew it must be a lot more modern now.

"What time is it?" Matilda asked Molly.

"It's a little after four." Molly was reading a book with Christopher. He was trying to read the words.

Tildy's family would find out anytime now that she was gone. She didn't want to think about that.

"He's such a good reader for a four-year-old," Tildy said over the bus noises.

"Thank you. I work with him a lot. He wants to grow up to be an astronaut." The young woman moved a curl off the boy's forehead.

"I'm going to build a house on the moon," Christopher said.

"Cool," was all Tildy could think to say.

***

Caroline came through the front door, annoyed. "Did you pick up Matilda? I waited at the school for half an hour."

"No, I she said you were picking her up," her mother said, wiping her hands on a dish towel as she came out of the kitchen.

Caroline sighed and went down the hall. She wasn't worried; it wasn't unusual for wires to get crossed about who was picking up her niece and when. She suspected the girl might mix things up on purpose sometimes as a way to sneak and spend more time with her friends. If Tildy wasn't in her room, a couple of phone calls would find her.

Caroline adhered to the "Please Knock!" sign her niece had artfully made and posted a couple years ago after Granddad had accidentally walked in to find her changing clothes. That had been a family crisis, with neither of them able to look the other in the eye for days.

But now Caroline only waited a second after rapping her knuckles on the old wood before opening the door.

That stupid stuffed frog or whatever it was smiled at her from Tildy's carefully made bed. Caroline grimaced. What had those old fools been thinking? Tildy hadn't been an infant for quite a while now, though the child acted like one sometimes.

Tildy was not there, and her desk chair didn't have the strap of her book bag over the back, so she probably hadn't been home yet. Caroline would call Missy's mom first. Tildy was probably over there listening to her new tape on her friend's stereo.

She'll say she told Granddad she was going to study for the chemistry test with Missy and he must have forgotten, and when I ask him about it, he'll back her up. Caroline knew how this worked. She was used to not being the favorite child.

She sighed and started to close the door, but her eyes fell on an envelope neatly placed in the center of the top of Tildy's bureau, leaning against the sea shell Tildy had gotten after her dad's parents has gone to Louisiana a couple years ago.

Caroline's name was on the envelope. She felt a chill. "No," she said to the empty room.

For no reason, a memory flashed to the forefront of her mind. Tildy, five years old, little bare legs jutting stiffly out from beneath her skirt as she tried to guide the small bicycle down the incline in the driveway.

Caroline had told her not to try to pedal. Just keep her feet out so she could catch herself if she needed to. *You can't fall, but try not to put your feet down. Just go down the hill. If you start to fall to this side, turn this way. If you start to fall to the other side, turn the other way.*

Tildy's little knuckles were white as she gripped the handlebars for dear life. She kept overcorrecting, turning too far to keep from falling, then having to turn too far the other way to stay upright. *It's not a turn, it's a nudge. Just a little nudge to keep your balance,* Caroline said, half running alongside the bike, forcing herself not to reach out and catch Tildy every time it seemed she must fall.

They got to the bottom of the incline without real success, but also without a crash. Caroline stooped to pick up the bike and carry it back up, but Tildy didn't let go. Tildy started dragging the uncooperative vehicle back up the driveway by herself. *I can do it,* she said, and on the next trip down, she did.

A dozen years later, Caroline stood in her niece's room with an envelope in her hand. She knew what was in it. She had read its like before.

Sissy,

By the time you read this, I'll hopefully be a few hundred miles on my way. I've decided to go ahead and take the trip that Mark and I had planned for our honeymoon along Route 66.

I have Mark's ashes in the passenger seat of Ophelia. When I get to a place we had said we wanted to explore together, I'm going to drop some out. When I get to the ocean at the end of the trip in California, I'm going to scatter the rest, and then I will come home.

I hope to only be gone a week or so. I took half the money from Mark's August check and I hope you'll use the rest to take care of anything Mattie might need while I'm gone. She's still with the Bankses, and they don't act like they ever want to give her back, so maybe you won't have to worry about it! Ha ha.

I'm sorry to dump this on you. I hope you will try to keep Mom and Pop from worrying about me. I just feel like I have to do this before I can figure out what I want to do with the rest of my life now that Mark is gone.

You have already been so good to me that I am getting teary eyed writing this. I know it wasn't good for you to have to come home during exams especially in your freshman year to help me out. I promise I will make it up to you even though you are a know-it-all bossy mean bully. Ha ha!

I love you and Mom and Pop and I promise when I come back I'll try to be a little easier to live with.

Sincerely, Nettie

Because she had to, Caroline opened the envelope and unfolded the sheet of notebook paper that was inside.

She had known. Oh, she had known.

She shrieked and threw the letter away from her, catching the edge of the dresser with her hand to keep from falling.

Again.

Caroline felt her back against the doorway of her niece's room, the room Annette had grown up in. Caroline's hands covered her face as she slid down to the floor, sobbing.

***

When the bus stopped in Tulsa, Tildy checked the bus schedule. The next westbound bus wouldn't be for hours. She waved goodbye to Molly and Christopher and decided to get a room for the night.

She walked across the street to a small motel that posted a low rate. The owner of the hotel watched her suspiciously as she over explained why, she, a teen, would be traveling across the country alone.

"I don't care." He handed her a ledger to sign. "You better not be bringing men back to your room." He handed her a key.

She had never spent a night by herself. She lay in the large bed and read the letter her mother had written to Caroline on the morning she left.

Matilda tried not to think about her family worrying about her. Sometime in the night she fell asleep.

The next morning she ate the peanut butter and crackers she'd packed and refilled her canteen from the sink in the bathroom of the hotel room. She walked back over to the bus station about a half hour before her bus was scheduled to depart.

She saw a policeman walking around the hub and was afraid that he was looking for her. Tildy ducked into the ladies room and didn't come out until the coast was clear. By the time she got out to the buses, hers had already started to fill up.

"Bus 325 towards Oklahoma City?" She asked the driver.

"Yes, ma'am. You made it in the nick of time. I was just getting ready to close the doors." The driver checked her pass as Tildy put her bag beneath the bus.

"Thank you," she said as she boarded. Matilda was worried when she saw that there were no open seats. As she walked down the aisle people made themselves look larger by spreading out or setting their bags into the seat beside them.

"Sit down, so we can leave. Someone make room," the driver said. Nobody shifted an inch.

The only open spot was next to a disheveled man sitting right next to the bathroom in the back seat.

"Can I sit with you?" Matilda asked him.

"Suit yourself." He scooted towards the window.

"Thank you," she said as the bus pulled away from the terminal. "I'm Matilda."

"Gus," he said. "Where 'bouts you headed?"

Matilda didn't want to rehash her story, so she said, "I'm heading to Chandler, Oklahoma. What about you?"

"Oklahoma City." Gus was straightening his denim shirt, and each time he moved the sour smell of body odor filled Matilda's sinuses. She tried to inch away as much as she could without making it obvious.

The blue sky she'd awakened to was full to bursting with fat gray clouds now as they headed west. Pulling some beef jerky out of her purse, Matilda offered some to Gus.

She was glad when he declined, because she only had two pieces to hold her over until her next stop.

Thunder began to grumble just as the bus came to a construction zone. Matilda opened the copy of *The Great American Road Trip*, and read up on her next destination.

Out of her peripheral vision she could see Gus wringing his hands. When the thunder rumbled or the heavy equipment made loud noises he would rock nervously.

"Is everything all right, Gus?" she asked.

"Yeah." A dump truck emptied a a load of chat right outside their window, and he yelped, looking around wildly. He saw what had made the noise and sat, stock still, for a moment, then glanced at his seatmate. "I'm sorry."

"It's okay." Neighboring passengers had started to watch them. Tildy tried to take control of the situation. "Are you sure you're all right?"

"Korea," he said as if she had asked a different question. "Sometimes it still gets me. I guess it's never too far away." Gus turned from her to stare out the window.

"My father was in Vietnam. I'm really sorry," Tildy said. "Is there anything I can do?"

He shook his head, still looking out the window. "Sometimes I feel like it was a million years ago." He sat back. "Where was your father stationed?"

"I don't know. He died right before I was born. Where were you stationed?" No answer he would give would mean anything to her, but Matilda felt like it might help for him to talk. If nothing else, it would pass the time.

Matilda had been ten years old when she had seen post traumatic stress disorder for the first time. She was helping her grandparents run the concessions booth at the VFW Independence Day celebration. Oscar Nichols began screaming within a few minutes of the initial volley of fireworks going off.

Grandma had run to him with a blanket, and reassured him that he was safe. Granddad had explained to Matilda that the brain hangs onto moments of happiness and horror, and that it will replay those moments whenever something jogs that memory loose.

"I'm sorry about your dad. Many a man better than me lost their life so politicians could claim a win." Gus was breathing easier as they talked. "I spent some time making my peace with the war, but now I'm fighting those same politicians who sent us to die just so I can get well."

"The VFW or American Legion are good places to network, and sometimes you can meet the right person that can help you," Tildy said, repeating things she had heard her grandma say before. She had nothing else to offer.

"I can't go to a VFW right now. Been dried out for over a month, and I have to avoid places where it's easy to slip into old habits. Thank you though." Gus pulled a coin out of his pocket. "My one month chip. I'm going to my sister's house in Oklahoma City to see if she'll let me stay this time."

"I hope she does, Gus. Everybody deserves a second chance."

"Be closer to my two hundredth chance, but it does feel different this time." He sat back in the bus seat, and watched as the bus started to inch forward through the construction zone.

Matilda picked up her book and tried to start reading again. After a while she noticed that Gus had drifted off to sleep. She wondered if her dad would have been like this when he came back from his war if he hadn't died. No, he would have been with his parents and her mom, and they all would have helped him recover from whatever it was that had happened over there.

She had never really thought about what had happened to her dad in Vietnam. Her grandparents on both sides said he had died fighting for his country. He had always been a hero to her, and in a distant way she was proud of him, but the specifics of his service and death were unknown to her. For all she knew, he had just accidentally eaten bad food or something. The idea bothered her. She wondered what she would have to do to find out the truth.

Then she realized she was setting herself up for another quest. *One parent at a time,* she thought.

Tildy tried to focus on watching for landmarks that the book mentioned. Twenty years had elapsed since the release of the book, and they were driving parallel to Route 66 and not actually on 66. She was having trouble locating anything of use.

The Chandler Hotel was circled in this section. She wondered if her mom had sprinkled her father's ashes there. Would she feel any kind of connection to the place? Matilda didn't believe in ghosts, but she hoped that if they were real that her dad's ghost would be somewhere that he loved.

Winds from the tail of the storm shook the bus, and Matilda steadied herself in the seat. She was glad that Gus wasn't awakened by the turbulence. A sign outside the bus caught her attention. "Visit historic Chandler this exit," it said.

She watched in anticipation as they approached the exit, but the bus didn't even slow down. As they passed beneath the overpass, she wanted to cry. Why had she assumed the bus would be stopping in Chandler? They seemed to stop constantly. She sank into herself.

When they stopped at the next hub she would ask to be sure they'd be stopping in Adrian, Texas. This journey was to find her mother, not to visit all the sites her mother had, but if she didn't find her mother, the whole damn trip would be worthless.

When they stopped in Oklahoma City she said goodbye and good luck to Gus. She gave him a hug and went to find some coffee before her next bus loaded. The coffee in bus stations was either grey water or black goo. Matilda was glad this coffee was black goo.

Oklahoma City was the biggest city she had ever seen, but from the bus station it didn't look much different from Springfield. There were the same long benches for waiting travelers, the same little TVs that charged a dollar in quarters for a half hour of viewing. The city probably had sights she had never dreamed of, but she wasn't going to explore them this way. She didn't care. Maybe someday she would come back and see what was worth seeing along Route 66, but for now her goal was to keep moving along her mom's path until she found her.

One day after being a little freaked out by all the people around her in a bus station, she had grown used to it. She had come to enjoy her anonymity a little bit.

No one in the world knows where I am right now. This might be the first time in her life that was true. It was a scary thought, but it also gave her a little thrill.

She carried her bag to the smoking section of the bus station and lit a cigarette. There were only five cigarettes -- four up, one down for luck -- left in her pack. Matilda would need to buy cigarettes at her next stop. She'd need to check her budget to make sure she still had enough money for the remainder of the trip. No matter what happened, the Discover America pass would be her lifesaver. She could board any bus in the fleet for thirty days — easily twenty days longer than she'd need. Even if she blew all the money, it was not possible for her to starve to death in the time it would take to get back home on a bus.

Matilda watched as a full bus emptied into the station. Dozens of people that had places to go were milling around, checking the departure schedule or rushing to the cafeteria. She wasn't antisocial, but she liked her space. She was glad no one came to occupy the other end of her bench.

Her cigarette had burned to the filter while she was people watching. An acrid scent made her wrinkle her nose, and she put it out in the ashtray in the midst of a hundred others just like it.

There were ten minutes until the next bus would begin loading, so she went to the restroom once more before she went to wait by the bus. There were a few others roaming around — veterans like her — hoping to be one of the first to load. The bus driver was ten minutes late. He made no excuse to the small, annoyed crowd.

Once he had loaded all the bags he began checking tickets.

"Excuse me," Tildy said after he glanced at her pass and motioned her forward. "Will we be stopping in Adrian, Texas?"

"What? No. We'll be stopping in Amarillo, and then Tucumcari, New Mexico. Did you get a ticket for Adrian?" He looked again at her pass. "If you are going to Adrian your best bet is to take a taxi or hitch a ride from Amarillo."

Matilda sat in the seat behind the unhelpful driver. Very little on this journey had gone as planned. She spun her father's ring around her finger with her thumb and tried not to let the feeling of defeat eat at her. She reminded herself that the letters were evidence her mother had gotten most of the way to California, so there was really no good reason for her to want to stop in Adrian. Still, it was a place her mother had gone, and she felt like if she could keep as close to her mom's path as possible she would have a better chance of finding her.

A young couple sat in the seat across the aisle from her and smiled at her as soon as she saw them. They were making out within seconds of the bus pulling out. She was thankful no one had sat next to her, but she didn't want to watch two hours of them going at it either.

Matilda focused on the horizon line as the sun moved directly in front of them. She sat her purse in the seat beside her and found her sunglasses. Pulling out her wallet, she counted her money. Her bus ticket, night at the hotel, and food and drinks had left her with $160 and some change. As long as she was careful, she would be fine. She tucked her money and bus ticket in her wallet, dropped it back into her purse, and went back to watching the road.

It was an uncomfortable six hour trip to Amarillo. Matilda's stomach growled the entire time. What she wouldn't give about now for some of her grandma's chicken and dumplings. She'd sipped at her water so that she wouldn't have to use the onboard restroom, which was gross. The dehydration, hunger, or the sun that had been in her eyes for hours had given her an awful headache.

She didn't want to spend the night in Amarillo, and it was only a few hours more to Tucumcari, New Mexico. Matilda got off in Amarillo after the driver announced a 30 minute stop. She ordered a hamburger at the cafe. She gobbled the burger down and drank a Dr. Pepper. She couldn't let herself get so hungry again. Matilda refilled her canteen and smoked a cigarette before returning to the bus.

The amorous couple were sitting across the aisle from her again. She considered moving before they noticed her, but it was too late, she'd been made.

"How far ya going, kid?" The man, who couldn't have been much older than her, asked.

"Tucumcari tonight, but as far as Holbrook, Arizona, at least," she answered. "What about you guys?"

"We're headin' to Las Vegas to get hitched," the woman responded with the worst stereotypical New York accent Matilda had ever heard.

"Congratulations. Where you from?"

"Dawn here's from Brooklyn. I'm from Iowa. James is the name, but folks call me Jimmy. What's yours?"

"Matilda, but people call me Tildy." She rubbed her temples.

"Well, it's good to meet ya, Tildy."

"You got a headache?" Dawn asked her.

"Yeah. Long day, I guess." Matilda stretched her neck.

"Here, I have some aspirin." Dawn dug in her purse. "I never get headaches."

"Ain't that the truth." Jimmy said, laughing.

Tildy pretended not to hear or understand the comment as she took the pill from Dawn. "I've never seen aspirin this large."

"They're extra strength," Jimmy said.

She took the pill and thanked them, then retreated to her seat right behind the driver.

She had left Tulsa at 10:20 a.m., and the bus had pulled into Oklahoma City a little before 1 p.m. It was after seven now. Tildy didn't understand how just riding in a bus could be so exhausting, but she felt herself getting sleepy as the bus continued westward.

Tucumcari was circled in her book with blue and red ink, and had hearts drawn all around it. It was also one of the places her mother had spent some time. There were at least two letters postmarked over a few week's time from there. She hoped Tucumcari would give her some clues to find her mother.

Matilda slid the book back into her bag, leaned her head against the bus window, and drifted off to sleep.

Chapter 5

"Miss? Hey, wake up. Everybody has to get off the bus." The bus driver was tapping her on the shoulder.

Matilda blinked her eyes. "What? Sorry, I guess I fell asleep."

"You think? I need you to get your things, so I can lock the bus up." His patience seemed to be in short supply.

Tildy stood up and reached for her purse. She panicked for a moment before seeing that it had just slipped to the floor. She felt a little dizzy and almost fell sideways as she bent to pick it up. *Get it together,* she told herself.

There was only one person still waiting to get a bag outside when she stumbled off the bus, still groggy. She apologized to the driver and to the passenger that was waiting for his things.

Before she got a room for the night she wanted to get some decent food. The sign for a 24-hour coffee shop right next to the bus station glowed brilliant in the night. She ordered a Dr. Pepper, but they only had Mr. Pibb. Grudgingly, she accepted the subpar beverage. It was too late for dinner and too early for breakfast, so she ordered fries.

"Is there a clean and affordable hotel you'd recommend?" she asked the waitress.

"Palomino, across the street, or the Blue Swallow a couple blocks down. Can't miss it." The woman refilled her soda. "Here's your ticket. I'll take care of it when you're ready."

"Thank you," she said through a mouthful of fries. Matilda fished around in her purse for her billfold. Nausea swept over her when she couldn't find it. She dumped the contents of her purse onto the counter.

"I've been robbed! Someone stole my wallet."

The realization was like a bucket of ice water dumped over her head. Any remaining sleepiness was gone. She wanted to cry. "That couple that gave me the aspirin," Matilda said aloud to herself.

"You need me to call the cops?" the waitress asked calmly. She looked skeptical, like she had had past customers come up with wild excuses for not being able to pay.

"What? No. Don't call the cops," Tildy said. Matilda didn't want any problems from the police. She emptied the change from this afternoon's lunch out of her pockets. "I have $2.63. How much is my bill?"

"$2.60." The waitress sounded beyond annoyed.

"I'm sorry that I don't have enough for a tip. I'll go back to the bus station and see if I can find the people that stole my money, and then I'll bring you a tip. I promise."

"It's fine. I been stiffed before, kid." The waitress cleared Tildy's plate.

Matilda checked to see if anything else had been taken, but it appeared that they had just taken the billfold. Grabbing her duffel, she ran back to the bus station.

There was only one person on duty, and he was watching *St. Elsewhere.* "Excuse me sir. I came in on the westbound tonight. A couple that got off the same time I did stole my wallet. I think their names were Donna and Jimmy."

He held up his index finger, and didn't look away from the tiny black and white screen for a few moments.

"Someone stole your wallet?"

"Yes. They were a young couple on their way to Vegas to get married. She gave me an aspirin for my headache, but I think it was drugs, because I passed out, and I never fall asleep in moving vehicles."

He held up his finger again. "First of all, how old are you? Secondly, don't take drugs from people you don't know. Third, I'll radio dispatch, and see if they know anything about your couple, but I wouldn't hold my breath. Your wallet's probably long gone."

Tildy fought back tears. "I'm old enough to know better than to take drugs from strangers, but I did it anyway, okay?" she retorted. "I messed up. And now I don't know what I am going to do." The dam broke and the tears began to flow.

Her bus pass had been in her billfold. *Now what am I going to do?*

The clerk's demeanor softened. "You can sit on the bench over there until we get this figured out, but I can't let you sleep in here," he said. "So what did these people look like?"

Matilda told him everything she remembered about the couple, described her wallet and its contents, and lied through her teeth about her age. She didn't want to give up now, when she'd come so far, and she definitely didn't want to call her family for help.

She sat on the uncomfortable bench as Lem, as his name tag read, watched the rest of his show, the late news, and Johnny Carson. Eventually, she fell asleep, rules be damned.

It was morning before a flurry of people arriving on the morning bus woke her and Lem up.

"Was there any word about the couple that stole my wallet?" She asked the ticket agent.

"Sorry, no." Lem answered her as he was relieved by a middle aged woman. Lem explained Matilda's problem to the lady, who bore a nametag with Meredith on it.

"I'm sorry that happened to you, but a young girl is lucky that they only stole your money," Meredith said, then started talking to other customers who had approached to buy tickets or get information.

Matilda went back to the bench. What was she going to do? She needed money, a bus ticket and a Dr Pepper so bad she could taste it. If she had her tape player or her electric keyboard she could pawn them, but as it was she had nothing of value to sell.

Matilda poured her purse out on the bench and took stock. Lip balm, her mother's letters, a pack of cigarettes -- three up, one down -- a lighter, two tampons, and half a pack of Freedent. In her duffel bag was clothing, an empty canteen, deodorant, and more tampons just in case.

"I'm going to have to go home," she said aloud, causing an elderly woman to scoot away from her on the bench.

Matilda slung her purse and her duffel over her shoulder. She went into the restroom to clean up and refill her canteen. Her hair had grown into a frizzy shrub on top of her head. Why hadn't she packed a comb or hair ties?

There was no hot water in the bathroom, so she washed up with gritty soap and brown paper towels. Her stomach growled as she guzzled the tepid water while trying to ignore the flavor of rotten eggs.

A flurry of women came into the restroom. Tildy grabbed her things and went outside. There were too many people in the small bus station for her comfort. She sat beneath a tree, lit a cigarette, and read the letter her mother had sent from Tucumcari.

Sissy,

Well, I thought I would at least be by the ocean now and ready to head back, but things don't always go like you plan them.

I'm stuck here in New Mexico, hoping this guy at the shop isn't just trying to rip me off. It's going to take a little money that I don't have to get Ophelia back on her feet. Tires, I mean, ha ha.

We were doing okay and making pretty good time until we got a few miles east of here. Ophelia made this weird screeching sound and started shaking like crazy, so I pulled over to the side of the road and looked. Her front tires weren't pointing in the same direction anymore.

I don't know much about cars, but I know that's kind of important, ha ha.

So I was stuck on the side of the road in this heat. I don't mean to whine because I know it was all my idea to take this trip, but it was so hot I wanted to crawl under the car just for some shade, but she doesn't sit very high off the ground and I got to thinking about rattlesnakes and how if one came I wouldn't even be able to run away because it would take me five minutes to get out from under the car.

I hope it's funny to you but I was about ready to give up and let the snakes have me by the time some guy in a truck came along and offered me a lift into town.

When I got there, the guy took me to a service station that had a tow truck, and the owner went and got Ophelia and brought her into town. It was maybe 18 miles round trip but I would be embarrassed to tell you what he charged me. It ate almost all my money.

Now I have to pay for repairs from the same guy, who it turns out is a cousin to the guy who gave me the ride. I could get mad, but what's the point? When they get you, they get you, and I'm just a dumb woman who doesn't know anything.

I don't want you to feel sorry for me, but I wanted you to understand that I might not make it back as quick as I hoped. I'm going to have to find some kind of job here to get the car fixed.

Please kiss my baby on that terrible nose and give Mom and Pop a hug from me. I will try to write more to let you know what's going on.

Love, Nettie

Matilda slid the letter back into its envelope carefully. Her mother didn't give up on her journey because she ran out of money. She found a job and made enough money to move on.

Now, this was 1984, not 1967. Finding a job without identification would be impossible, and even if she could find a job, that would take too much time. Matilda didn't want her family to worry any longer than necessary.

She looked down at her hand, at her thumb spinning the ring out of nervous habit. The gold glinted in the sunlight. Her stomach clenched at the thought of losing her father's ring, but she wasn't willing to give up on finding her mother yet.

Where could a seventeen year old pawn something? She thought she knew who might be able to answer that.

Walking back inside the bus station she smiled at Meredith, the ticket lady. "Hello. As you know, I was robbed on one of your buses last night." Tildy spoke loudly enough that everyone nearby could hear her. "And your company wasn't able to find the thieves or my property."

"Hey, keep it down," Meredith said. "We tried to find your stuff. It's just not there. Those people are long gone."

Tildy bowed her head, acknowledging the truth. "I need to see how much it would cost to replace my ticket that was *stolen*? It was a Discover America pass."

Meredith leaned toward Matilda, and lowered her voice. "A thirty day pass will be $67 plus tax."

"Where can I go to pawn the wedding ring of my father, who died in Vietnam, so I can replace my *stolen* ticket?" Tildy asked loudly, locking eyes with Meredith, who looked increasingly uncomfortable and now a little angry.

"There is a pawn shop down past the motels on 66," Meredith said. She didn't separate her teeth as she spoke.

"Thank you. I'll be back." Matilda turned to walk away and walked face first into a very tall man.

"My brother fought in the war. Let me help you. It's not much, but I hope you'll take it." The man handed her a five dollar bill.

"Thank you, but I don't know when I'll be able to repay you."

"It's not a loan. It's a donation." The man smiled. "Good luck getting where you need to go."

Another lady came to Matilda, and handed her a fistful of bills and change. "We all want you to have this." Tildy looked at the people behind her and several nodded.

She was at the verge of tears. "Thank you," she said.

Matilda had wanted to guilt the bus company into replacing her ticket. She hasn't wanted to take money from hard working people.

When she counted the money, there was almost twenty bucks. It wasn't enough to buy the Discovery Pass, but it would probably get her to Holbrook. She put the money in her front jeans pocket so nobody could steal it.

Matilda still had business here in Tucumcari. Her mother had worked at Walt's Coffee Shop waiting tables. In a letter she mentioned working with a Larry Noble and a Juanita with no last name.

"Do you know where Walt's Coffee Shop is?" she asked a young man that was watering the lawn in front of the gas station next to the bus stop.

"Never heard of it. We have a Del's, but no Walt's." The boy went back to watering the brown grass.

Matilda went back to the cafe from the night before. She asked several people if they knew of a Walt's, but it was fruitless. Most of the customers were tourists, and the staff was too young to remember.

She sat down in a booth in the back of the cafe, and a waitress brought her a menu.

"What's the cheapest thing on the menu?" She felt nauseated by her hunger.

"Toast or coffee, They're both under a buck."

Matilda turned the coffee cup on the table over. "Can I have one of each, please?"

"Certainly." She said scribbling something on her ticket pad.

Chapter 6

Matilda listened to her stomach growling. Had she become a panhandler? She had taken money from people who might be not much better off financially than she was.

Her grandfather would have been appalled. After he had the stroke, church members and neighbors often dropped off casseroles or desserts to help out. He refused to eat any of the "charity food" even though he and grandma always had helped out people who were down on their luck.

Matilda ate her toast with as much jelly as she could pile on it. She poured half-and-half into her coffee until it looked more like milk. Adding as many calories to her meager breakfast as possible, she hoped, would make her feel full longer.

"Did you find the person you were looking for?"

Matilda turned to find a booth with three women behind her. "Not yet. Thank you," she said.

A thin, red-headed women smiled at her. "You new around here?"

"This is my first morning."

"Can we join you?" the redhead asked.

Tildy shrugged. "Sure, I guess."

The women carried their coffee cups over. "I'm Carrie," the redhead said. "This is Monica and Sherry." Carrie slid into the seat next to Matilda, and the others sat opposite them.

The waitress came back by to fill up coffee cups. "Are you ladies doing all right? Is there anything else I can get you?"

"Thank you," Matilda said to the waitress. She felt bad eating her jelly laden toast in front of these women, who might be hungry. They didn't look very well off.

"I'm Matilda," she said. She took a bite of her toast. Her stomach continued to growl.

Carrie said, "Are you just traveling through, Matilda, or will you be staying with us for a while?"

"I guess I'll be here for a few days at least."

"You should stay with us," Sherry said in an eager voice.

"What?" Matilda said, pulling her purse closer to her.

"Sorry," Carrie said. "What Sherry was trying to say is we live at a women's boarding house just off of Main Street."

"Oh. I was nervous there for a second. I don't have much money." Matilda took the last bite of her toast and washed it down with a swig of coffee. Her stomach decided it was enough for now and settled down.

"That's fine. We have a work-for-rent program. Monica does laundry and is a cleaning goddess, and Sherry cooks and does the dishes. We all have something to contribute." Carrie said.

"That's pretty cool," Matilda said.

"Debbie, can we get the ticket?" Carrie said. "We'll take you to see the house, so you can decide for yourself. No pressure."

The waitress brought the ticket over.

"As a welcome to Tucumcari gift, we'd like to take care of your breakfast," Carrie said to Tildy.

"Thank you, but I can get it." She dug a five out of her purse, handing it to the waitress.

The waitress nodded. "I'll be right back with your change."

There was an awkward silence as they waited for the waitress to return.

The waitress handed Tildy the change. "You have a nice day, now," she said.

"Can you give one of these to the waitress that was working around eight last night? I didn't have enough money then for a tip."

"I'll check the schedule. Thanks." Debbie tucked the money into her apron as she walked away.

Matilda grabbed her duffel from under the table and followed the three women to the parking lot. Carrie climbed into the driver seat of a rusty blue Chevy Luv, and the other women climbed into the bed of the pickup.

"You get shotgun," Monica said to Matilda.

Tildy felt bad about taking the only other seat. "Are you sure? I don't mind riding in the back."

"Don't be silly," Carrie said. "Guests always ride in the front."

Matilda climbed into the pickup, and held her purse and duffel bag. She could see the pavement through the rusted hole in the floorboard.

Crazy Train by Ozzy slammed Matilda in the senses when Carrie started the truck. Carrie turned the music down. "Sorry."

"No problem. I like music."

Carrie killed the truck a few times before getting it out of the parking lot. "I hate stick," she said, shaking her head.

"Me too. My grandma forced me to learn on a standard though. She said that learning automatic first was like learning to make a soufflé before learning how to crack the egg."

"That's funny. Your grandma sounds like a smart lady." The warm wind blew into the cab, and tendrils of Carrie's long red hair fluttered out her window as they drove.

"She is." Matilda thought about Grandma, and how scared she must be. Tildy loved her family so much, and she never wanted to cause them pain. She missed them despite that it had only been a couple days.

Matilda looked at the truck's side mirror. The women in the back of the truck reminded her of a country music video. Willie Nelson probably drove around a rusty pickup full of women at least once.

Carrie turned off the main road, and nothing looked familiar now. In the distance Matilda could see the red butte that loomed over the city of Tucumcari. In the dark last night it had looked like a giant tombstone.

The pickup shook as Carrie turned into a small, pitted parking lot. The huge house had seen better days. "It used to be a motel in another life," Carrie said.

Matilda followed the other women into what might have been the lobby. The room was furnished with several mismatched chairs and a stereo system, and the front desk had been turned into a makeshift bar of sorts. Most of the light filtered through thick green drapes and shined down through dust motes.

Matilda was not a snob, and she was grateful for a free room since she was so low on money. "Where can I put my stuff?"

"I'll show you around," Carrie said as she shooed a tabby cat off a chair.

She led Matilda through an archway to the right of the bar and down a short hallway. On the right was another archway that showed a large dining room with a single long table surrounded by high-backed chairs. The formal setting seemed at odds with the peeling wallpaper and grime in the corners.

Carrie unlocked a door on the left and pushed it open for her. Matilda hesitated.

"This is kind of a guest room. We'll get a room upstairs with the rest of the girls ready for you in a day or so. The bathroom is at the end of the hall. The water takes a minute to start flowing when you flush or run the sink. I'll let you get settled in and come gather you in a little while."

"All right," Matilda said and walked into her room. A twin bed, a desk and a chair were the only furniture. She jumped when the door behind her latched.

She set her things on the bed and checked to make sure that she could open the door. When it opened easily, she felt more at ease, but she wondered why Carrie hadn't left her the key. She wouldn't be able to lock it when she went out.

There was a small needlepoint of the Ten Commandments above the bed and a window to the side. She pulled back the thick curtains and tried to open the window for some air, but the frame was cemented in with a half century of paint. Through the grime on the glass she saw there were bars on the outside.

For no good reason, a line from a Robert Frost poem occurred to her: *Before I built a wall I'd ask to know what I was walling in or walling out.* She shook her head to clear it of random thoughts and walked down the hall to find the bathroom.

The bathroom was sparse but cleaner than the rest of the house. A white porcelain sink, tub, and toilet sat in a white tiled room. The only color was from the bare yellow bulb that was mounted on the ceiling.

Matilda wished that she didn't have to share a bathroom because the door didn't lock. She washed her face, but there was no mirror to see if she looked as forlorn as she felt.

Matilda went back to her room and sat on the bed. It was firm but not uncomfortable. She lay down, and pushed her belongings to the foot of the bed. The ceiling, once white, was water-stained right above her bed, and the plaster had a soft pithy look. *Good luck sleeping while the ceiling caves in on me,* she thought, but within minutes she drifted off.

She dreamed of eating watermelon on the back porch, of her baptism, and of her first kiss.

Her baptism had happened in The Gasconade River when she was nine years old. It was in July after she came home from her first church camp. Brother Bowman had walked her through the process; he had said a few words, she had said yes, he had put a handkerchief over her mouth and nose, and then he'd briefly dunked her in the water.

She had worn a daisy yellow sundress to the river, but Grandma had told her to put a change of clothes in the car so they could go out to lunch to celebrate afterwards. It wasn't until she was belly deep in the murky water that she remembered that she hadn't packed any extra underwear.

Would Grandma be mad that they would have to go home before they could go eat lunch? What if she didn't tell? She could wear her wet underclothes, or pretend she had on underwear and quickly put some on when she got home.

These were the things going through her mind while the preacher said his prayer. When he asked her the question she nodded her head. The water filled her mouth and nose when he dunked her. She'd forgotten to hold her breath. Now she was clawing and kicking as she gulped the water into her lungs.

It was hours later when she finally felt well enough to stop crying. She cried because it hurt; cried because this was supposed to be an important event and she'd screwed it up; and most importantly cried because she hadn't understood what *saved* meant in the first place and this felt more like a punishment.

She was eleven when she'd overheard Aunt Caroline and Granddad arguing in the garage. Watermelon was dripping down her chin and arms. Caroline kept saying, "She needs more in her life than school, church, and the VFW. If you don't let her experience the world, she'll run off too."

Granddad had yelled at Caroline to get out of his house. She took off in her truck, and it was a week before Matilda saw her again.

Her first kiss happened at the skating rink when she was thirteen. He was a year older, and they were both on the speed skating team. The dark skating rink was crowded, and *All Out Of Love* by Air Supply came on. He leaned in to kiss her just as she started to say that she hated the song. His kiss landed firmly on her lower lip and chin, and even worse, he didn't notice.

The dream woke her up. She was laying in the bed trying to sort through her thoughts when someone knocked on the room door.

"Hang on," Matilda said, hopping out of the bed as the door opened.

"Are you allergic to anything?" Carrie asked.

"Shrimp, I think." She wasn't sure if she was allergic to shrimp, but she hated it so much that she'd always claimed she was.

"No worries there. Did we tell you that dinner is at six?"

"Yes. I'll be there."

"We need to go over the rules here," Carrie said as they walked into the hall. "First rule is that you are responsible for keeping your room clean. That means making your bed as soon as you get out of it."

"I can do that," Tildy said.

"There are no visitors after eight in the evening, and bedroom doors must be closed at that time. Room and board must be paid for with cash or service, and must be paid in full before you leave."

"Other than that last one, the rules are the same as at church camp," Matilda said.

Carrie smiled. "Let me show you the rest of the place." They stood in the hall. "This area is for boarders only, and no visitors are allowed back here." She pointed to a door marked EMPLOYEES ONLY. "Kitchen. You'll probably be working in there a lot. Like I said, we have dinner at six, and everyone here must attend." She pointed to another door at the end of the hall next to the restroom. "That's my and Ray's rooms. Off limits."

"Okay," Matilda said, having tuned out already. "Is there a phone I can use to make a collect call?"

"No phones in the house. Ray says they're a distraction. There is one at the service station about a quarter mile down the road."

"I'm going to run down there to make a call. I'll be right back."

Carrie nodded. "See you at dinner. Six."

Matilda went upstairs to grab her purse. She lit a cigarette as soon as she got outside.

"Don't go," Monica said from the side of the building. "Sherry has already gotten in trouble for scaring off new girls, and I don't want her to get in trouble again."

The sun was directly overhead, and it was over seventy degrees. "I'm just going to the phone up the street. I'll be right back." She tried to change the subject. "How can it be this warm in March?" Matilda rubbed her shoe against a brown stub of grass.

"You get used to it." Monica said. "Will you please stay?"

"Yeah." She examined her cigarette, so she didn't have to make eye contact. "I need to do some things in town. I'll be back after that."

Monica grasped her and hugged her.

Matilda felt like she was being manipulated, but she wasn't good at confrontation, so she just smiled at Monica. The woman looked much older to Matilda than she had that morning. Her hair was bleach bottle blonde, but there was gray coming in at the temples.

"Would you like a ride?" Monica asked.

"Need the exercise." Matilda had only smoked a few cigarettes in the past day and a half, but by the time she'd made it to the phone booth she'd finished the last three in the pack. Nobody answered at her grandparents' house, so she decided to walk to the bus station.

"How far west can I get on eighteen dollars?" she asked the ticket agent.

"Westbound, Albuquerque is twenty dollars. Eastbound, Amarillo is sixteen dollars."

"I don't need to go east. Do you know where Walt's Cafe was?" Matilda asked, defeated.

"No, but I bet the owner of the cafe across the street does. He knows everything in these parts. He owns the bus station, the cafe, and a few other businesses."

She'd already asked all around at the cafe, so Matilda resigned herself to walk back to the boarding house. On the way she stopped to get a pack of cigarettes -- another seventy-five cents gone -- and try to call home one more time.

The buildings in Tucumcari must have been something special in their day. They were brightly painted, and some of them were designed to look like teepees and sombreros. It was like a world lost in time, but once you got past the main drag you could see the difference. Mobile homes, mini malls, and fast food franchises dragged you right back to the 20th Century.

There was a different truck sitting in front of the boarding house. It was a little newer and a lot nicer than the Chevy Luv it was parked beside. Matilda put out her cigarette and left it in the outdoor ashtray by the front door.

Inside the front door stood Carrie talking to a large man. He must have been well over six feet tall.

"Matilda, this is my husband, Ray."

Ray looked Matilda up and down. "How old are you, kid?" he asked.

She didn't want to admit to being a runaway. "I'm eighteen."

"Good answer. Tell that to anyone that asks." He leaned down and kissed Carrie. "Looks like I've got business to scare up. I'll see you later."

"Did you have a nice walk?" Carrie asked, lighting a cigarette and offering it to Matilda.

She took the cigarette, and Carrie lit another. "I guess, but I didn't find out anything that I didn't already know."

"You should ask Ray. He knows everyone in town, and a lot of other folks too. He's a people person."

Matilda nodded. "Thanks. I will." But she wasn't sure she wanted to ask him about anything. "I think I'm going to lay down for a while. I'm getting a headache." Matilda excused herself and went to her room.

Her door was standing open, and everything but her clothes was spread out on the bed. "What the hell?" She looked around for her clothes, but there was no place to put them in this tiny room.

"I noticed that some of your clothes were dirty, so I put them on to wash." Monica said from the doorway.

"You really didn't have to do that." The intrusion was too much. "Thank you, but I can take care of my things."

"I was just trying to be nice." Monica sounded near tears.

"It's okay. I'm just not used to somebody touching my things."

"I won't do it again."

"Thank you," Matilda said, gathering her toiletries. She was glad she'd kept her letters in her purse.

She probably should go down and see if there were any chores to help with, but she felt too violated to face anyone right now. Matilda opened *The Great American Road Trip,* and sat on her bed to read it.

Tucumcari, New Mexico: A Small Town with a Swinging Vibe!

Route 66 runs through the center of this town. Whether you're looking for dinosaurs, aliens, or a funky room for the night, try Tucumcari tonite. With hundreds of hotel rooms and dozens of unique dining options, Tucumcari has something for everyone. With shopping for mom, the library for big sis, dinosaurs for little brother, and aliens, museums, and car shows for dad; Tucumcari offers activities for the whole family.

"Stereotype much?" Matilda said out loud.

Beneath the article was a list of hotels, restaurants, and activities. A photo of Route 66 showed the Tucumcari strip. She studied the photo for a long time. One of the signs in the background looked like it might say Walt's. The picture quality was too poor to be sure.

She read the descriptions of each of the locations. There was a number there for Walt's.

Matilda went to find Carrie or one of the others to tell them she was going to run to the phone booth, but that she'd be right back. Sherry was setting the table in the dining room, but nobody else was to be seen.

"Hey, I am going to run back up to the phone booth. I'll only be gone a few minutes," she said. The woman looked immediately alarmed.

"No, you can't. Dinner will be called in a few minutes, and you have to attend dinner." Sherry looked around. "Mr. Ray won't tolerate missing dinner."

"Wow. All right. I'll go after dinner." Matilda wondered what the big deal was about dinner. Grandma was kind of a stickler for everyone showing up promptly at the table, but she never freaked out about it. Besides, it was still over an hour until the scheduled meal. Matilda decided she would leave this crazy boarding house tomorrow at first light.

The laundry room was accessible through a swinging chrome door in the kitchen. Monica was standing in front of a large industrial dryer folding sheets.

"You need a hand?" Matilda asked.

"No thanks. Carrie is a real tight ass when it comes to how the sheets are done," Monica said.

"Yeah, I never got that," Matilda said. "I don't know why people fold sheets in the first place. It's not like you're going to wear them to church."

Monica smiled. "Well, you don't want a wrinkled up bed if you have a gentleman caller, do you?"

Matilda felt her face heat and Monica laughed out loud. "Why don't you help Sherry peel potatoes for dinner?"

"Sure," Tildy said. She went back to the kitchen. *Gentleman caller? Not likely.*

Now Sherry was standing at the wooden table in the center of the room with an open bag of potatoes on one side and a large pot with a couple peeled potatoes on the other. Sherry handed Tildy a paring knife, and moved the scrap bowl towards her.

"My grandma had a little vegetable peeling thing. It made things a lot faster for me as a kid since I wasn't cutting myself every few seconds."

"Carrie is pretty particular about how she wants things done. She doesn't like a lot of waste, so be careful peeling," Sherry said.

Carrie must be kind of a tyrant once you get to know her, Matilda thought. *Everybody acts like she's going to beat them with a stick.* "I'll be careful. Where is Carrie?" Matilda asked.

"I'm sure she's with her husband. She definitely doesn't like nosy people, so you'd best get a handle on that." Chastened, Matilda went to work in silence. After a few minutes, Sherry finished her last potato and put it into the bowl. Matilda had made it through most of one potato.

"What else can I do to help?"

"You can help me pluck the chicken for tomorrow's dinner."

Matilda looked at her with horror. " I know that I'm from the Ozarks, but I'm going to admit that is something that I have never done."

Sherry pulled a chicken out of the fridge. It still had its feet and all its feathers. Matilda wanted to cover her eyes. She never wanted to see a chicken like this, and would prefer if they only came nugget shaped. She had watched Grandma do this once and had always made herself scarce after that.

"I'm willing to help, but I am more than a little freaked out right now."

"It's easy." Sherry held the chicken by its feet and plunged it into a large pot of boiling water. After a few seconds she pulled it out and laid it on a metal sheet pan. "Just grab a handful of feathers with one hand, hold the chicken steady with the other, and yank."

People had been doing this for centuries, but it was the most barbaric thing she'd ever witnessed. And the smell!

"Come on," Sherry said, tearing out another clump of feathers.

Tildy grabbed a wad of feathers, steadied the bird and pulled, but nothing happened.

"You have to pull hard and fast. It's dead. You aren't going to hurt the bird." Sherry sounded more than a little annoyed.

This time she closed her eyes and tore the feathers out. She wasn't sure if it was the handful of wet feathers or the smell of the dead bird was making her ill. "This is the grossest thing I've ever done."

"How old are you?" Sherry stared at her unblinking. "You have no idea what gross even is."

Matilda didn't know what to say. "I'm sorry. I didn't mean any disrespect."

"Matilda, you are fine. Sherry is just a little grumpy." Carrie said from the doorway. "Why don't you go get a clean shirt for dinner? I'll help her finish cooking."

"I'm sorry," Matilda said again. She walked straight to the bathroom and scrubbed her hands, then went back to her room.

Matilda stood with her back to her room door. She felt worthless and helpless. She renewed her determination to leave this place tomorrow. The vibe was just weird, and she couldn't see any way she would be able to fit in, even for a short time.

A knock startled her. Matilda turned and opened the door to find Sherry, red faced. "I'm sorry if I made you uncomfortable," the woman blurted. She looked angry and afraid at the same time.

"What? You don't need to be sorry. I'm sorry that I was so immature," Matilda said.

Sherry smiled, and Matilda saw that she had several cavities and some teeth missing. "It's a while until dinner. Liz will take you to get some clean clothes."

"I can just wear this," Matilda said, gesturing toward her dirty marching band t-shirt and jeans.

"Don't be silly. Go with Liz." She stepped to the side so another woman who must be Liz could step in. The woman was probably about 30, short and a little heavy, wearing too much makeup and dressed in a green pantsuit that screamed disco.

Liz led Matilda down the hall to the lobby, then up the stairs. The walls in this wing were painted a clean white and decorated with generic framed artwork.

"This is nice," Matilda said. It was odd that the hall with the tenants' rooms would be so much better kept than the main floor of the building.

Liz opened a door with a key. "If you're here long enough then you can get a room in this wing."

"Oh, I won't be here long. I'm just traveling through."

Liz laughed. "That's what I said. I've been here over three years."

"I have to be back home as soon as possible, but I'm thankful for having a place to stay."

When the door opened Matilda had to blink. The room was the same size as hers downstairs, but it was one giant closet. Metal pipes hung from the ceiling supporting women's clothes on hangers. The whole room smelled musty.

"What size dress do you wear?" Sherry asked.

"I don't know. Who wears dresses in the eighties?" Matilda laughed nervously. "Please, just a shirt."

"You're probably an eight or ten in a dress." Liz went to the middle of the rack, and handed her a red dress made of a slippery material Matilda probably couldn't pronounce.

"Oh. I can't wear this. I don't even wear dresses, and my bra straps would show, and the only shoes I have are my Cons."

Liz looked at her feet and handed her a pair of red heels. "You don't need a bra with this."

"Ha." Matilda laughed too loud. "I am not comfortable wearing this."

"Everyone dresses for dinner." Liz ushered her towards the door. "Now, hurry and get ready. I put shampoo and towels in the downstairs bathroom for you."

It's like Sunday dinner at Granny Margaret's, she told herself. *Some people dress for dinner, so maybe it isn't that weird.*

Sherry left Matilda at the archway that led to her room. "I'll come get you in half an hour."

The shower head had been disconnected, so Matilda filled the bathtub with rusty water. She peeled off her clothes, and climbed into the bath. The water was tepid, but it still felt pretty good. Sherry had left a bottle of no name shampoo and soap beside the tub.

Washing her hair was difficult. The curls had a tendency to knot up if she didn't have conditioner, and the only thing she had was shampoo that smelled like flowers and kerosene. Once she had cut her hair short, hoping it would be easier to manage, but with no weight to hold it down it looked like she was the bride of Frankenstein.

Matilda drained the water and dried off. The dress Liz had given her would have been great on *Saturday Night Fever*. She pulled it on and felt like she was playing dress up. It was absurd. The shiny red material hung to her knees. There was an elastic waist that sat right below her sternum, and spaghetti straps held the bodice up.

The dress was probably considered pretty at one time, but now it was outdated and laughably feminine. It did fit though. Liz had a good eye. The shoes were strappy sandals with a very short heel. They were a little big, and Matilda felt ridiculous clomping down the hall to her room.

She shook out the clothes she'd been wearing, and hung them over the back of the desk chair to air. She dreaded having people see her in this getup, but she could hear footsteps in the hallway.

Matilda opened the door just as Monica began to knock, startling them both. Monica was wearing a short black Lycra outfit that clung to her curvy body.

"It's time to eat," Monica said. "You look real nice."

"I'm as ready as I'll ever be," Matilda muttered, following her to the dining room. She had worn heels to her eighth grade graduation but had kicked them off as soon as she could. They made her feel uncoordinated and attention-seeking.

Dinner was already on the table when she entered. Sherry and Liz were seated at the large table, and they were all dressed up too. Liz had on too much coral rouge, and her lip liner was a completely different color than her lipstick.

The whole scenario put Matilda in the mind of when she and Missy had dressed up in fancy clothes and makeup to play tea-party when they were in elementary school.

Monica sat down at the table, and Matilda sat at the remaining place setting, trying not to look directly at anyone. Would she ever be able to eat meat again? She tried not to think about yanking the poor bird's feathers out or she might be sick.

Sherry took up the plates, and served the meal. She put a tiny helping of meatloaf and potatoes and a big pile of lettuce on a plate, and dropped it unceremoniously in front of Liz.

When everyone had a plate Sherry sat down and started to eat. Matilda wished she had received Liz' plate instead of hers heaped with gray, flaccid meatloaf.

"Where is Carrie at?" Matilda asked, pushing the meat around on her plate. What she wouldn't give right now for a bowl of Cheerios.

Nobody spoke up, and when Matilda looked up from her plate they were looking at each other conspiratorially.

"Carrie and Ray have a charity fundraiser tonight. They'll be back sometime this evening," Liz answered. "Where's the tea, Monica?"

Monica got up and went into the kitchen, returning in a minute with a pitcher. She poured iced tea into everyone's glasses.

Matilda sipped the beverage, and decided that it wasn't horrible. It tasted a bit like licking pennies, but everything she'd drunk since arriving had. The tea made it easier to eat the awful food. She didn't even chew it, but instead swallowed it like pills.

When she wasn't pushing the conversation nobody spoke, so she just concentrated on getting the meal over with.

When Liz pushed her chair back the other women did too. Matilda felt like she was in the Army. This made her laugh. The others joined her in her laughter.

Monica insisted on taking everyone's picture in their fancy clothes with a Polaroid. They posed like they were Charlie's Angels. After dinner was going so much more smoothly than the rest of the day had. They all laughed and joked around while they cleaned up dinner.

Matilda felt good but not normal. Colors were brighter and jokes were funnier, and she found herself fascinated by an old stain on the carpet of the dining room. Somebody said they should all play a board game, and someone else suggested cards, and then a good-natured argument broke out that ended with everyone yelling "Go FISH!" at each other, and later Tildy couldn't remember if they had ever gotten around to playing a game or not. She didn't remember exactly when she went to bed, but she remembered Monica helping her into a nightgown.

Chapter 7

Matilda was vaguely aware of someone speaking to her, but she didn't open her eyes until they touched her.

"Get up already!" It was Liz, and she seemed pissed.

"What the hell?" Matilda said grabbing the hand that was tapping her shoulder. "Don't touch me."

"It's an hour until dinner, and you are still in bed. You need to get your ass up before Carrie gets here."

Matilda sat up, discombobulated. There was daylight leeching around the hideous drapes. "We just had dinner."

"Are you high? We haven't seen you since last night. Sherry and I have been covering your chores." She yanked Matilda's covers off the bed. "Get yourself cleaned up."

Matilda didn't recognize the nightgown she was wearing. It was pink cotton with bleach spots. Had she really slept, what was it, more than twenty hours? *Did they drug me?*

There was a white yoked dress, and black patent leather shoes on her desk, but there was no way in hell she was dressing like she was in elementary school. Her marching band t-shirt and jeans were laying in the floor by the door. They didn't smell the freshest, but she was wearing them, anyway.

She leaned against the door while she got dressed, because it didn't lock from the inside. How had she not noticed that yesterday? She put her Cons on sockless and ran to pee before it was too late.

She got into the hallway just as Carrie, Ray, and Monica came in. Two other men followed behind. Carrie frowned at Matilda and took her by the arm, half pushing her into the dining room.

"It was nice of you to dress for the occasion, Matilda," Carrie said under her breath. "I can see you and me are going to have to have a talk."

Matilda pulled her arm away. Her head still felt fuzzy from sleep, but she was ready to go grab her things and get out of this place. She had no doubt the other women had put something in her food or in the tea last night that had made her loopy.

"The table looks nice, Elizabeth," the older of the two men said.

"Thank you, sir," she said, bringing a pitcher to the table. "Would you men like some of Monica's famous iced tea?"

"Wouldn't miss it," the younger man said. He pulled out a chair for Monica.

Ray sat at the head of the table. "Mr. Edwards and I'll have a beer, Liz."

"Matilda, this is Mr. Edwards and his son, Donnie," Carrie said, sitting across from her husband.

"It is nice to meet you, darlin'." Mr. Edwards said, taking his hat off and handing it to Liz to hang up.

Tildy took a step backwards. She didn't like this man. It wasn't even what he said. It was the familiar way he looked at her. "It's nice to meet you," she said, but she didn't move any closer to the table.

Liz put the food on the table and handed the men bottles of beer. "I'll go get the others."

What others? Matilda wondered. The only person that she could tell was missing was Sherry.

"Have a seat," Carrie said to her as a command more than a suggestion. She pointed to an empty chair across from Monica.

"Sorry." Tildy said, taking the seat at the huge table. She was too far from the door to slip out unnoticed.

There were five seats on each side of the table, and one at each end where Carrie and Ray sat. Matilda was trying to do the math to determine the likelihood of the awful man sitting next to her.

Liz returned after a couple minutes with three women that Tildy hadn't met and Sherry.

"Mr. Edwards, you know Cheryl, Brenda, and Amelia. Ladies, this is Matilda. She's a new boarder."

None of the women including Sherry looked up from the floor until Ray cleared his throat.

"It's nice to meet you. I am Ami." Amelia was hispanic and had a very strong accent.

"It is nice to meet you. I am Brenda." Brenda was bone thin, with short shaggy brown hair. "This is Cheryl. She don't talk."

Cheryl was the biggest of all the women. Her eyes, unsynchronized, darted around the room, landing on the chair next to Carrie. She was afraid of something.

"Sit ladies, so we can get started," Ray ordered.

Liz sat a chair away from Matilda, so Mr. Edwards sat between them. When everybody was seated, Carrie stood and served Mr. Edwards, his son, and Ray, and then the tray was passed around the table to the women.

Sherry was the last person seated at the meal, and there was no table setting in front of her. Matilda hoped that she hadn't gotten in trouble because of her.

"Whaddaya think of New Mexico?" Donnie asked Matilda.

"It's beautiful. I've never seen anything ..." Matilda began.

"That's an interestin' accent you got there. Where you from?" Mr. Edwards asked, tearing the meat off a chicken leg with his fingers.

"Missouri," she answered. She leaned away from him.

"Don't be shy, Missourah," he said, pushing her hair away from her eyes with his greasy fingers.

"I'm not shy," she said stiffly, turning toward Brenda a little more. She felt like everyone was watching her.

"Have some tea," Carrie said to her, pouring her glass full of the muck brown beverage.

"Thank you," Matilda said. She took a large drink of the concoction, and it burned all the way down her throat. It wasn't the same tea as last night's, whatever that had been.

"What is it?" Matilda choked. She was trying not to sound judgmental, but the stuff was awful.

"Tea, quaaludes, and gin," Liz said, smiling without humor.

"Oh. That is strong." Matilda had sneaked champagne at weddings and drunk more than a few wine coolers, but she'd never had hard alcohol.

"You're eighteen. Live a little," Edwards said, filling her glass again.

Matilda picked at her food and listened to the dinner conversation around her. The men were talking about baseball and the Dodgers' chances of taking the division in the coming season. For the most part, the women were quiet, only responding when asked a question.

Still, it wasn't awful. Matilda figured she could get through the meal, then pack her stuff and head out immediately afterward. She didn't think they would try to physically stop her, but she hoped to get out without having to explain anything to anyone.

Liz set a large red jello mold in the middle of the table.

Matilda picked at the wiggling dessert on her plate, finding it to be the best thing she'd eaten in days. Drinking whenever someone at the table encouraged her to was making her tipsy.

Dessert seemed to be some kind of signal. The next time she looked up from her plate, she gaped at some of the bizarre things the others were doing.

Monica was kissing the neck of Donnie, and Liz had her hand in Mr. Edwards' lap. Miss Wickman would have slapped them all with PDA demerits long before Liz had her hand slipping through the zipper of Mr. Edwards' jeans.

Not okay. None of this was okay. Everything happening around her was freaking her out. "I need to go to my room," she whispered. *I need to get out of this place right now.*

"It's rude to leave the table before the host," Ray said.

She sat stockstill. It occurred that everything around her was being done for her. It was all some grand bacchanalian show for her benefit. Every set of eyes at the table was focused on her, except Cheryl's, which seemed to be focused on two different points in the room.

"No, I have to go to my room. I'm not feeling well." She slid her chair back, arose and stumbled for the arched doorway.

Someone grabbed her, and spun her around. It was Mr. Edwards. He was laughing. "Come here, you," he said. He grabbed her by the back of the head and stuck his tongue into her mouth. Matilda pushed against him, trying to scream. Someone, a woman, laughed.

There were more hands on her now. Ray, Carrie, and Monica were groping her, and pushing her back towards Mr. Edwards.

For one terrifying moment things became clear. The greasy food in her stomach rolled, and she pushed backwards just as she vomited onto Edwards. He cursed and let go of her, then knocked her sideways with a backhanded slap. "Bitch!"

Monica screamed. Matilda staggered away and ran toward her room.

Edwards was yelling. "I paid for that girl!"

When she got to her room she pushed the desk chair under the door handle, shaking. She didn't know if that would really keep anybody out, but it seemed like it worked in the movies. Grabbing her purse, she looked around the room and realized she was trapped.

Several thuds shook the door in its ramshackle frame. "Get a screwdriver," Ray yelled to someone outside her door. "Open this door, or you're gonna be sorry when I take it off the hinges. You don't want to make me angry, Matilda. Ask Sherry how well that works out. You can do this the easy way, or we can do it the hard way. You'll enjoy one much more than the other."

The only exit from the room was the window, and it was painted shut. Even if she broke it, there were bars outside. No way to know how strong they were.

She could hear the sound of scratching as Ray attacked the hinges.

There was no way out. In moments the men would get through the door and into the room, and then they could do anything they wanted to her.

Matilda pulled the drawer out of the desk and swung it by the handle with all her terror-fueled strength. The window exploded outward. Matilda swung the drawer again at the bars outside, and the jolt rattled back through her arms and into her skull. Maybe with time and tools, she could get out that way, but she had neither.

She screamed and fell back against the bed, sobbing. Ray was going to punish her. Edwards ... They were going to hurt her so bad, and there was nothing she could do.

Matilda sat up, shaking and crying, looking desperately around her room. There had to be something. But there wasn't. The scratching at the door stopped and she jerked her head in panic, but the door still stood. Suddenly with a BOOM! the door lurched inward an inch, shoving the chair. That wouldn't hold.

Matilda balled her hands into fists and raised them to the sides of her head. She felt pain. She opened her left hand and blinked through her tears to see the shard of glass embedded in her palm. From the window. She had an idea.

She couldn't imagine they would hurt her if she already had hurt herself.

In seconds she had found the biggest piece of window glass she could. I *could die. Either way it's a way out.*

Her fear still threatened to take her sanity, but now she had a plan. She lay down on the bed. She took the shard in her right hand and pressed a jagged point against her left wrist. One quick swipe. Then the other side. She could do it.

The door shuddered inward again, but she didn't look. Even if they got in now, they wouldn't have time to stop her.

She looked at the stained and sagging ceiling and took a deep, shuddering breath, pressing harder with the glass.

And she saw a pudgy finger, and then a pink, fat hand, poke through the damaged plaster above her.

Chapter 8

Half an arm was showing before Matilda got over her shock. The arm waved frantically. Who..? It had to be Liz or Cheryl or somebody she hadn't met yet. Matilda dropped the glass she had been holding against her wrist.

The arm disappeared through the hole, then more broken plaster fell onto the bed. She was enlarging the hole. The arm came down again, the wrist snapping in a beckoning motion. Whoever it was wanted her to do something. Climb up?

Somebody was trying to save her. Matilda didn't need to be asked again. She jumped onto the bed, slung her purse strap over her shoulder and grasped the hand she could barely reach with both of her own. She heard a soft grunt, and then the arm began to pull her up.

Below her in the room, the door lurched inward again and Matilda heard the chair fall over.

"What the fuck? Get her!"

She was halfway through the hole now and could see it was Cheryl, the large mute woman, red-faced and straining, her left hand grasping Matilda's as her right anchored them both to an old-style radiator. In her extremity, both eyes were focused on Matilda, seeming to plead with her to hurry.

Something touched Matilda's foot and she kicked reflexively, eliciting a yowl of pain. She let go of Cheryl with her right hand and grabbed the edge of the floorboard next to the hole. She pulled herself up as hard as she could and seemed to rocket up into Cheryl's room.

Ray's howl of rage followed her. Cheryl jumped up from the floor and grabbed two boards that were leaning against the wall, replacing them over the hole. Then she sat on the floor and covered her face in her hands, sobbing.

Matilda didn't know whether to hug her or scream. In about 30 seconds, Ray was going to be through Cheryl's door, and now he would be angry enough to kill both of them.

"We have to go!" she said. "Cheryl, we have to get out!"

The woman shook and sobbed, rolls of flesh wobbling. Matilda knelt beside her. "Come on," she said. "Let's get out of here. We can go to the police."

Cheryl dropped her hands, shaking her head, no. She heaved herself onto her knees and pointed.

Her room's window was open, and there were no bars.

Matilda felt hope. "Let's go!" She jumped up and ran over to the window, sticking her head out. The broken sidewalk looked very far away. It looked like it wanted to break a couple of her legs. But that would be better than staying here.

Booted feet were pounding up the stairs. Matilda pulled her head in and saw that Cheryl's door was closed, but there was no way to know if it was locked. She found that the other woman had moved and now was standing beside her, making indecipherable gestures and then pointing to herself, then repeating the pattern, faster. Her eyes kept darting toward the door.

"I don't understand!" Matilda cried. "You want to go first? You --"

Cheryl shook her head violently and mouthed, no! Then she reached out and picked Matilda up. Matilda's instinct was to resist, but whatever the woman's idea was, there was no time for anything else. Cheryl pivoted and swung Matilda's feet and legs out the window, and Matilda felt panic.

"No! It's too far!"

Cheryl shook her head again. Matilda now was resting with her stomach on the windowsill, her legs dangling outside. Cheryl grabbed both of her hands. Behind her, there was the click of a key turning in a lock.

Matilda understood. She scooted backward on her stomach until the only things supporting her were Cheryl's sweaty hands. The woman's grip was iron as she lowered Matilda as far as she could. Matilda looked up in wonder at the angel who was saving her, the one who would not escape Ray's wrath, and saw Cheryl was smiling through her tears as she let go.

Matilda landed on her feet and absorbed as much of the impact as she could by bending her knees, but when her butt hit the sidewalk she still howled. It knocked all the wind out of her. Matilda knew she had to get up. Her whole body hurt when tried to move, but she jumped to her feet and ran. It was dark, so she went toward the neon lights of town. Behind her she could hear doors slamming and motors being started.

Cheryl! There was no way to help her friend that didn't include getting away right now.

The alcohol and drugs slowed her down, and it felt like every frantic step forward was accompanied by two or three staggering steps to the side. Her purse, never heavy before, now repeatedly dragged her off course. But the image of Edwards' greasy fingers touching her hair stayed with her, and she welcomed it, using it whenever her legs wanted to fall out from under her. She could not stop, could not be caught.

I'm not going to outrun them. They have cars. I have to hide.

The idea was simple, but in her panic she had been running right down the middle of the street. Without slowing, she veered to her right through someone's yard. Frantic, she looked around, but the lot was close to a streetlight, so there was no darkness to help conceal her. She kept running until something stopped her and she fell down.

A small chain-link fence lined the back of the yard, probably marking the property line. Matilda thought she heard a revving engine from the direction of the street. Biting back a scream, she jumped up and leapt over the fence, but her sneaker caught and was ripped off her foot, falling back into the yard.

Tildy burst into fresh tears, which made her angry. She started to turn away and keep running, but then she thought she wouldn't get far with one shoe. She stumbled back to the fence and leaned over it, grabbing her beloved Converse just as Ray's truck pulled into the house's gravel driveway.

Now she did scream. But she didn't freeze. Matilda jammed her foot back into the shoe and ran, her breath coming in sobs. She was in another yard, this one darker, but it was too close to her pursuers to try hiding now. She ran past the side of the house and came upon another street, turning right, but that would take her back in the direction of the old hotel. Her feet pounded the cracked and pitted sidewalk. Across the street was an alley.

Thank God, thank you thank you …

She flew into the mouth of the alley just as headlights appeared at the corner of the street she had just left. They couldn't have seen her, but they might have. She ran.

The alley ended in an empty, unlighted parking lot. Matilda crossed it and found a street. She turned left, hopefully toward the main part of town.

Now her legs were beginning to fail, and her breath was coming in hoarse gasps. She slowed and found it was even harder to walk straight than it had been to run. She had no momentum to help.

What did they give me?

Hiding behind a gas station, long since closed, Matilda rested in the high weeds and assessed her situation. She had cuts on her hand and wrist from the glass from her window. Her face hurt from being struck by that crazy bastard Edwards. Her arms felt like they had been yanked out of their sockets. She was sure that her ass was going to be as bruised as her psyche.

Car lights grew closer to her and she realized that sound she kept hearing was her own whimpering. There was only one tree and the low brush behind the station. Matilda got onto her hands and knees, and crawled deep into the sharp brush. She lay down flat with her purse beneath her head.

It seemed like hours before the night grew silent. Matilda was too scared to get up and look around. The insects and other native New Mexican creatures that were climbing around on her were not important. There was no way she was going to stand up. Maybe ever.

Either the alcohol or the trauma caused her to slip in and out of sleep. She may have only slept for a moment, but it was long enough for her to dream. Her head was filled with graphic visions of Mr. Edwards descending on her; his mouth open and his zipper down.

How had she gotten herself into this situation? She knew better than this.

She had acted against everything she believed. The police needed to know what was happening, but she was a runaway. Matilda didn't want to be arrested, but even more than that she didn't want her grandparents to know what had happened to her. And what had almost happened to her.

The sun was just starting to rise as she headed toward town again. Her clothes were torn from the briars she had been laying on. What would she do? Where would she go?

Matilda walked towards the bus station, staying close to the buildings in case she needed to hide again. She worried about the women, especially Cheryl, that were staying in that house of horrors. What would they do to the woman who had helped her escape? What had they done to Sherry? How many times had they done this to women?

Her eyes filled with tears and she squeezed them closed. "You do not get to cry over situations that you wouldn't be in if you would have stayed in Missouri," she said aloud.

She was grateful there was nobody in the bus station other than Meredith.

"What in God's name happened to you?" Meredith asked as soon as Matilda stumbled through the glass doors.

"Can I please hide in here?" Matilda begged. She looked out the large picture windows, feeling like right now when she was so close to being safe was when Ray and Edwards would show up to take her back.

Meredith nodded. "Of course you can, honey. Is someone chasing you? Are you all right?"

"I don't know if I'm all right, but I will be," Matilda said. "There was someone chasing me, but I hope they gave up."

"Do you need me to call the police?"

"No, I'm okay." Matilda said.

Meredith still looked alarmed and a little angry. She too looked through the large windows as if to find the people who had hurt Matilda. "Why don't you go try to get cleaned up a little, child? You know where the restroom is."

Matilda felt like she weighed tons, but she dragged herself into the ladies' room.

The vision she saw looking back at her from the mirror was alien. Her lips and chin were stained red from the gelatin she'd thrown up. Her left cheek was swollen and purple. There were leaves and debris in her hair.

Worst was her eyes, now done with crying, dark and hollow. She looked into her own face and saw a corpse, but she was too exhausted and damaged to be appalled.

Matilda filled her hands with soap and scrubbed at her skin, but she couldn't scrub it away. The soap burned in the cuts and abrasions on her hands and wrists, and pieces of glass and gravel clinked in the bottom of the sink. The red stains on her face blurred into the irritation caused by her nails and the soap. Still she scrubbed. She felt like she would never be clean again.

She ran her fingers through her hair, and shook it out. Her shirt was torn and strewn with vomit and blood, and her jeans had blood and filth on them from her jump from the window.

She didn't want to leave this bathroom. It wasn't the cleanest she'd ever been in, but it felt safe.

Someone knocked at the door and Matilda almost screamed.

"I'm almost done," she called. Her hand shook as she reached for the door handle.

Meredith was standing outside the door. "Are you all right?"

She nodded her head, but her eyes betrayed her when they filled with tears.

"Did somebody hurt you?"

"I'll be okay. They took my clothes." She tugged on the tail of her shirt. "I don't know what I'm going to do."

"We'll get you sorted." Meredith put her arm around Matilda, and gave her a gentle squeeze.

Meredith went to the counter and made a phone call. "Come watch the station for a minute, please. I have a little emergency to deal with."

A few minutes later a tall, middle-aged African American man wearing an apron came in. "Everything all right, babe?" he asked Meredith.

"I just need to run ..." She looked at Tildy. "Matilda? Right? I need to run her to the house for a little bit."

"Okay. Take as much time as you need. I have two line cooks this morning, so the cafe is covered."

"Thanks, Larry. We'll hurry back." Meredith grabbed her purse from behind the counter and led Matilda out the rear door to her Lincoln behind the building. Tildy winced as she sat down in the car, thinking of the grime she would be leaving on Meredith's passenger seat, but Meredith apparently didn't give it a second thought.

Meredith turned left out of the bus station lot. Matilda sank into the comfort of the seat, looking out the window as Tucumcari started its day. The little city had seemed like a circle of hell just a few hours ago, but now it looked like people were just going about their regular lives as if there were no such things as evil and horror. The contrast confounded Tildy. *People should know,* she thought. *They should know the things that are happening right outside their doors.*

She dared not lean her head back, knowing she would fall asleep instantly.

"Thank you for this," she said softly. Meredith huffed.

"Matilda, there are bad people out there. I don't know what you're running from, but there has to be a safer way to get there."

Matilda couldn't disagree with that. Still, she didn't want Meredith to think she was just some spoiled kid who ran away from home.

"It's kind of hard to explain," she said. "My mother disappeared in 1967. I'm trying to find her. She spent a few weeks in Tucumcari late that year."

"Oh my," Meredith said. "I'm so sorry."

"Where are we going?" Tildy asked, apprehensive. This neighborhood looked a lot like the one she had escaped last night. "Please, don't go this way."

"Is it the old motel?"

Matilda nodded.

"Son of a bitch!" Meredith said, turning a few streets before the motel. "Every town has their undesirables. I'm just sorry that you met ours. Are you all right? They didn't hurt you, did they?"

"I escaped before they could do much." Matilda blushed, looking down at the scabs starting to form on the palm of her hands.

A few minutes later, Meredith pulled the car into the driveway of a Spanish style ranch home. Mesa Tucumcari was visible behind it.

"You have a beautiful home," Matilda said politely as she got out of the car.

"Thanks. It took a lot of hard work, but nothing worthwhile is ever easy," Meredith said.

Tildy followed her to the front door and into the house. The house was decorated much like Meredith -- elegant and understated. There weren't knick-knacks or dried flower arrangements covering the terracotta walls. Instead there were abstract paintings scattered throughout the entryway and into the living space.

"Wow!" Matilda said, admiring a painting by the front door.

"My son, Joe. We sent him to business school, so of course, he became an artist instead."

"Did he paint all of these?"

Meredith sat her purse down. "Yes, we were his best client while he was struggling. Now he has his own gallery in Taos. Come on. Let's see what I have for you to wear."

Meredith led her down the hall to a bedroom. "This is Tony, my younger son's, room. He is in the Air Force." She dug through a closet that was full to bursting with clothes. Meredith tossed some jeans, sweats, and shirts onto the bed.

"These will be too loose on you, but we'll try." Meredith left the room, then came back with tube socks and a pair of boys' boxer shorts, of all things. For a second, despite her exhaustion and grief, Matilda had to stifle a grin.

"There is a shower in my room. Use anything you like," Meredith said, directing her to a room at the end of the hall.

"Thank you," Matilda said. "I don't know how --"

"You're welcome," Meredith said brusquely. "I'll give you some privacy."

Matilda locked the bathroom door behind her and peeled off her filthy clothes. She looked at the bruises on her backside in the mirror. When she climbed into the powerful shower, the dirt and dried blood on her turned the water rusty brown before it flowed down the drain. Matilda turned the knob to its hottest setting and let the shower scald her.

She squirted strawberry scented shampoo onto her hair and lathered her hair into a fruit frenzy. She felt ten pounds lighter when she climbed out of the shower.

The clothes didn't fit, but they were close enough. At five foot ten, she hadn't found many jeans for girls that were long enough, but these were too long. She rolled them into a cuff. Matilda didn't know much about sports, but the Lakers t-shirt felt like the softest, most comfortable thing she'd ever worn. The boxers, not so much.

She picked through her hair with her fingers and borrowed a ponytail holder to tie it back. There was a hairbrush in a green plastic holder on the sink counter, but she would feel weird using someone else's brush.

Before exiting the bathroom she threw her clothes into the trash.

Meredith must have heard the door open. She met her in the hallway. "You look just like my Tony. Well, if he were shorter, female, and white." Meredith laughed.

Matilda smiled. "Thank you for this." She gestured to her clothes.

"It's no problem. I wish I could have been more helpful to you that first day we met, but I've been conned so many times that it makes a person skeptical."

Matilda nodded. "I understand. I'll try to get out of your hair as soon as I can."

"No, I don't mean you, child. I feel … I could kick myself for not doing something about you that first day. Maybe things wouldn't have been so hard on you."

Matilda thought about it and kind of agreed. Meredith was under no obligation then or now, but a little Christian charity could have gone a long way and might have spared Tildy a ton of pain. But no one could have known that. Still, Matilda couldn't picture her grandma ever turning away someone in need no matter how many times she had been "conned" in the past. Although Grandma wouldn't mind telling the person every single mistake they had ever made to get into "such a fix."

"It's okay," she said to Meredith. "There was no way for you to know I was going to get into so much trouble."

The woman still looked pained as she led Matilda into a bright yellow kitchen. Two large, steaming mugs of black coffee were on the kitchen island, and Matilda didn't remember the last time she had seen anything so beautiful. Meredith waved her to a stool and sat across from her. Matilda gulped, burning her tongue, then gulped some more anyway. The cup was more than half empty when she found her voice again.

"Do you think you could help me find out where Walt's Coffee Shop was at? I just want to find this guy, and then I can get out of this town," Matilda said. She dug into her purse for *The Great American Road Trip* and pulled out a slip of paper. "I need to find a Lawrence, or it might be Larry, Noble or a woman named Juanita. I don't know her last name. They were friends of my mother's while she was here."

Meredith stared at her with her eyes wide, and her mouth agape. "Matilda, are you sure it's Larry Noble you're looking for?"

Tildy nodded. She pulled out her mother's letter from Tucumcari, and found the part where it mentioned Larry. She pointed out the paragraphs and handed the letter to Meredith.

Working at Walt's is pretty easy. I make alright tips waiting tables. I made a few friends that you'll have to meet when I drag you back to this town in a few years. Juanita is the head waitress. She's funny. She says if somebody complains about their order, just tell them I don't speak no good English. She says it always works for her!

Larry Noble is the dishwasher. He and his wife let me crash on their couch when Ophelia broke down. He was a mechanic in the Army, so he's going to help me fix her once I can buy the part. That should be Monday when Walter, the cafe owner, pays me.

Meredith's hand went to her mouth. "My Lord," she said. "How did I not see it? You're the spitting image. Come on, there is something you need to see."

She walked to her bedroom, beckoning Matilda to follow. There she pointed to a picture hanging on the wall. It was a black and white portrait of an African American couple dressed in formal clothes. It appeared to be their wedding day.

"On January 7, 1963, at the Tucumcari courthouse, I married Lawrence Noble," Meredith said.

Matilda gaped. She felt like she was going to pass out. "You knew my mother?"

"Only as a casual acquaintance. Larry worked with her at Walt's. She spent a few nights on our couch when she ran out of cash. The boys loved her. And she … She's still one of our favorite people. But that's not my story to tell. Let's go talk to Larry," Meredith said.

Chapter 9

The man she now knew was Larry Noble carried a coffee pot over and filled Meredith's cup as they sat at the counter. "I had heard someone was asking about Walt's?"

Matilda didn't say anything for a minute. Her eyes dropped to her glass of Dr. Pepper.

"Go ahead," Meredith urged her. "You didn't come this far to get cold feet now."

"Yeah. Annette, my mom, used to work there back in '67."

The man stood across the counter from Tildy, expressionless. He flipped over another cup on its saucer and poured himself a coffee, then reached behind himself without looking to set the coffee pot back onto its cradle. He raised his cup halfway to his mouth, then seemed to forget what he was doing.

"My God," he said softly. "You're her, the baby she left behind."

Matilda felt her face reddening. To hide her discomfort, she dug into one of the envelopes and rummaged around until she found her mom's photo.

Larry took it from her, his eyes widening. "Yes, I knew your mother. How is she?"

Tildy's heart went into her throat. "I don't know how she is, because she's missing. I was hoping you might have information that could help me find her."

Before he could answer the waitress came over. "Can I get you something?"

"Toast, please." Matilda answered.

"That's not much food," Larry judged.

"Don't got much money."

"What is it about the women in your family rolling into a town penniless?" Larry asked in mock irritation, but his eyes were twinkling. "Debbie, please, bring our guest the special."

"Sure, Mr. Noble." She looked at Matilda. "How would you like your eggs, ma'am?"

"Scrambled," Matilda said.

"Sausage, ham, or bacon?" the waitress asked.

"Bacon." She wanted this women to leave her alone, but she also wanted food.

"Hash browns or home fries?" The waitress smiled.

"Hash browns, I guess."

"Toast, biscuit, or pancakes?"

"Toast is fine. Thank you." She wanted this, the longest conversation she'd ever had about breakfast, to be over so she could talk to Larry.

"Thanks, Deb. We'll have it over there," Larry said, nodding toward a booth by the window. He led Matilda over and sat across from her, scooting over to give Meredith room to sit beside him.

"How long has your mother been missing?"

"The last letter we got from her was dated November 30, 1967. Is there anything that you know that might help me find her?"

"Your mom took out of here 'roundabout Halloween. I'm sorry that I don't remember the date, but that's been near ..."

"Seventeen years ago," Matilda said, finishing his sentence.

"You must have been just a baby," Meredith said. Matilda nodded.

The bell tied to the front door jingled, and a group of women came in. Meredith stood up so Larry could get out and go seat them. Matilda watched him call the customers by their names and say something that made them laugh before guiding them to a table. Tildy noticed Meredith looked amused.

"He's still got it," Meredith said. "Charmer."

After a few minutes, the waitress brought Matilda an enormous plate of food.

"Thank you," she said. Her mouth watered, and she didn't believe she had ever smelled anything so good. Tildy was surprised to see her right hand shook a little as she reached for her fork. Her stomach protested as she bit into the crispy bacon, but after a moment it settled down.

Larry came back to the booth. "Sorry about that," he said. "I try to help out when I'm on the floor. We're a little busier than usual today."

"It's all right," Matilda said. She scooped some scrambled eggs onto a piece of grape-jellied toast as Meredith watched, apparently somewhere between amused and unnerved.

"Sir, what can you tell me about my mother?" Matilda asked.

"Call me Larry. She was a hard worker. She was brave, and she was one of the most stubborn woman I'd ever met. Not counting my wife." He smiled and put his hand over Meredith's.

His wife rolled her eyes. "Kiss-up," she accused.

"The letter said that you both worked at Walt's Cafe," Tildy said.

He nodded. "That's right. I washed dishes and cooked on occasion. Your mother, she was a waitress. She was a good one. She didn't treat anybody any different because of what they looked like. Just did her work and went on her way."

"That's good. My grandparents raised her right."

"That who's raising you?" he asked.

"Yeah. Them and my aunt."

He sipped his coffee. "A while after she lit out a man came around looking for her. He said he was a private detective. He asked everyone at Walt's about your mom. I tried to tell him what

I knew, but he told me that he didn't have any interest in talking to a ... black man."

"What? My aunt said that my grandparents spent all their money trying to find my mother."

"I finally wrote what I knew on a napkin and had one of the waitresses give it to him. We never saw him again, and as far as I know nobody else ever came looking for Annette."

"I'm sorry that man disrespected you," Tildy said. "I know the man my grandparents hired. He goes to our church back home. I've never liked him."

"That makes two of us," Meredith chimed in. "I didn't meet him, but Juanita said he gave her the creeps."

I'm going to have some questions for Russell Claxton when I get back home, Tildy thought. "Her car broke down here? That's what she said in the letter."

"Well, your mom was here about three weeks. She left in a hurry, and didn't have a chance to get her final check."

"Why was she in such a hurry to leave?"

"It's a long story. The sixties were a much different time." Larry looked into his coffee. "It was all a huge misunderstanding, but that's all it took back then."

"What happened?"

"After work one night I was trying to work on your mom's car. I had been a mechanic in the Army," Larry said. He was interrupted by the return of the waitress.

"Are you guys doing okay? Can I get you anything else?"

"Get Matilda another Dr. Pepper," Larry said, taking the ticket, signing his name on it, and handing it back.

Meredith made a shooing motion to her husband to let her out of the booth. "I am going back to the bus station. I've heard all these stories before, and 35 is due from Kansas City," she said. "But they're always late."

Larry stood up so she could take her leave. She kissed him on the cheek and gave Tilidy a little wave as she left.

When she was gone, Larry was quiet for a minute. Matilda was dying to hear the story, but she didn't prod.

"The springs needed work and she had a busted tie rod end, so after work one night I was looking at it with her. It was sitting in the back parking lot at Walt's. When she couldn't afford to have it fixed, Nelson -- the mechanic -- towed it over there and dumped it," he said.

Debbie deposited a fresh soda, refilled Larry's coffee cup and took Matilda's empty plate. Matilda wondered if Debbie was a little bit of a brown-noser. She couldn't remember the last time a waitress had been so attentive to her needs.

"One of the diner's regular customers, Gary Turner, confronted us. He thought I was going to attack your mother because I was black. We tried to reason with him, but there was no use. Annette decided she probably should go ahead and leave town to avoid any more trouble."

***

Larry Noble wasn't about to tell this child what really happened the night her mother fled from Tucumcari, thinking the police were right behind her and ready to arrest her for murder.

It wasn't the dry season, which was winter, but it still had been a surprise earlier in the day when it had rained for a solid hour. That happened only a couple times a year, usually in the spring, but it was just Larry's luck.

The Bug -- what did she call it, Ophelia? -- was jacked up by the front bumper as the only mechanic Annette Banks could afford wallowed beneath it in the mud of the diner's back parking lot. The unsteady bumper jack worried him, but he didn't have any blocks handy and didn't intend to be under here for very long, just long enough to see what needed fixing. He might be able to find what Annette needed at a junkyard and get her back on the road.

214

The moon was just a sliver hidden by the clouds, and the lot was unlighted. Larry used a small flashlight to inspect the damage. The tie rod was busted through. It was a miracle the girl hadn't flipped the car when it went. The shocks looked like they were original equipment -- well past their useful life -- and the springs were in decent shape except for one of the mounts.

I'm going to have to weld a plate there, he thought. Drill and tap a couple holes ... Larry cussed to himself. This wasn't going to be a quick or cheap fix if he did it right, but he couldn't have the woman taking off down the road in a deathtrap.

The freezing mud got through his black polyester pants, which hadn't put up much of a fight. Larry would have groaned if Annette hadn't been standing right by the car. The cold and wet had him in a mood, and the car's owner wasn't helping.

"Can you see anything? How much is it going to cost?" Annette asked. He could barely see her white sneakers shuffling nervously next to the jack's base. *God, don't hit that,* he thought.

"Don't know yet," he answered shortly. It wasn't the first time she had asked. He was trying to be patient, but Lord.

Then someone else was there.

Larry couldn't have said how he knew. In Vietnam, sometimes the guys who made it back didn't survive because they saw, heard or smelled the enemy. It was a matter of feeling the enemy.

He was already scrambling out from beneath the car when a voice whip-cracked through the night. "What the hell is going on here?"

Annette gave a little shriek. Larry's head cleared the vehicle's undercarriage and he saw Gary, one of the regulars at the diner, about ten feet away and stumbling toward them. Larry got to his feet slowly as Annette backed away around the front of the car.

"What you doin' out here in the dark with a white woman, boy?" the man said.

Larry concealed his immediate anger. "Just taking a look at the car here," he said.

Gary seemed like he had been drinking some, and he wasn't a nice guy when he was sober. Juanita regularly cussed him in Spanish because of his lousy tips, usually a few pennies if anything. And the man complained about everything, sitting at the counter for a couple hours each morning, expecting to be served like he was a king.

"You better be sure that's all you're doin'," Gary said. "Some of us been thinking you're a little too friendly with this white girl. We seen you joking around all the time in the restaurant." Gary jerked his head toward the closed diner as if they wouldn't know where he was talking about.

Larry didn't know Annette all that well, but he had seen flashes of her temper. Now he saw it in full bloom.

Annette marched back around the front of the car, her white shoes sinking into the mud as she stomped. "He's just looking at the car, you bumpkin asshole," she hissed. "Why don't you crawl back into whatever hole you crawled out of and leave us alone?"

Larry could barely make out the man's features in the dimness, but he could almost feel Gary's instant rage.

"I'm going to get you fired for that, bitch," Gary said. "You can't talk to me that way." He took a step toward Annette, fists clenched, but she wasn't backing down.

"That's right, why don't you go and tattle on me to Walt?" Annette said, now close enough to poke a finger in Gary's chest. "You're nothing but a damned coward. And a lousy --"

Gary swung his right arm from his side and struck Annette on the left side of her head, knocking her against Ophelia. The jack slipped out from under the front of the car and the Bug crashed into the mud.

Larry acted on instinct, grabbing Gary's jacket sleeve and pivoting, spinning him away from Annette. Gary stumbled and fell on his butt, grunting.

"You touched me," he said, looking up at Larry in shock. "You put your hands on me, you black bastard."

Now we're in it, Larry thought for the first time since leaving the jungle.

"Look," he said, holding up his hands. It was probably way too late to defuse this situation, but he tried anyway. "I ain't messing around with a white woman or any woman who ain't my wife. I don't need any trouble."

"I don't give a rat's ass what you need, boy," Gary said, struggling to his feet, then reaching into his corduroy jacket. "All I know is what you're gonna get."

His hand came out with a small automatic handgun.

Larry froze as the muzzle pointed at his heart. This redneck son of a bitch was going to kill him. Larry slowly began to back away. He was calm. He didn't want Annette to see this happen. She also had regained her feet, but he couldn't see her behind the enemy.

"You touched me," Gary said again, his voice on the edge of hysteria. "That was your last mistake. Ain't no jury in this county going to convict me for killing a nigger who knocked me down."

"This doesn't have to happen," Larry said. Meredith. The boys. *Meredith. I'm so sorry.*

Gary barked a laugh and raised the gun to eye level, his arm fully extended. "Oh yes it --"

The sound was like a hammer hitting meat. Gary dropped the gun, his eyes rolling up in his head, and collapsed to the muck.

Annette stood behind his crumpled body, holding the jack handle, her face moon white.

Oh my God, Larry thought. He took two uneven steps and fell to his knees beside Gary. It was too dark, too dark to see the blood, but he could smell it.

Annette dropped the iron bar. It landed point down and stuck in the mud, standing at a crazy angle. Annette screamed and covered her face with her hands, stumbling away.

Gary wasn't moving. Larry was pretty sure he wasn't breathing. He held the back of his cold hand in front of Gary's nose and felt nothing. Gary's eyes were open.

The wind, strong and bitter cold all day, now whipped into a frenzy. Larry shuddered and Annette sobbed.

"We got to get you out of here," he said, looking up. Her feet were braced, but she looked like she might blow away. Gone was the naive but funny waitress who had taken to reading to his boys every night, making up ridiculous new twists to the stories they had heard before just to hear them giggle. Gone was the sad but determined traveler who would not give up her journey no matter what obstacles she faced. Now she was frail and in shock and totally without hope.

Larry stood up and got moving. He looked for the gun and felt an instant of panic when he didn't see it immediately. Then his foot kicked it. He picked it up and pulled back the slide, ejecting the chambered round, then dropped the seven-round magazine from the bottom of the handgrip. He released the slide and flipped the safety switch on the left side downward, all without thinking about it. They all worked pretty much the same. This one was old enough to have a swastika and eagle emblem on the side. The sight of it made Larry's blood run cold. This weapon likely had killed before.

He reinserted the ejected bullet into the spring-loaded magazine, then pocketed the magazine and the gun.

Annette was still crying, still looking defeated, but she was watching him.

Larry picked up the crowbar. He couldn't see anything on it, but there was probably blood and hair, and certainly it held Annette's fingerprints as well as his own. He squatted by the body and used a a flap of Gary's jacket and wiped it as clean as he could. It would have to disappear.

Now. Now what? "We have to get you out of here," he told Annette again. He dug in his pocket for his keys and held them out. "Go wait in the truck, and get the heater going. No lights."

For a moment he didn't think she was going to respond, but then she held out her hand and he dropped the truck keys in them. She turned and headed toward his aged International pickup, and Larry turned back to his work.

In the soup, he had been calm enough during a firefight. It was afterward that he hid from his buddies to get through the shakes. He could feel the shakes coming on, but there was still too much to do.

If this happened here, it wouldn't take a genius to point the finger at Annette and him. So this had to happen somewhere else.

That meant this whole mess needed to be cleaned up, and Gary had to be moved.

When Larry thought about all the footprints in the mud that would need to be wiped away in the pitch dark, he almost cried. But first things first. He couldn't leave a car without front tires sitting in the mud without a jack, and he couldn't just jack it up and leave it on the jack with no jack handle there. It would look weird to anybody who walked by.

So he had to put the tires back on. First things first.

It took an hour to get everything done, and it probably still wasn't perfect, but it was the best Larry could do in these conditions. He had thought about asking Annette to help erase the footprints, but she had been staring, motionless, out the pickup's cracked windshield when he had gone to rummage for fresh flashlight batteries in his glovebox. He didn't think she was going to be much help for anything for a while.

The panic and adrenaline had faded by the time he dragged Gary to the truck and lowered the tailgate. Larry was so tired he could barely lift the man into the bed of the truck, but he got it done. Gary's head flopped lifelessly on his neck during the maneuver, and Larry went to the side of the pickup and threw up everything he had ever eaten.

Wiping his mouth on his mud-caked sleeve, he clambered into the driver's seat. Annette still wasn't moving or reacting. Larry leaned his head back for a minute, closing his eyes.

He had no idea what he was going to do with the body.

The truck was warm, maybe too warm. Larry opened his eyes and found the temperature gauge. The truck had been idling all this time, but the gauge still wasn't much above the middle of the dial. He sighed with relief.

Larry stomped on the clutch and grabbed the gearshift, muscling it into first. He waited until he got to the edge of the parking lot before turning on the headlights as he made a left turn onto Route 66 and headed west.

And straight into a miracle.

Sparks flew and light flashed to his right and Larry stood on the brakes. The truck engine died unnoticed as Larry and Annette gaped at the sight of the Wild Heron Motel's neon sign crashing to the asphalt parking lot. The gusty winds had been too much for it.

And just that fast, Larry knew exactly how Gary had died.

***

"She took off that night, and I never heard from her again," Larry said. "I'm sorry that I don't know what happened after that. The VW sat in the back a while, but I eventually got it fixed and kept it safe. I had hoped that your mom would come back so I could give it back."

220

"Thank you. Thanks for telling me what happened, and for being my mom's friend. Do you know what happened to it?"

"The car?" he asked.

"Yes. Did you sell it or scrap it?"

"It's up on blocks in the back of my garage."

"Holy shit! You still have Ophelia?" Matilda said, louder than she intended. A few of the restaurant patrons' heads tilted toward them momentarily, then returned to their own business.

"I'll get Ophelia off the stands, change her oil, and she'll be ready for you to take to go find your mom. If that's all right with you."

Matilda nodded, tears threatening. "Thank you, that would be so wonderful. I only have fifteen dollars and some change, so I don't have anything to repay you, but I can try when I get back home."

He held up his hand. "Consider it a donation to the cause. When you find your mom, drop us a line so we know how everything goes. I can have the car ready this evening, but why don't you wait until the morning to leave? That way you won't be driving into the sun."

"I don't have anywhere to stay." She didn't make eye contact.

"Meredith has a ticket agent coming in at five, and then she can get you set up in the boys' old room for the night."

Matilda felt tears threatening. "I don't know how to thank you and Meredith. You … I'm a little overwhelmed."

Larry smiled. "You know what? You don't need to thank us for anything. Your mom ..." He paused so long Tildy wondered if he had lost his train of thought. "Your mom was good to us at a time there weren't a lot of white people being good to us."

Matilda smiled. "I'm glad. That would make my grandparents very proud."

"They should be," Larry agreed. "I thought about trying to write to her after she didn't come back for her car, but then that private eye showed up. I figured if she wanted to be found, she would be. Then it got to be years gone by."

Matilda didn't understand that. Why would her mom not want to be found? She wondered if there were something Larry wasn't telling her.

"Is there a pay phone nearby?" Matilda asked. "I need to make a call."

"There is a phone in my office you can use." He pointed her toward the door marked PRIVATE.

Matilda looked at the photos on the office wall. It was Larry and Meredith posing with famous people and in front of fancy cars. President Carter smiled in one photo; Paul Newman leaned against a vintage Porsche in another. Larry stood in front of a Route 66 sign with Burt Reynolds and a sports car she didn't recognize.

Matilda was floored by the generosity of some of the people she'd met on her journey. But she was also horrified by some of the others, and it was time to do something about it. For Cheryl's sake. She sat down to make her call.

"Hello operator. Please get me the Tucumcari Police Department. Yes, I'll hold."

A dusky male voice answered the phone. "Tucumcari Police. Sergeant Dale speaking."

She swallowed hard. "I want to report some women being kept against their will at the Tucumcari Arms Motel."

A long moment of silence ensued. Then, "Ma'am, let me transfer you to a detective."

The line clicked. There was no hold music. A minute later, the line clicked again. "Hello."

Matilda said it again, exactly the way she'd practiced it all night while she lay in the briars behind the dead gas station. "I want to report some women being kept against their will at the Tucumcari Arms Motel."

"That's a pretty serious accusation," the detective drawled. "Why don't you tell me where you are so I can come take your statement, Missourah."

Edwards.

Matilda slammed the phone down onto its cradle, shuddering. It was going to be a long time before the idea of that man didn't fill her with panic. Could he have traced the call? No, on TV it always took a few minutes. And he asked her where she was, so he probably didn't know. Still, it was a full minute before she could stop shaking.

Matilda picked up the phone again. She dialed the number with trembling hands. It hadn't finished its first ring before someone picked up.

"Hello." The voice sounded foreign yet familiar.

"Aunt Caroline?"

"Matilda! Oh thank God. Where are you?" There were tears in her voice.

"I'm safe."

"Where are you?" she demanded.

"I only have a couple minutes. It's long distance. Are you guys all right?"

"Everyone is worried sick. Your grandfather spent the night in the hospital. You have to end this foolishness and come home now!"

"Stop! I love you. I love Granddad and Grandma, but I have to finish this. I will be home as soon as I can."

"You have never been whipped the way I am going to whip you when you get back," Caroline started.

Matilda sighed. Her aunt went on for a couple minutes, piling guilt on guilt. Finally Matilda interrupted her. "I am sorry I have hurt everyone, but I am getting closer to Mom. I know I am."

Caroline paused. "That doesn't seem like it can be true. Please come home, Tildy."

"I can't. Not yet."

"I do not support this. You are being a selfish bitch! You are destroying this family!"

The words lashed her. "I'm sorry," Matilda mumbled and hung up the phone. What had she expected? They would forgive her in due time. She hoped.

She was so tired. Matilda sat at Larry's desk with her elbows propped on his desk calendar, her chin resting on her palms. She could go to sleep right here.

To keep from doing so, she looked around the small office again. Larry Noble certainly had come up in the world since his days as a dishwasher, it seemed like. The things he had chosen to keep and frame told a lot about him, and because he had been her mom's friend, they kind of told Matilda something about her as well.

Her eyes fell on a framed newspaper clipping she hadn't noticed before. It was from the Tucumcari News and dated Thursday, Nov. 2, 1967.

The headline read: *Local man survives falling hotel sign.*

Tildy wondered what was so interesting about this article to Larry. She could get why he had saved all his photos with celebrities, but this seemed out of place. And the article was dated just after her mom left this town.

By Carl Revis

Staff writer

A man who was apparently knocked into a coma by a falling hotel sign Monday evening awakened early Wednesday.

Gary Turner, 52, of Willowcreek Drive, is listed in stable condition, the hospital said Wednesday.

Turner was found at approximately 8:22 p.m. Monday partially under the collapsed sign of the Wild Heron Motel on Route 66, according to a police report.

Police believe Turner was walking home after spending several hours at a local tavern when the sign fell on him, striking him in the head, the report said.

The report indicated that unusually high winds Monday might have contributed to the sign's collapse. Other minor damage occurred throughout the town, according to the police, but no other injuries were reported.

Gary Turner was the name of the man Larry said confronted him and Annette. And it happened right around Halloween.

Matilda didn't know what was going on, but now she was sure Larry hadn't told her the whole story. But she couldn't think of any reason he might lie to her.

Weed the row you're standing in, she thought. Another of Grandma's Greatest Hits. Her cheek still ached from where Edwards had struck her. She lifted her hand to the bruise and cupped it. It felt hot.

One way or another, she would see that somebody knew what was happening there. She had one last call to make.

"Hello operator, connect me with the Tucumcari local newspaper." She would Woodward and Bernstein their asses.

"Tucumcari Times, Tracey speaking. How may I help you?"

"I want to report some women being kept against their will at the Tucumcari Arms Motel. The people holding them are named Ray and Carrie. Detective Edwards and his son, Donald, are in on it."

"Oh my gosh. Please repeat the names, so I can get them to the news desk. Also, can I get your name?"

Matilda repeated the information, and added any details she could remember including the women's names that were being held. "I'm sorry, but for my safety, I can't give you my name."

There was a knock at the door. "I have to go. Thank you." She hung up the phone as Meredith opened the door.

"Jamie showed up for work for a change, so I'm taking the rest of the day off," she said. "You ready to go to our place?"

"Yes." She had done what she could for Ray and Carrie's victims. She grabbed her purse and followed Meredith to her car.

"Is that Larry's car?" She asked Meredith as they passed by an old steel gray Chevy.

"Yes. That's his 1952 Bel Air. It was the first car he rebuilt and sold. He didn't find it again for a long time."

"It's beautiful." Matilda admired it as she got into Meredith's car.

"Everything we have today is because of that car."

"What? Why?"

"Larry bought that car a couple years after he got out of the Army. He'd been pretty badly injured over there, and he spent a long time trying to find his place." Meredith backed out of the cafe, and headed back towards her house.

"He rebuilt that car one piece at a time while washing dishes. When he got it done, he sold it for a hefty price. After he did that five times he bought the cafe, then our home, five more times, bought the bus station, and so on. Our original plan was to buy businesses we could work at with our kids, but our kids had bigger plans."

"That's the American dream, I guess," Matilda said.

When they got back to the house Matilda helped Meredith put fresh sheets on the waterbed in the boy's room.

"I can't thank you enough for the help you've given me," Matilda said.

"You're welcome, Matilda. You know what? Sit a minute. I need to talk to you a little bit."

The women sat side by side on the end of the waterbed. Matilda wasn't comfortable, because it was almost never good news when a grownup decided they "needed" to talk to you. For a minute, Meredith was quiet, and Matilda expected the woman was gathering her thoughts and would soon launch a stern lecture about everything Tildy had messed up that led her to relying so much on the kindness of strangers. *Well, get in line behind my aunt,* she thought.

To her surprise, however, when she snuck a sideways glance at her hostess, she saw tears streaming down Meredith's face.

"He was ..." Meredith began, and then she just busted out bawling.

Matilda scooted a little closer and put her arm over Meredith's shoulders. "It's okay," she said lamely. "It's all going to be okay."

"I know," Meredith said. "Just today. It's brought back so many ..."

She couldn't keep talking. Tildy let her cry. Meredith would get around to what she needed to say, but some things couldn't be rushed. Matilda hugged the woman and for some reason remembered Granddad saying the reason turtles don't golf is it's too fast paced. And then he would laugh, and Matilda hadn't understood the joke, bad as it was, until a couple years ago.

"He was ..." Meredith sniffed and drew her sleeve over her eyes. "Larry was so hurt in the war. He came back the same but so ... I guess he just got old in Vietnam. He tried. For the boys' sake and for my sake he tried."

"My dad died in Vietnam," Matilda said.

"I know. I think that's maybe why Larry felt like we had to help Annette. I think he felt guilty for coming back."

Matilda couldn't understand that, but she could. She thought about Cheryl still trapped at the motel not three miles from where she now sat in safety. *You do feel guilty when the worst things happen to someone else and not you. But I think sometimes the reason you feel guilty is that you're ashamed that you're glad it's them instead of you.*

She would never say that to Meredith, but that was what her own experience had taught her. She still wasn't sure how she was going to live with that.

Meredith had regained some of her habitual composure and leaned a little away from Matilda, so Matilda withdrew her arm.

"You know him now," Meredith said. "He is a strong, capable, beautiful man, the same as the man I married, but better in some ways. But when he came home in '65, he was sick and hurt and trying to be strong but he was being eaten up. He tried so hard, but he just lost something over there. It was like he didn't have any faith left that anything could be good or that anyone could ever be good. Or even if they were, that being good ever meant anything."

Matilda tried to picture Larry that way but couldn't. Meredith was right; her husband was kind, generous and formidable. *Like if Santa Claus and Rambo had a kid.*

"It wouldn't have been a surprise for the Larry who came back from the war to be beat up or shot in the diner parking lot by some redneck because he was with a white woman," Meredith said. "In his mind, that was just the way the world worked. So when your mom stood up for him, it meant … It meant the world could be different. Good people could still do good things and make a difference."

Oh my God.

Larry had glossed over the seriousness of the "misunderstanding" with Gary Turner. *She thinks he told me what really happened.*

"I'm very proud of her," Matilda said, and her words felt hollow as she said them. She didn't know what else to say. *Mom did what?*

"Your mama lit a fire under him that was just ashes before," Meredith said. "Everything the war took, she gave back just in that one minute she snatched up that crowbar and hit that man. It was like --" Meredith snapped her fingers -- "snap! He started paying attention to the boys and was able to take some joy in them. He started building those old cars and I figured, well, he seems like he's happy, and then he started selling them and I thought, oh boy!

"Just about everything good I have in my life is because of what your mama did. So I don't want to hear any more thanks. And if I tell you I am sorry I didn't help you the first day I met you, don't you tell me it's okay, because it's not. I will do better."

Matilda started to cry, and Meredith started to cry again.

Larry appeared in the doorway and stared. He cleared his throat. "I can come back later," he said.

Matilda laughed. She let go of Meredith, who stood up and wiped her eyes on her sleeve again.

"None of your business, Larry."

He smiled. "I guess I can come back later," he said again.

"It's okay," Meredith said. "We're about done in here. Putting on the sheets."

"Sheets can be a sad thing," Larry observed. "I know I can start sniffling up just putting on a pillow case."

Meredith punched his shoulder and pushed past him out of the room. Larry looked like he was about to bust out laughing, but he controlled himself. "Matilda, do you want to look at your mother's car?"

"Yes!" Matilda leapt up, reminding herself in the process that every muscle in her body ached. She followed her host in a much more sedate manner.

He led her through the backyard to the largest garage-slash-workshop Tildy had ever seen. Inside were a dune buggy and a few all terrain vehicles in various states of repair, as well as several large cardboard boxes labeled with his sons' names. *Granddad would love this place,* Tildy thought.

Larry went to the far side of the huge building and pulled a painter's tarp off a blue Volkswagen Beetle.

"Ophelia," Matilda breathed. She felt like she was going to vomit again. Matilda leaned against the wall. She felt faint. "Can I touch it?"

"Of course. It's yours. I almost got rid of it a few times, but I'm glad I never did."

Matilda walked to Ophelia like she might approach a wild animal, her hand extended. She ran her fingers across the glossy blue finish and down to the chrome door handle.

"That's Pacific Blue paint. In case you ever have to match it. Do you know why she named her Ophelia?"

Matilda nodded and reached for the door handle. Ophelia was locked.

"I have the keys around here somewhere," Larry said.

"My dad's uncle, Rowdy, bought this car new," Matilda said. "He had been teaching his wife to drive it a couple years later when she lost control and drove it into a pond. Rowdy told my dad that if he fished it out he could have it."

Matilda paused, letting the memory wash over her. Grandpa Wyatt had told her the story at least a dozen times.

"My grandpa said that it took my dad a long time to get her out of the water. He was a bad swimmer, and the pond was at least 12 feet deep. Finally he got a chain around the bumper and hauled her out with my grandpa's Farmall. When he did it took even longer to get her dried out and repaired."

She let her fingers trail lightly over the passenger side window, looking into the car to get another look at the interior.

"My dad was reading Hamlet in high school, and when he read about Ophelia drowning, he knew that when she got fixed up that's what he'd name her. Ophelia returned from the dead."

"I have fixed up a ton of cars, and I never get tired of a good origin story," Larry said. He handed her a set of keys. "I'm going to change clothes and then put some fresh oil in her and put her wheels back on."

"Can I look through it?" she asked Larry when headed back to the house.

"Of course," Larry said. "Your car."

Matilda unlocked the car door gingerly, afraid for no reason that the key might break. It didn't seem possible that this was her mom's car. Her dad's car. *Her car.*

She closed her eyes when she opened the door, and let the scent of molded plastic, vinyl, and paint flood over her. Matilda had seen pictures of her dad and mom with Ophelia, but she never thought she'd meet her.

She climbed into the bucket seat, rubbed her hands across the smooth steering wheel, and fiddled with the gear shift.

Matilda turned the dial on the A.M. radio, and opened the tiny glovebox. There were some papers, probably the car title and registration, and odds and ends. Chewing gum wrappers. A rubber band that was so dried out it looked like it would fall apart if she touched it. One small wrench. A small brown paper bag, neatly folded but with what looked like grease stains on the outside.

She found something else that made her heart jump -- a letter.

The envelope said:

Annette Sterling Banks
General Delivery
Tucumcari, New Mexico

Inside was a letter.

Nettie,

We all miss you so much. Matilda has grown a lot since you've been gone. She rolls onto her tummy now, and she eats all the time. Probably gets that from you, ha ha.

Mom and Dad are worried about you, but I have faith. Whatever it is you need to find out there, know that you have my full support. I'm taking a semester off so I can help with Mattie and bills. I got my job back with Ned's.

You take your time, and come back when you're ready. We'll be here for you when you do. I am enclosing some money. Don't worry about paying me back. Use it to fix Ophelia, eat a real meal, or buy yourself something pretty.

I love you and can't wait to see you after you do what you have to do.

Love, Caroline

Matilda read the letter again. Caroline had never returned to college. She gave up her own American dream to help raise her niece.

In the envelope was a picture of Caroline and Annette as gangly teens in front of their dad's ancient Buick. They were arm in arm, crooked smiles and pigtails. How long had it been since Caroline had been happy?

"You like pizza?" Meredith called through the garage door.

"Yes," Matilda called back, holding the photo to her chest.

Meredith gave her a thumbs-up and closed the door.

Matilda finished searching the glovebox. She found an empty pack of Lucky Strikes, a toll slip and a few receipts.

The Luckys pack reminded her that she hadn't had a cigarette in a while. She took the letter to add to the ones in her purse, and returned the rest of the contents to the glovebox.

Matilda tried to open the trunk of the car to look for more mementos, but discovered that the back of the car actually housed the motor. Tildy didn't know much about cars, but this engine looked brand-new. She wondered how many hours Larry had spent out here, honing every part of this car. It was probably like a shrine for the whole family, a symbol of the woman who had been with them for such a short time but seemed to mean so much to all of them.

It would have made sense for Larry to give one of his boys this car. It was a classic and would have scored them major points with the other teenagers a few years ago. *But he kept it. It's almost like they knew I would come someday.*

Getting to the front of the car took a little time. There were old wagons, bicycles, and go carts parked in the front of the car. Matilda stood in the seat of a go cart to get close enough to pop the trunk.

There wasn't much inside. A thin flannel baby blanket that was moth chewed, a cloth sack that had been folded up, and a few steel Dr. Pepper bottle tops, bent slightly in the center from the opener. Not quite as powerful as finding Ophelia herself.

Matilda closed the trunk carefully and made her way back to the house. She didn't want to leave Ophelia, but she was craving a cigarette now. She added the letter to her mother's and tied the ribbon that held them together. She needed to find a better way to store them, because the edges were getting bent and worn.

She fished around in her purse for her lighter but couldn't find it.

"Hey, do you have a lighter I can borrow?" she asked Meredith in the kitchen.

"In the sunroom through the sliding doors." Meredith pointed to a set of sliding glass doors that led towards the back of the house.

Tildy went through the doorway, and down a few steps to a glass walled room. There was a lighter and an ashtray on a small table between wicker chairs.

She didn't like to smoke inside. It felt like an intrusion, but the ashtray, while empty, had been used for cigarette butts. Matilda sat on the love seat, and propped her feet on the ottoman.

Stretching her neck and shoulders, she leaned back and fell asleep before she could light up.

"Pizza's here." Matilda sat in the front row of church beside her grandma. "Pizza's here," Brother Bowman said again, tapping her on the shoulder.

"Matilda, come eat some pizza, and then you can go get some rest." Meredith said, standing over her.

Matilda yawned and stood up. She looked around for her cigarette but decided she'd find it later. Even out here that pizza smelled awesome.

Matilda followed Meredith into the main part of the house and into the kitchen. Larry was nowhere to be seen. Tildy suspected he was out saying goodbye to Ophelia.

The pepperoni pizza was delicious. "I've eaten more real food today than I have in a week," Matilda said.

"That's not good. You have to be taking care of yourself out there," Meredith said, her mom instincts obviously taking control. Tildy silently agreed; she hadn't done such a great job of taking care of herself so far, but that would change.

"Where is Larry?" Matilda asked to change the subject.

"He's getting your car put back together. It won't take him long. I used to think that Bug out there was going to sit in my garage forever. I trusted my husband, but everyone else thought that he was pining for your mama. We had two toddlers and a tiny little house when she stayed with us." Meredith chuckled.

"He hid that car in our backyard for a year, and when we got a house with a garage it moved indoors. Our kids grew up and moved out, but that car stayed the same."

"Thank you for taking care of it all these years," Matilda said grabbing another slice of pizza and another napkin. The pizza was good, which meant it was also a little greasy, and the sight of her own greasy fingers nauseated her a little. Mr. Edwards was still fresh in her head.

"It's going to be strange to get used to her not being out there, but I'm glad she's going back home," Meredith said.

The sound of a motor starting made Tildy's heart race. "Do you think that's her?"

Meredith smiled. "Let's go see."

The two women hurried out the front door to see Ophelia pulling around the house. Larry looked so out of place in the tiny car. His height and broad shoulders took up most of the front seats.

He climbed out, and held the door for Matilda. "I want to show you a few things in here." She climbed into the driver's seat. "She's a four speed. Can you drive a stick?"

"Of course. It's what I learned on."

Larry showed her the car's eccentricities, leaning down beside the open driver's side window to talk to her. "This doesn't have an oil filter, so you will need to have the oil changed more often," he said. "I wouldn't go more than a couple thousand miles without getting it done. Also, your valves are going to start to clatter some, but any good mechanic can adjust them. You've got forty horsepower to play with, which is really not bad with the four-speed, but you won't be going up many hills with any speed."

Matilda nodded, not caring much if the little car had some quirks. She loved it.

"Also, your heater is terrible," Larry said. "If you drive this in the wintertime in Missouri, you'll want to bundle up."

Matilda nodded again. "Change the oil, check the valves, wear a sweater," she said. "Got it!"

Larry laughed and stepped away from the car. "I think you just want to drive it. Go ahead and have fun."

Matilda eased off the clutch, slightly revved the motor and was relieved she didn't stall Ophelia on her first attempt to drive her. She headed down the driveway, pizza forgotten.

***

"There is something you need to know," Larry said, sitting at the table. "Your mom took out of here in such a hurry that she left some things behind."

"I found a few things in the glovebox." Matilda said.

"She slept on the couch in my living room for a little while. Her family, your family, sent her some cash, but when she took off it was still on my kitchen table. $200 was a lot back then. About eight months after she left I got an opportunity to buy a 1952 Chevy Bel Air. It needed some work, but I knew I could fix it up and sell it for a profit." Larry took a bite of his pizza, and got a photo album from a nearby bookcase.

"I was almost $200 short, so I borrowed it from the money your mother left behind with plans to pay it back as soon as the car sold." He flipped the album open to a photo of a beautiful vintage car. "Well, turning that car over led me to be able to do it many more times." He fluttered through the pages of the album. There were before and after shots of dozens of vehicles.

"Your mom never came back for that money. I'd like you to have it."

"Holy crap!"

He handed her two one-hundred dollar bills. "This should make your traveling a little easier."

"Wow!" was all Tildy could say. She felt tears threatening and looked down at her hands on the table. "You should … You should keep it to pay for all the work on the car. I know it must have cost more than that to fix her."

Larry barked a laugh. "That wasn't work. It was a labor of love. I'll bet there's not another 1962 Bug in this country in as good shape as Ophelia is now. As many cars as I have rebuilt, that one was the most fun. You don't owe me anything."

Matilda put the money under her pillow before she went to sleep that night. It took a long time before she could close her eyes without seeing Edwards. Bad dreams woke her through the night, and each time she checked to make sure the money was still there.

It was dumb, because these bills probably hadn't even been printed when Caroline sent the money to her mom, but when she clutched them, it felt like Aunt Caroline was holding her hand, and that made the nightmares bearable.

The next morning Meredith had packed her some clothes and snacks. She also made sure she ate breakfast.

Matilda turned the key, and the car came to life. She put on her seatbelt, and pressed the clutch. Waving to Larry and Meredith she put the car in gear. The car died as soon as she let off the clutch.

"Forgot how tight that clutch was," she said, her face hot. The Nobles just smiled. The second time she started the car she waved and drove away.

Matilda merged onto westbound Interstate 40, and drove towards Holbrook, Arizona.

Chapter 10

Ophelia was so small compared to her grandma's Buick that it was like driving a toy. Diesel trucks roared past her as she putted towards Holbrook.

A rainstorm moved across the desert towards her. It filled the western horizon. It occurred to her that it was just a little more than a week since she'd left. It felt like an eternity had passed since she'd sat at her kitchen table.

Now, instead of being surrounded by family, she was utterly alone. Her only company as she drove was the radio. The only radio station she could get was in Spanish. Most of the songs were in English though. Listening to the country music made her miss her Aunt Caroline, who loved the Judds, and would have been singing along with Wynonna as she exclaimed to her mama about her crazy boyfriend.

She passed a sign saying Albuquerque was fifty miles ahead. Bugs Bunny always said he'd taken a wrong turn at Albuquerque. Matilda hoped it was just a topical joke aimed at the adults who watched with their children, and not a warning to drivers about complicated highways.

Road work slowed her down as she entered the city limits of Albuquerque, but she was able to get through the city unscathed. She pulled in to a gas station.

"Fill it up, please," she said to the attendant. The station was tiny with outside restrooms. The attendant gave her a key fastened to a hubcap. "Thanks," she said, embarrassed.

"Gas and soda will be six dollars. That's a cute car," the attendant said when she brought the hubcap back.

"Thanks. It was my mom's."

"Be careful driving it on expired tags. Smokey is going to give you a ticket if they catch you."

She hadn't thought about that. "Crap." Opening her wallet she realized she only had hundred dollar bills. Matilda handed one to the clerk.

"I'll have to go to the office to get change," he said, annoyed.

"Sorry."

Once she was back in Ophelia, she felt more at ease. She scanned for radio stations, and found a heavy metal channel. Judas Priest echoed through the car as she got back onto the interstate.

She wasn't planning on stopping again until she got to Holbrook. That was a little over two hundred miles. Matilda eased her car into traffic, and held her breath as a diesel sped around her.

Ophelia didn't like driving over fifty, and as they drove higher into the desert mountains there was no need to worry about that. The car was struggling to do thirty.

An angry man in a pickup flipped her the bird as he passed her. There was nothing she could do about it. The little Volkswagen was not made for speed.

Mountains grew up around her as she crossed into Arizona. The Ozarks had hills, but she'd never seen anything like this. There were a lot of signs for tourist traps as she neared Holbrook. The Painted Desert and Petrified Forest were advertised on a sign inviting her to the 'legendary' Route 66 Motel.

The Route 66 Motel had a vague resemblance to its glorious photo on the billboard. It no longer had pink stucco walls, a swimming pool, or a giant dinosaur to welcome visitors. Instead the motel had white aluminum siding, a big fenced-off hole in the ground, and an overflowing dumpster.

Matilda decided to stay anyway. It was the only place she'd seen that looked like she could afford it, and she needed to stop for the night. Her whole body ached as she climbed out of the car. The last seventy miles of road work had almost shaken Ophelia apart. Tildy's hands were numb from holding the vibrating steering wheel so tightly.

There were things she needed to accomplish in Holbrook, but more than anything she needed a hot shower. The car had been so clean and shiny when she'd left Tucumcari, but now a thin layer of red dust covered every inch of Ophelia's blue exterior and Matilda too.

The motel clerk, Theresa, gave her a room key and an armload of towels. "I haven't had a chance to get the towels changed today. Can you drop a set off at unit three on your way to your cabin?"

"Sure," Matilda agreed. "Where can I get dinner around here?"

Theresa couldn't have been over fifty, but she moved like an eighty year old. "I'm having a TV dinner, but I only have the one."

"Oh. Umm. No. I didn't want your dinner. Is there a restaurant or grocery store nearby?"

She handed Matilda an old pamphlet. Through the water rings and sun damage she could make out the words, but the pictures were faded to yellow. "Navajo Joe's? Is this place still open?"

"Should be." Theresa took the pamphlet, and looked for the hours of the place. "Should be." She shrugged, and put the pamphlet back in the cobwebbed window sill.

"Well, I better go deliver these towels," Matilda said, making her exit, amused that she had allowed the woman to draft her into helping out.

The door on unit three was standing open. "Hello. Anybody here?" She could see that nobody was in the room, so she stepped inside, and lay one of the sets of towels on the desk.

"Can I help you?" A male voice asked behind her.

240

Matilda jumped. "Just delivering towels," she said to the tall man standing in the doorway.

"Great. Thanks. Hey, my air conditioner isn't working. Can you take a look at that?" the man said.

"I don't know anything about air conditioners." She held her towels and purse tight to her chest. The image of Edwards coming at her with his tongue out and zipper down flashed in her mind. Matilda blinked away the horror.

"Well, do you have a handyman or maintenance man?" The man stood with his hands on his hips.

"I don't work here. I'm just dropping off towels." She wanted out of this room and away from this man.

"Sorry about that." The man said stepping into the room further. "You going to the Grand Canyon?" He wore red running shorts, loafers and knee socks.

"I don't think so." She moved towards the door. "Enjoy your stay." Matilda exited the room, and rushed to the standalone cabin at the end of the sidewalk. It took several tries before she got the door unlocked. As soon as she stepped inside Tildy locked the door, and hoped the man hadn't seen which room she'd gone into.

Then she shook for a long time, hating it and hating Ray and Edwards for making her afraid of some guy who just wanted his AC fixed.

I'm not going to let them turn me into a coward, she thought.

The room was bright. It wasn't just because of the light streaming through the large windows. Blaring seventies floral patterned curtains clashed with plaid upholstery and bedding and a swirling abstract carpet. Everything was in vivid hues of orange and yellow.

Matilda didn't hate it. The utter absurdity of it made her feel better.

After peeing and checking out the room, she got out her mother's letters, and found the ones that were postmarked

Holbrook. There were two of them, and a postcard. The last letters she'd sent.

November 2, 1967

Sis,

I hitched into Holbrook early this morning. There are some real kind people in this world, but there are also some absolute turds.

I have to tell you about what happened in New Mexico, but I am not going to do that in a letter. I am a little shook up even though it's been a few days since I had to leave. I didn't have time to get Ophelia fixed and I left all my money and clothes there too.

Since I got here so early there was no place to stay, so I dozed off on a bench at the bus station. The wack job that worked there hit me with a broom, and yelled at me to leave. I wasn't hurting anybody, but it's okay now.

A nice woman invited me to their church shelter. I told her that I wasn't homeless, but that I'd had to leave my money and car behind. Her name is Crystal. There were a lot of women around my age at the Church of the Blue Oracle. They made me feel at home.

A real sweet lady from Mexico showed me how to make homemade tortillas. I will teach you when I get back home. Mattie will be old enough to eat them soon. It makes my heart happy to know I'll see her soon.

Mom and Dad still pissed at me? I'm sure they are, but the fact that you aren't makes me feel like I'm on the right path. Tomorrow after church I'm going to go to the painted desert and sprinkle some ashes.

Thank you for everything you've done for me and Mattie. I know that we quarreled a lot when we were younger, but I want you to know that there is nothing I wouldn't do for you.

I gotta go, because Father Paul is here to read devotional with us. I love you.

Love, Annette

Matilda dug the phone book out of the desk drawer. There was no Church of the Blue Oracle or Crystal Stardream.

Maybe she'd have better luck asking around town. The map in the back of the phone book showed that were several shops and cafes on 66. They were close enough that she decided to walk and give Ophelia a well deserved rest.

The first restaurant she came to was a bar and grill. Her stomach growled at the smell of burgers and fries in the air. Matilda sat at a booth, and the waitress poured her a glass of water in a red plastic Coke glass.

She wanted to hug the waitress. The familiarity of everything made her think of going to the Bell Restaurant with her grandparents. Matilda always ordered the same thing.

"A cheeseburger, fries, and a Dr. Pepper," she said to the waitress.

"All right." She tucked the menu back under her arm, and jotted down Matilda's order. "You want everything on that burger?"

"Everything." Matilda sipped the water at her table, and read through the business card holder on the table to see if she found any Crystals or Pauls.

When her food came it was hard for her to wait to eat. "Excuse me," she said to the waitress. "Do you know a Father Paul, Crystal Stardream, or Church of the Blue Oracle?"

"None of that sounds familiar," the woman said, said setting down the plate of food.

"Thanks," Matilda said half-heartedly. Perry Mason always got the information he was looking for without having to question every single person in a town. Then she thought about her incredible good luck finding Meredith and Larry. Maybe she shouldn't expect things to be so easy all the time.

Matilda covered her fries in ketchup and picked the onions off her burger. She had put herself in danger getting the information she needed in Tucumcari. This time she'd be more careful. There would be no going back to somebody's creepy house.

Matilda needed some necessities, but she also knew that she needed to ration her money. She needed to buy tampons and underwear.

Matilda scarfed her food down, and drained her soda. There was so much she needed to do in Holbrook; find a church, a preacher, and a hippie.

With her belly full, Matilda got directions for the library and set out walking. Fortunately the librarian there didn't look like a pterodactyl.

"Excuse me, do you have any phone books from the sixties?" Matilda asked the librarian.

"Yes." She led Matilda to the reference section. "We have the 1969 Bell Telephone book."

"Thank you. Do you have anything earlier than that? I'm needing to find a church that was here in 1967."

"We have some church directories. Which church is it?"

"The Church of the Blue Oracle."

The librarian screwed up her face. "Is that Presbyterian?"

"I have no idea. All I know is that I'm looking for Father Paul from the Church of the Blue Oracle and Crystal Stardream."

"Stardream? Is that the last name?" The librarian thumbed through the phone book. "No Stardreams or Blue Oracle churches. Check your source. Stardream sounds like a made up name."

"Thank you." Matilda said. Her source was a letter written seventeen years ago.

She walked back towards the Route 66 Motel, stopping to shop at a dollar store. Tildy wandered through the aisles of the store, throwing a few necessities into the cart. Peanut butter and crackers would be a filling snack. Shampoo and deodorant would make her less objectionable to anybody she questioned. She didn't plan on being in this town more than a day or two.

"Have you ever heard of The Church of the Blue Oracle, Father Paul, or Crystal Stardream?" she asked the clerk.

"We have some rock music tapes behind the counter. What was it called again?" The old woman looked at the wall. "Blue Oyster Cult?"

"Close, but I'm looking for a place it was called the Church of the Blue Oracle."

"Hippie place off old 66?"

"Yes! That's it. That's it. Do you know where I can find it or any of the members?" Matilda bounced.

"It was in an old service station. Cops ran off the hippies and shuttered it. Think it burned a few years after that. The police department can tell you about it."

Matilda didn't want to go to the police. "Did you know anybody that was a member there?"

"Not by name. You could always recognize them, because they all dressed the same."

"Thank you so much. Is it okay if I come back to see if you remember anything else?"

"I reckon, but who you need to talk to is Clay Wheeler. He's county commissioner of this ward. That fellow knows everything that happens in this town. You can find him having coffee at the All Day Diner most mornings."

"Thank you so much. I can't tell you how much I appreciate this."

"You're welcome. Don't forget your purchases." She handed Matilda the paper sack.

Matilda walked back to the motel as fast as she could. She got out her journal, and wrote everything she remembered from the library and the dollar store.

She sat her notebook on the desk, and went to take a bath. She'd been wearing the boys' underwear she got from Meredith. Those went straight into the trash.

Matilda poured a capful of Prell into the water to get a nice Mr. Bubble effect. She sank into the tub. The water was too hot, but after a few minutes she got used to it. If she was at home she'd have shaved her shaggy legs. Her legs were bonier than she remembered. She had lost a significant amount of weight for the short amount of time she had been gone.

Tildy had never been a twig, but since she was so tall nobody seemed to take much notice. When she had sufficiently scrubbed her body Matilda slid down in the tub. Her hair floated in the water around her.

After shampooing, rinsing, and repeating she slathered her hair in the generic conditioner she'd picked up at the dollar store. Matilda drained the tub, and brushed her teeth before rinsing the conditioner out in the sink.

She used the shampoo to wash out the clothes Meredith had given her, and then threw them over the shower rod to dry. The nightly news played in the background as she picked through her hair, and braided it down her back to dry.

She felt more alone than she had in a long time. But she also felt like she was more in control of her own life than she had ever been.

At home, Grandma and Granddad would be griping about something Dan Rather said and making predictions about the weather. Matilda usually laid in bed reading and listening to the radio, comforted to know they were just a wall away.

Finding her mother had never been a priority for her before because she couldn't pine for someone she didn't know. Grandma and Caroline had always taken turns filling the mother role. They kept Matilda fed, clothed, and loved. Granddad held her to a high standard, one that she seldom met, but he never gave up on her.

Matilda lay back in the bed, and tried not to think about what a monster she'd been. She rebelled against everything that meant anything to her. The smoking, drinking, and messing around with boys didn't make her unlovable to the people that it affected the most.

Matilda prayed that when she found her mother it would be a big enough gesture of apology for all she'd put them through.

Sometime in the night her self reflection waned enough for her to fall asleep. When she woke the next day it was storming. She was sick of the rain. This was supposed to be a desert, damn it.

Meredith had given her several outfits that her sons had left behind. Today Matilda wore a loose Run DMC shirt over jean shorts. With her tall socks and Converse she looked like she could be the lead singer of the Beastie Boys.

She looked up the address for the diner and headed out to find Clay Wheeler. Ophelia didn't like the rain either. It took several tries to get her started. Muddy brown water splashed around them as they pulled onto the road.

The All Day Diner's parking lot was full, but inside there was only a single group of customers. A bunch of men were drinking coffee and talking. They didn't pay any attention to Matilda until she spoke.

"Excuse me. I'm looking for Clay Wheeler," Matilda said.

"What you want with Clay?" asked a heavyset man wearing overalls and a John Deere cap.

"I'm looking for information about the Church of the Blue Oracle, Father Paul, or Crystal Stardream."

"Hippies," said a man wearing a dirty gray cowboy hat. A couple of the others laughed.

The original man spoke again. "I'm Clay. What ya need to know about the place? That must have been twenty years ago."

"Almost seventeen. It was November of 1967 when my mother attended the church. She disappeared. I have come a long way to try to find out where she is."

The man looked at her levelly, then sighed. "I can't imagine you're going to find her if she was part of that bunch. It wasn't a church. It was a bunch of hippies selling dope out of a gas station. Sorry, kid," he said. Wheeler turned back to his breakfast, dismissing her.

Matilda hadn't realized how much she was counting on him to give her good information until he didn't. But she wasn't going to cry in front of all these men. "Well," she said. "Even a bunch of hippies don't just evaporate. They must have gone somewhere."

"Hippies evaporate," one of the men said, and guffawed. But another man spoke up. "Ease up, Jake. It's her mom."

Wheeler looked around at the group, then gave Matilda his attention again. "I don't know what else I can tell you. The cops raided the place a bunch of times. It burned down. That's about all I know about it. Theresa Jimenez at the Motel 66 could probably tell you more than me. She ran around with the hippies."

"Thank you," Matilda said, writing down the information in her little notebook. The men turned back to their coffee as if she'd never been there.

Theresa the desk clerk? Tildy could have asked her the first day before delivering the woman's towels.

She hoped Theresa had information. She had been the first person Tildy had spoken to when she arrived in Holbrook, and Matilda prayed she'd be the one to lead her to her mother.

There was a young man in the office of the Route 66 Motel. He was probably in his early twenties and cute in a dorky way.

"Hey, do you know when Theresa will be back?"

"Theresa that works here?" he asked.

"Yes. I needed to ask her something personal."

"She doesn't work again until the weekend."

Matilda's heart sank. Maybe she could find her in the phone book, or --

"But she lives in cabin twelve if you need to talk to her before then," the man added. He pointed across the parking lot to a cabin a few doors in front of Matilda's.

Tildy could have hugged him, but she stayed casual. "Thanks," she said over her shoulder as she headed out the door.

Wheel of Fortune blared at an insane volume inside the cabin. Matilda knocked on the door.

After a couple minutes and some more knocking, Theresa opened the door. "Can I help you?" She wore a floral house dress that appeared to be none too clean, and it struck Matilda again that with the woman's sun damaged skin and bleached hair she looked eighty at least.

"I wanted to ask you about the Church of the Blue Oracle."

The woman looked shocked. "How do you even know about that place?"

"My mother stayed there for a while. With Father Paul and Crystal Stardream."

"Huggins," Theresa said.

"What?"

"Her name was Crystal Huggins, is still Crystal Huggins."

Matilda pulled out her notebook and jotted down the information. "Is there anything you could tell me about the church. Did you know Annette Banks?"

"Name doesn't sound familiar. I don't know a lot about the place. I didn't spend as much time there as Crystal did."

"Do you know where I could find Crystal Huggins? My mother is missing, and she was one of the last people to see her."

"Crystal lives in a trailer park out towards Petrified Forest. She may not be much help." The woman gave Tildy an address.

"Thank you for your help," Matilda said sincerely. She went back to her own cabin and jumped into Ophelia.

Matilda wasn't snooty about trailer parks. There were plenty in the Ozarks, several in and around Landover. She had visited a couple friends in them as she was growing up, so there wasn't much about the squalor, the wild, unkempt lots and the accumulating piles of trash that fazed her. Still, as something of a connoisseur, she recognized that this one exceeded all the ones she had seen in terms of outright depravity.

None of the cars and trucks parked haphazardly around the ten or twelve occupied residences seemed less than fifteen years old, and she doubted that half of them ran. She had to laugh a little as she drove under the crookedly hanging metal sign announcing she was entering the Petrified Mobile Home Park. If she lived here, she'd be scared all the time too.

The garbage piles might delight a future archaeologist with a strong stomach. She was trying not to see, concentrating on finding Unit 8, but dirty diapers, old tires and decaying food seemed to be everywhere. She had a crazy thought that she would have to wash Ophelia's tires when she got back to town because they had touched the place.

Still, when there's nothing you can do, do nothing. She had to talk to Crystal Stardream, Crystal Huggins. She felt like all she had been through — getting robbed, almost being raped — had been steering her to this point where she might finally start to find some answers about where her mom might be.

And she had learned that good might happen along the most unlikely paths. The nightmare in Tucumcari that led her to meeting the Nobles convinced her that pushing on, however uncomfortable or painful, could be worth it.

I wonder if that's how my mom felt, she thought, and then she immediately decided that it wasn't. Annette's arrival in Holbrook had been totally different. She had just lost her car and money and clothes and had every reason to think the police were looking for her for hitting that Turner guy.

She must have been so desperate and afraid. And then these Blue Oracle people took her in.

Matilda decided she was grateful to Crystal and the rest of the hippies no matter what had happened here. Her mom had survived, and they had helped her get back on her feet.

Unit 8 wasn't marked, but Unit 6 was. It had a tiny rusted metal sign that read simply "6" on the border of the lot facing the half-gravel, half-dirt driveway that looped around all the trailers. Tildy guessed that Crystal lived two doors down.

She parked Ophelia gingerly, conscious of the broken glass everywhere, next to a Ford Maverick that looked a little better cared for than most of the vehicles around here. The only glass broken out of it was the rear window, and Tildy guessed that in the desert, that wouldn't be too much of an issue most days.

She was nervous but steadied her hand as she reached toward the door of the small mobile home. White paint flecked to the ground as she knocked. The sound of a yapping dog seemed to shake the whole structure.

She waited an eternity before hearing "Who is it?" in a hoarse voice croaked through the door.

"My name is Matilda. I'm looking for Crystal Huggins, or Crystal Stardream." She held her breath until the woman spoke again.

"What do ya want?"

"I need to speak to Crystal…"

"What do ya want with her?"

"She knew my mother in 1967."

The door opened just far enough that the occupant could peer through the doorway. The face was thin and orange. "Who was your mother?"

"Her name is Annette Banks. She was eighteen in 1967. Are you Crystal?"

The door pushed closed again. The woman unhooked the chain lock, and opened it fully. "I'm Crystal. Excuse the mess. I wasn't expecting company."

Matilda stepped inside the trailer door. The mess Crystal mentioned was piles of magazines, old food, and animal droppings. Matilda acted like she didn't notice, but the smell of rancid garbage was overwhelming.

Crystal couldn't have been more than eighty pounds. Her tanned skin looked like leather, and her frizzy blonde hair hung past her waist. She wore a purple sun dress that was probably meant for an elementary girl.

"Did you know my mother?" Matilda asked again.

"Yes. We met at the church," the woman said. She turned away and threw a hand over her shoulder in what Matilda interpreted as a beckoning motion. The woman went into the small living room where there was a couch piled with old laundry and trash bags. The only available seat was a metal-vinyl kitchen chair with a faded floral pattern. Crystal sat as Matilda stopped a pace away.

"That's right. She mentioned the church in her letters," Matilda said, standing uncomfortably.

"What happened to her?" Crystal asked, reaching for a cigarette pack on the coffee table, which also supported an overflowing ashtray and an assortment of small rocks. Matilda wondered if they were supposed to be decorative. They looked like something someone might pick up during a walk in the desert.

Crystal pulled out a crumpled looking cigarette that Matilda immediately recognized as a joint, then grabbed a small lighter and lit it. Her wrinkled face went slightly smoother as she inhaled and then offered Matilda a hit.

"No thanks," Tildy said, a little amused. She wasn't a prude; she had tried pot a couple of times with Missy and Ray, but she wasn't going to smoke with a stranger here in the backside of Hell.

"I don't know if anything happened to her. She never came home," Matilda said.

Crystal took a deep drag and didn't speak for long moments. Then she exhaled a cloud and spoke in a croak. "She was alive and well when I dropped her off in Santa Monica," she said. Her red-rimmed eyes focused on Tildy. "Annie said something about dumping her husband's ashes, so I drove her to the pier. That's a crazy place. She was fine when I left her."

Crystal leaned her head back and coughed violently. "Emphysema."

"I'm sorry." Matilda said, wishing she could bathe in Lysol. "So she made it to Santa Monica? The last letter she mailed was from Holbrook, and she said she was going to sprinkle the remainder of my father's ashes at the end of Route 66 in Santa Monica, and then come home."

"She wasn't with Lorne." Crystal spit on her finger, and pinched the ember on her joint before setting it on a dinner plate overflowing with cigarette remains.

"Who's Lorne?"

"Her lover."

"You must be thinking of someone else. My mother was a war widow."

"Oh darling. Women don't stop taking lovers just because their husband died. If anything, that gives them more excuse."

Heat stung Matilda's cheeks. She was angry. Who the hell did this woman think she was to talk about her mother that way?

"I'm sorry to have wasted your time," she said stiffly. She turned to go back out the trailer door, which Crystal had left open.

"I still have my photos from my time at the Blue Oracle. Let me see if I can find them."

Matilda's head spun as she followed Crystal to her bedroom; both from the smell and the new information. Every step she took was treacherous. She passed by bones that looked like they were from an old fried chicken. She hoped they were from fried chicken.

Crystal's hallway had two doors. They were both wedged open with garbage. The hallway smelled of old urine and rot. A milky eyed chihuahua growled at her from the only clear space in the house; a wallowed out spot on a mattress. Clothes covered the rest of the bed, as well as the rest of the room. There were vast piles of clothes.

Crystal began excavating beneath a window that was partially covered with aluminum foil. She began handing Matilda metal boxes of photos. "They should be in here." Crystal stood up, and wobbled on the clothes pile a few times before catching herself.

Once again Matilda followed her. This time Crystal led her out the front door to a rickety picnic table beside Ophelia. Crystal started rummaging through the boxes. "Here we go. There's old Blue, and maybe your mama from the backside."

Crystal slid the photo to Matilda. There was a polaroid of a bearded man holding a bottle of beer, and the back of a woman with short brown hair. The man's eyes glowed red from the camera flash.

"Oh, here's some more." Crystal handed her a stack of Polaroids. "That's Blue, Annie, Lorne, me, and my sister, Theresa."

Blue and Lorne were shirtless, but all the women wore what looked to be white nightgowns.

"What are you wearing?"

"Blue thought that when Jesus came back he would only take the people wearing cotton to heaven. He said an angel came to him while he was tripping. That's why he started the Church of the Blue Oracle. He was Blue, the oracle."

Tildy got lost in the pictures. Crystal kept finding new ones, commenting, "There she is" and "Here's another." Her mom, pretty, young, carefree, smiling from the edge of some lake or pond, covered mostly by the water but obviously not wearing any clothes. Her mom, eyes red from the flash beside a forgotten campfire, laughing. Her mom, scrubbing a shirt on an old style scrub board, sweaty, looking a little miffed at having her picture taken. Her mom, dressed in virgin white, solemn in a circle with several others on the grass, listening with apparent adoration to a man in their center.

She was happy here.

Matilda came to a picture of her mother sitting in a man's lap. His arms were wrapped around her, and she was kissing his cheek.

"She didn't love him," Crystal said before she went into another coughing jag. "He just blunted the pain. It was the sixties. We were all just trying to blunt the pain."

Matilda put the picture aside and burst into tears. *How could she? How could she?*

For the first time, she regretted this trip, trying to find her mother. The mystery had been better. Matilda felt her own hands on the sides of her head, trying to hold in something she couldn't name. She rocked on the cracked wooden bench of the picnic table, crying because she didn't know what else to do.

Her parents' love had been like something out of a story. She had known that since she was a toddler, that she was the product of something special and wonderful. Her dad had died in the war, and her heartbroken mom had disappeared, unable to live without him.

No part of the story prepared her for the idea her mom had been able to move on.

So she cried. After a little while, Matilda felt a light hand on her shoulder and opened her streaming eyes. Crystal was standing behind her and had placed a picture on the table in front of her. Matilda closed her eyes again, trying to get herself straight, and a small, weathered hand rubbed her shoulder, patted, then rubbed again as if it didn't know how to comfort her but wanted to.

"This is her and I at the Santa Monica pier. That was right before I headed back to Lorne and Blue," Crystal said. Matilda opened her eyes and looked at the picture. Two young women, arms over each others' shoulders, happy.

She wiped her eyes. It was a minute before she trusted herself to speak, and even then she sounded tremulous and unsure to herself. "Is he still around here? Lorne, I mean." She hated saying his name. She hated him. But had he helped her mom heal? *It's going to be a while before I'm able to look at this like a grownup.*

Crystal didn't seem to hear the question. She went back around the end of the table and collapsed as if she were exhausted on the bench. "Cops ran Blue out of town for selling weed to the tourists. That was a few months after Annie left. A few years later he overdosed in his van. At least that's what the cops said, but you can't trust pigs.

"Everybody still in the church scattered then. It broke Lorne's heart when Annie left. She needed closure, and he wanted somebody to love other than his crazy wife."

"He was married?"

"Yeah, but they had kind of an open marriage. He lives outside town. Works at Palmer Gas and Go. Ask for Lorne Huggins."

"You're related to him?"

Crystal met her eyes, seeming sober for the first time since she had opened the trailer door.

"He's my husband. Got married in 1964 when he was on leave," she said. "Guess it was kind of a whirlwind thing. I don't know. I know he looked damned good in that uniform."

Matilda stared, shocked. "I'm sorry, Crystal." Matilda put her hand across the table on Crystal's arm. "Did my mom know you guys were married?"

"It wasn't a secret. I was seeing Blue. Besides, everything I liked about Lorne got left in Vietnam."

"Do you think he would have hurt my mom?"

Crystal looked shocked at the question. "No. He was still passed out when Annie and I headed to California. She and I went into town to cash her widow's pension, and then we left town. I was always ready for an adventure, which is what brought me to Blue in the first place. You're dumb when you're young, but you outgrow it."

"Do you remember when that was?"

"Must have been around the first week of December, because that's when benefit checks were mailed."

"The last letter I have from her was dated November 30, 1967. She never came home. Why didn't she come home?" Matilda tried to swallow the sob that escaped her lips.

"Ah, Sugar, I don't know. She was all in a tizzy to finish her journey, and go home. I don't know why she didn't make it home. I told all of this to the private dick that came looking for her."

"He never found her."

"Not a surprise. Blue wouldn't let him into the church, and they ended up in a big fight. That fat ass P. I. cracked Blue over the skull with a billy club, and he wouldn't let Theresa or I tend to him unless we told him what we knew about Annie. Lorne was off getting clean or sulking, so it was only us girls left there to protect our church and Blue. So I told him everything."

"What did he say?"

"He said she was a whore who wasn't worth another minute of his time, and that her family couldn't pay him enough to keep looking."

"That son of a bitch took all my grandparents' money, and didn't even try to find her. He lives a few miles from us, and he knows that my family was destroyed when she didn't come back," Matilda said. Anger roiled in her belly.

"Life is tragedy," Crystal said, coughing loudly.

"Thank you for your time. Is there anything else you could tell me about my mother?"

"She loved you. There wasn't a day that went by that she didn't talk about you."

"She thought pretty highly of you too. In her letters she said you helped her learn to really live."

Crystal croaked a laugh. "Maybe we did, a little," she said, then started piling up all the photos she'd pulled out. "I want you to have these."

"What? I couldn't take them."

"Nonsense." She coughed again. "This is your mother, and listen, Sugar, I don't need them. Doctor says I have less than six months before I kick it anyway."

"What?"

Crystal pointed to a large oxygen tank leaned against a stack of trash bags by the tongue of her trailer. "That's why they said I had to carry that monster with me."

"Oh God. Crystal."

"I'll see God soon enough. There is a favor I need from you in return."

***

A half hour later Matilda was driving back to the Route 66 Motel with a stack of photos, a record album, and the meanest, stinkiest blind chihuahua she'd ever seen.

Matilda found the Gas and Go and went in to ask about Lorne. A middle-aged bald man turned from stocking cigarettes. He stared at Matilda in shock.

"Lorne?"

"Annie?" His small voice trembled.

"Annette is my mother."

"You're the spitting image of her."

"Thank you. Have you seen her?"

"What? I haven't seen her since the sixties. How old are you?"

"I'm seventeen."

He was doing the math in his head. "Are you Matilda?"

She nodded. "Crystal said you were my mother's ... friend."

"Well, Crystal is crazy. I haven't seen your mother since the day she took outta Holbrook. That was the autumn of '67, I think. Is that your dog?"

Matilda looked outside just in time to see the chihuahua walk into the glass door and then fall down.

"No. Well, yes. Crystal gave it to me. I left my windows down, and I guess it jumped out." She ran outside, and picked up the dog as it growled and snapped at the air.

"You can't bring that hellhound in here," Lorne said. He pointed at the No Pets sign.

"I'm sorry." She held the smelly dog away from her. "Do you have a box tall enough that she can't jump out of?"

He dumped a couple of cartons of cigarettes on the counter, and handed her the empty box. "How was Crystal?"

"Well, I don't know how to tell you this, but ... she's dying of emphysema."

"No she isn't."

"Really." Matilda set the chihuahua in the tall box.

"Crazy isn't terminal or she would have died a long time ago."

"Well, She has an oxygen tank and she coughs a lot. And she gave me this dog."

"She'll have another psycho dog within a week or two. I'll drive out and check on her, but I promise you that she's fine.

Crystal lives on weed and drama. My daughter went out there on the first to take her shopping, She said it sounded like there was a new dog."

"How old is your daughter?"

"She'll be nineteen in July."

"My mom didn't mention you in her letters. She talked about Crystal and Father Paul."

"I was nothing worth mentioning." He looked sad.

The dog started scratching at the box. "I'm sorry if my mother broke up your marriage," Matilda said.

"My marriage wasn't anything worth mentioning either. That's not true, I guess. We've been married nearly twenty years, and it got me April, my daughter."

"Was your daughter in the cult … I mean church too?"

"April lived with my mother until she was five. It took me that long to put my life back together after 'Nam. You ask a lot of questions."

"My mother never came home from her trip to sprinkle my father's ashes. Her last letter was sent from Holbrook around the time she was with the church."

Lorne's jaw tightened and he looked afraid. "Did Crys tell you that she drove her to Santa Monica? That's what she told me."

"Yes, but nobody has heard from her since that day. Do you think Crystal could have harmed her?"

"I got a letter from Annie. It was mailed the day she left."

Matilda's heart raced. "Do you have it?"

"It's been seventeen years. Of course not. I think I burned it as soon as I read it."

"What did it say?"

Lorne looked down at the cartons of cigarettes still on the counter. He picked them up, then stooped as if to put them underneath. He muttered a curse and straightened, the cartons still in his hand. He set them back on the counter.

"It said she didn't love me."

He turned and busied himself with the rack of packs behind him, not accomplishing much that Tildy could see.

"I know this is … weird for you," she said. "But I have to know. Did the letter say anything else?"

"That was enough for me." He met her eyes. "One other thing. She didn't write 'Dear Lorne' or 'Hey Lorne' to start the letter. She wrote 'For Lorne.' It was kind of a private joke we had."

"'For ..?' Oh, I get it," Matilda said. "Forlorn."

"Yeah."

Matilda stopped hating him. She pulled out her mother's letters, and laid the last envelope on the counter. "When she mailed your letter she must have mailed this one too."

Lorne picked up the letter, and looked at the date. "Good lord." His eyes misted with tears. He pulled out the Polaroid of Crystal and Annette. "I loved your mother. If I hadn't been stupid enough to tell her about it then I might still have her."

"What do you mean?"

"Blue's Church, if you want to call it that, was cozy quarters. Everybody knew everybody's business. When Crystal and Theresa began sleeping in Blue's bed, Annie felt sorry for me." He rubbed his finger across the picture. "Annie took care of me. We talked about war and loss and the children that we missed and the children that we were.

"She was at my side; day and night. The night I told her that I loved her she cried. I was her escape, but not her love. It was so fucked up."

"What was?"

"Crystal was all about peace, pot, and free love as long as we were her lap dogs. I told her that I loved Annette, and that I wanted a divorce. She took Annie from me."

"What did she do?" Matilda was afraid of what he was going to say.

"Crystal disappeared for a couple of days, and when she came back she just told lies. She said Annie was pregnant and ran away."

"Did you believe her?"

He shook his head. "When I got Annie's letter it was an apology. She said she was leaving to sprinkle her husband's ashes, and that she was going home to raise her daughter. I blamed Crystal for a long time, but I don't think she forced her to leave."

"I'm sorry that you lost her too. When I find her I will let you know how she is doing."

"Thanks. Are you going to keep that dog?"

She looked down at the horrible creature that was laying in its own pee. "I honestly don't know. Do you want it?"

"No. We're already raising three sad sacks that April brought home from Crystal's. I think my old lady would have my neck if I took that." He pointed at the box that was shaking as the hound scratched.

"I guess I'll keep it then. Thank you for talking to me."

The front door buzzed as a customer came in. "So what's your next step?" He asked Matilda while setting two bags of chewing tobacco on the counter for the customer.

"I guess I'm heading to Santa Monica." She picked up the chihuahua. The dog snapped and barked at her. "Do you have a different box?"

He sighed and swapped a clean box for the soiled one. "Good luck, Matilda."

Chapter 11

Matilda sneaked the dog into her hotel room. It took less than a minute to pack her belongings. She sat down, and planned out the trip to Santa Monica. It would take eight hours if she could drive at highway speed, so it would take her ten hours at least.

She toyed with the idea of staying another night, and heading out at first light, but she couldn't. She'd learned too much new information today, and she was ready to see this mystery to its conclusion.

Besides, it was unlikely she was going to be able to sleep. Crystal's words kept coming back to her: *We were all just trying to blunt the pain.*

Why wasn't I enough for her?

Matilda spread the pictures of her mother on the desk. She tried to imagine what it might have been like in the '60s, sitting around a campfire and singing folk songs and smoking pot, then going somewhere private to make love with someone, maybe someone you just met. The pictures were the proof that her mom had grown into that lifestyle in the short time she had been here.

I think I have too much Grandma in me, she thought. Matilda didn't want to judge her mom, but it was hard. She didn't know much about hippies and flower children and the whole peace movement of the 1960s. She did know, however, how her aunt and her grandparents would react if they ever saw these pictures. It would not be good.

Still, Annette did look like she had found something here, maybe a way to heal from the hurt of her husband's death and to recover from the ordeal that led to her leaving Tucumcari.

If I had a time machine I would go back and find out what all this was about. I would talk to her.

But that wasn't going to happen outside *Star Trek* reruns.

The dog bumped into her ankle and nuzzled her leg. Matilda picked up the filthy animal. It growled as it rubbed its head against her.

"You need a name." She looked at the dog's underside. "You're a girl." The dog turned its head, appearing to listen to her. "Definitely not naming you Princess. You aren't a Fluffy." She made her decision. "Morag! You could easily be a Scottish swamp monster."

Matilda carried Morag to the bathroom sink and gave her a bath. The motel soap had a strong floral scent that was only mildly less offensive than the terrible smell emanating from the dog. Morag growled the whole time she was being bathed but didn't try to escape.

Before they left, Matilda picked up the phone, and dialed zero. "I want to place a collect phone call to Landover, Missouri."

The operator took the information, and tried the number. The phone rang six times, and right before Matilda gave up a gasping Caroline answered.

"Hello. Yes, I'll accept the charges." Before the operator disconnected Caroline was apologizing. "I'm so sorry, Tildy. I was a little --"

"It's ok. I understand." Matilda was on the brink of tears for the millionth time today.

"I was just scared. It would destroy me and your grandparents if anything ever happened to you." Caroline's breathing was coming at a regular pace now. "Can you tell me where you are?"

"I'll be home once I find mom. There are so many things that I've discovered about her. My journey is almost over, and then I'll be home with or without her."

"Are you going through Nevada?" Caroline asked.

Tildy felt like any answer she gave could be leading her into a trap. "Why?"

"If you are near Nevada you need to talk to a man there. Get some paper and write this information down. I'll wait."

Matilda dumped her purse onto the TV stand, and grabbed her journal and a pen. "All right. I'm ready."

"I want you to go to Mesquite Flat, Nevada. It may be out of your way, but do it. You need to find Jim, maybe James, S-i-y-u-g-a. Don't ask me to pronounce that, because I'd butcher it. He has information about your father and maybe your mother too. If you're going on this asinine adventure then you should not miss an opportunity to speak to a man whose life your father saved."

Matilda looked at the old battered journal in her hands. This unpronounceable name was a link to her father, and maybe to her mother too.

"Did you write it down?" Caroline asked.

"Yes." She felt a little overwhelmed. "Thank you, Caroline."

"No thanks needed. Oh, and um, hey. I've got some news. You know Jonah Wilkey?"

"Yeah," Tildy said. "I saw him at the bus station the morning --"

"I know, he told me," Caroline said. "Well, he was at church Wednesday night and found out about you running off, so he came over to the house on Thursday morning to tell us he had seen you. We got to talking and I guess we kind of hit it off." Caroline laughed lightly.

"What?" Matilda was amazed. "Oh my God, he's perfect for you! That is so cool!"

Caroline laughed again. "Well, it's still pretty early to be counting on anything, but it's ... It's just nice. It's been a long time since anybody has been this nice to me."

Matilda was speechless for a moment. She was so happy for her aunt she felt tears threatening. "You totally deserve someone being nice to you," she said. "I should have run off ten years ago."

"Brat," Caroline snapped back, but there was no heat in it. "I love you. Please, come home soon."

"I love you too, and I will be there as fast as I can." As they said their goodbyes Matilda felt a sense of peace and purpose.

When she and the dog were sufficiently dry they loaded into Ophelia. Matilda said goodbye to her home of the last few days. She had almost a hundred dollars left, but she needed supplies.

Matilda drove to the Farm and Home she'd passed on the outer road. She carried Morag under her arm and went inside. The smell of popcorn made her stomach ache. She kept forgetting to eat.

"Where is the dog food?" she asked a clerk.

"Aisle seven." The woman pointed to the far corner of the store.

Morag sniffed at the air as they passed by a livestock tank with fluffy yellow chicks hopping around inside.

Matilda grabbed a small bag of dog food off the shelf.

"That won't work," said an employee from behind her. "Dog's got no teeth. You need soft food."

She looked into Morag's mouth, and indeed, she had very few teeth, and none of those looked very healthy. "Thanks. Any suggestions?"

"I'm supposed to tell you to get the most expensive brand, but the store brand is just as good."

"We also need a water bowl that will work while traveling," she said. The young man nodded and directed her further down the aisle.

Within a few minutes Matilda was ready to pay out.

"$4.28. Would you like a bag of popcorn?" the clerk asked.

"How much is it?"

"It's free," the clerk said.

"Can I have two?"

Matilda ate handfuls of popcorn while Morag walked around in the grass. It had been three days since she'd smoked a cigarette, and it hadn't really bothered her until this moment. She tried to distract herself by talking to the dog, but it didn't work.

They said goodbye to Holbrook and set out west on the highway. They were twenty miles away before the craving passed.

When they saw the sign for Winslow, Arizona, Matilda sang the song *Take It Easy* to Morag, but she didn't appear to be an Eagles fan.

Tildy drove with the windows down, allowing the dry desert air to whip through the tiny car as she chugged westward. She cranked the radio and sang along when she knew the words.

Why can't you see me standing here I got my back against the record machine ...

Oh my God! Van Halen. *Jump. Was that only two weeks ago I got the tape?* The song felt like an oldie to her now, something she had liked a lot in her younger days. *Younger days. In my younger days I played with dolls and had a poster of Shaun Cassidy too. Wasn't that long ago.*

Matilda realized she was having fun. The open road, the sunshine and the music had her in a good mood. It was exciting not to know what might crop up on the horizon at any given moment, and she felt a thrill that no one knew where she was and what she was doing. The freedom was intoxicating.

This is what Mom and Dad wanted to do, she thought. *The only way this could be better is if you were doing it with the love of your life.*

Her mom must have been so sad to take the trip alone. *She shouldn't have tried,* Matilda thought. *She wasn't going to find him again.*

Morag began whining in her box, so Matilda lifted her out and let Morag cry on her lap. What would her life have looked like if she hadn't lost her parents?

After a few hours she stopped to gas up and walk the dog. It was almost three in the afternoon before Matilda pulled back onto the highway, and spring storms rolled in the distance. Morag trembled at the sound. Matilda had spread paper towels from the gas station in the bottom of Morag's box. The little rust-colored dog cried again as soon as Matilda put her in it. "Oh all right, fine," Matilda groused.

She drove into the rain with the dog tucked up inside her shirt. The shirt hadn't smelled great beforehand, but now it had an extra note of floral dog stink that gave it that extra something it was missing.

She stopped at the first service station that she came to and bought a map of Nevada. Maybe Mesquite Flat wasn't too far out of her way. She needed to meet this man and see what he could tell her about her parents. Had her mother made it to see him?

Chapter 12

The route to Mesquite was desolate. It scared her that there hadn't been a service station in an hour. She was afraid of what would happen if she ran out of gas in the actual desert, and Ophelia did not seem to like driving for long stretches in the heat.

Matilda pulled off at the first small convenience store she passed. Morag whined incessantly as she walked around on the barren terrain. Tildy bought a hot dog of questionable quality and a Dr. Pepper after she gassed up. There were a ton of pamphlets and advertisements for Las Vegas in the store.

"Is there any way that I can get to Mesquite Flat without having to go through Las Vegas?" she asked the store clerk.

"I don't know where Mesquite is, but it's easy to get lost turning onto back roads around here." The clerk opened a map that was for sale on the counter. "Looks like your safest route is through Vegas."

She'd heard all sorts of terrible tales about Las Vegas. The city of sin had everything from gamblers, drunks, and prostitutes to the mob. It was the kind of place that she'd had a morbid curiosity about, but wouldn't want to go alone.

"Thank you for your help," she told the clerk, then headed back to the car.

Morag was asleep, in her box for a change, and Matilda hoped she'd stay that way for a while. Billboards began popping up as she got closer to Vegas, and traffic increased as well. She pulled over to check her map several times to be sure she was on the right route.

Traffic began to move in bursts as she entered the city limits. Large flashing signs for the Flamingo and Circus Circus amazed her as she inched her way through the town past tour buses, limousines, and tractor trailers. Women dressed in all manner of clothing congregated at an intersection that Matilda had to sit still at for an uncomfortable amount of time.

"Looking's free, honey," a woman called to a car in back of Matilda.

By the time she'd made it through Vegas, she was exhausted. She was grateful when she saw the sign announcing that Mesquite was just ahead.

It had taken just over five hours to make it to Mesquite. She stopped at the first phone booth, and looked up the name Jim Siyuja. It was there with the address. She put two dimes into the phone, and dialed the number.

When a man's voice answered she forgot how to speak for a moment.

"Hello?" the voice said again.

"My father was Mark Banks. Is this Jim?" Matilda blurted.

"Dad, I think it's for you," the voice called. "Hang on. My dad is coming."

There was silence on the other end of the line for a minute. "Hello."

"My father was Mark Banks. Is this Jim Siyuga?" She pronounced the last name like Sigh you gay.

"This is Jim Siyuga." He pronounced it "See you ha." "Mark Banks, huh? I haven't heard that name in a long time."

"My name is Matilda Banks. I wanted to talk to you about my father."

A metallic voice told her to insert another dime to continue her call.

"Crap. The phone is going to cut me off! I'm at the Texaco on first and..." The dial tone vibrated in her ear. "FUCK!" she yelled, slamming the phone onto the cradle.

Matilda tore through the car looking for more change, but all she found was pennies, and pay phones didn't take pennies. Morag started whining as Tildy shifted her box.

"Hey," a voice behind her said.

Matilda backed out of her car, and turned around slowly.

The man standing across from her had long black hair, brown skin, and a metal claw on one arm.

"Are you Jim?"

"Yeah. Are you Mark Banks' daughter?" he asked.

"I am. You got here fast."

He pointed across the street. "I live right there. Please, come meet my wife."

"Can I bring my puppy?" she asked.

"Of course. Pull your car into our driveway. I'll meet you there." Jim walked back across the road.

Matilda got in her car, and drove the short distance to the Siyuga home. She rolled the windows up and cradled Morag so she wouldn't be scared.

"Please come inside," Jim said as he met her in the driveway. "My wife won't believe this." He opened the door, and called for his wife. "Jessa, come here. There is someone here I want you to meet."

"Hello ma'am," Matilda said as a petite woman dressed head to toe in hot pink entered the room. "I'm Matilda. I love your outfit."

Tildy turned to Jim. "My Aunt Caroline said you had contacted her about my father's death. I was hoping you would be able to tell me more about it."

"Of course. Come to our table. You can put your … puppy down anywhere, if you like."

Matilda sat Morag on the floor beneath a chair, and she stayed there cuddled up to Tildy's legs. "Did my mother come speak to you about my father?"

"No. Did she say that she did? I sent her a few letters over the years, but never heard from her. Your aunt called me. I told her that if your mother ever showed up that I would contact her immediately. Would you like some tea or lemonade?" He opened the refrigerator, and waited for her answer.

"Lemonade would be great," she said.

Jim used the metal claw to hold the door open, and got the lemonade with his intact arm.

Matilda tried not to stare. "My mother disappeared in 1967 while traveling Route 66 to sprinkle my father's ashes. I was hoping that she had come here to meet you."

"You poor child." Jessa said. "You had to grow up with no parents? Would you like a Pop Tart?"

"No, thank you. I'm all right, I guess. My family loves me. I'm just trying to put some pieces of my past back together."

Jim set a lemonade for each of them on the table.

"I'll tell you everything I can remember." He sat across the table from his wife and Matilda. "In February of '67 our outfit was the first unit that came upon the aftermath of a firefight just over the border into Cambodia.

"There were many dead and wounded from both sides of the battle." He took a deep breath and exhaled the memory. "Mark and a few others began to triage the wounded, so our commanding officer could call in a chopper to get them to a field hospital. Another crew was tasked with identifying the dead. I was one of them."

Jessa reached for Jim's hand, squeezing it in support.

"I moved one of the bodies to see if its dog tags had been displaced due to the nature of his injuries. As soon as I lifted the remains I knew I was fucked, because I heard a click."

"Big Jim, watch your words," Jessa said wagging a finger at him.

"Excuse my French." Jim said.

"It's fine. I've heard much worse," Matilda said.

He started again. "I knew I was in trouble, because there was a loud click when I lifted the body. Before I could release the body Mark had knocked into me diving onto it." Tears ran down Jim's face.

"Our corpsman said the explosion killed him instantly. I only lost my arm."

"He really was a hero?" Matilda whispered.

"He is our hero," Jessa said. "Without him I wouldn't have my husband or my children."

The front door of the house opened as if on cue, and a bunch of people came into the house.

"Who's here?" a young girl, asked running into the kitchen.

"Speaking of family, this is our daughter, Hala and our son, Little Jim," Jim said.

Little Jim must have been over six feet tall. He had his father's bronze skin, his mother's almond eyes, and long black hair. He wore a Black Flag shirt and tight black pants, and he was gorgeous.

Matilda blushed when she made eye contact with him.

"Nice car," he said. "Dad, we're going to jam in the garage."

"Oh! My! Dog! Look at the little dog!" Hala squealed. "Can I pet it?"

"Yes, just be careful. Morag is old, blind, and cranky," Matilda said.

Hala lay on the floor and slowly inched toward Morag while cooing at her. Morag growled for a moment, pressing closer to Matilda, before allowing Hala to woo her with scratches.

"What kind of name is Morag?" Hala asked, picking up the dog.

"I think it's Scottish for swamp monster. I heard it in a poem in middle school, and it stuck with me."

"You named your dog after a swamp monster?" Hala asked.

Matilda laughed. "You would understand if you would have smelled her before I bathed her."

"Hala, why don't you take Morag to the backyard to play while the adults talk?" Jessa said.

Matilda couldn't have been more than five years older than Hala, but she already longed for the days when she was shooed outside so the adults could talk.

Hala grabbed some granola bars, and headed out the back door. Hard rock music blared when she opened the door.

"Close it fast, Hala!" her mother yelled.

"I'm sorry for all the interruptions," Jim said.

"It's no problem at all. Makes me miss my family. I can't wait to finish my trip and go home." Her heart ached at the thought.

"Is there anything else you can tell me about my father, Mr. Siyuga?"

"Call me Jim." He got up and poured more lemonade. "Your father was a good man. Vietnam had a way of carving the heart out of a man and filling him with bile. I never saw your father treat anyone with less than respect. My parents are American Indians. Banks would go toe to toe with anyone that disparaged me or my family."

Matilda smiled. "That makes me happy."

"I have a few old film reels from Nam. Would you like to see them?"

"Yes, please!" Matilda said with her heart in her throat.

"Jessa…" Jim began.

"In the garage." Jessa finished.

Jim stood and headed towards the back of the house. Matilda and his wife followed him out to the garage. In the backyard Hala was running in circles around Morag singing M-O-R-A-G to the tune of BINGO. Morag's tongue was lolled out, and she looked happy.

Little Jim was hammering away on a bass as the other guys played the guitar and drums. They were awful, but they were enthusiastic.

"Dad! We're practicing," Little Jim said, stopping mid song.

Jessa applauded. "You sound great. Did you write that song?"

"Mom, that's the Clash," Little Jim said.

"Hi, Mrs. Siyuga, my mom told me to ask you are you still having a bake sale this weekend?" The drummer asked, pushing his long hair away from his eyes.

"Saturday after soccer. Your mother needs to make churros," Jessa said.

Jim was looking through a box marked *Home Movies* on a shelf loaded down with a lot of other labeled boxes. The tableau made Matilda miss Granddad.

"Found them," Jim said, holding up some battered film canisters. "LJ, grab the projector for me."

"Dad, we're practicing," his son protested again before setting his bass on the garage floor. Little Jim climbed onto a chest freezer and grabbed the projector from an upper shelf. "Want it in the living room?"

His father nodded. "Do you boys want to come in for lemonade and home movies?"

"Sure," the drummer answered, laying his sticks to the side.

"Mike! We're practicing," LJ grumped.

When they were all in the living room, Jessa handed out oatmeal cookies while Jim weaved the film through a projector even older than the ones that were pushed around on carts at Tildy's school.

"Where you from?" the drummer asked Matilda, who sat on a loveseat with Hala and Morag.

"I'm from Landover, Missouri."

"Is that near St. Louis?" the guitarist asked, munching a cookie.

"Nowhere near it. It's about four hours from St. Louis, KC, Tulsa, or anywhere else in the developed world." Matilda fed a bit of the cookie to Morag and wondered if she could sneak the rest under a cushion. *Doesn't anybody else in the world like chocolate chips?*

"That blows," LJ said.

"Jimmy, do not say 'blows,'" Jessa said.

"Sorry, Mom." LJ rolled his eyes a little, and smiled knowingly to Matilda. "My mom is pretty old fashioned," he whispered. "It's a Filipino thing."

"I understand. My grandparents are the same way." She stopped. "They aren't Filipino, but they're pretty strict. I know they mean well, though."

"They let you drive across country. If I drove past the city limits I would have to listen to the story of my mother being whipped for walking on the same sidewalk as a boy when she was a kid," LJ said.

"Well, my family doesn't know exactly where I'm at, or that I have a car ... or a dog." She rubbed Morag's head.

"You're a runaway?" Hala said, eyes wide.

"Not exactly. I'm going home. I'm just not going until I find out what happened to my mother."

"Shit. That's badass," LJ said.

Matilda tried not to blush.

When the film reel started, Jessa dimmed the lights. She ran the teen boys off the couch so she and Jim could sit together.

The boys sat on the carpet in front of the loveseat. They were close enough that Matilda could feel LJ's body heat through his t-shirt.

"That's my sergeant, Sergeant Greene. He was terrifying. This is the river near Fort Leonard Wood."

"The Gasconade?" Matilda asked. "That is half an hour from my house."

"Maybe. I don't remember. It's been too long. Okay, this is in Fort Drum, New York. Well, it was Camp Drum then."

The film was silent, and within minutes of it starting the room grew silent as well. Jeeps rolled by on the film in a parade of waving soldiers.

"This was my garrison," Jim whispered. "There he is!" He jumped up, and the film played on his metal arm as he pointed out Mark. Mark was dressed in winter gear, and his annoyance at being filmed was evident as he smiled and waved at the camera.

Matilda held her breath. That was her Dad. He was standing beside a man that was a young Jim. There were other shots of men shining their shoes in their barracks.

The whole video didn't last twenty minutes, but it was long enough to break Matilda's heart. "He looked happy. He was a world away from my mother. How could he be happy?"

Hala leaned against Matilda's shoulder. "I'm sorry you lost your dad."

"Thank you," Matilda said.

"There are moments of happiness even at the worst of times." Jim loaded another film reel. "He was just trying to do his time, and get home to his family."

LJ leaned back against the loveseat, brushing against Matilda's legs. The closeness made her think about the first time she'd made out with a boy. She'd longed for something in the farmboy's embrace that she'd never been able to achieve, a sense of wholeness.

"Hala, go out to play," Jim said.

"Can I take Morag?" she asked.

"Sure. Don't let her get into any trouble," Matilda said, handing the dog to Hala, who was climbing over the boys to get out.

"Christ. You stepped on my hand," LJ said, standing to let her by. When he sat back down it was in the spot next to Matilda.

"Jessa, you may not want to watch this one."

"I am fine," she said nervously.

The next video began to play. Soldiers were removing trees and brush with machetes. Men were laying still on the ground. Matilda watched closely for signs that they were breathing as the camera panned across them. A body lay on its back with its mouth and eyes unnaturally wide.

Matilda dropped her eyes. A sick feeling rolled in her stomach.

"Sorry, guys. That was the reality of Vietnam. This was a few weeks before Mark was killed. We were working our way into Cambodia, and we could only move inches at a time."

The film went dark for a moment before her father's face covered the entire screen. It looked like her father, but there was no smile. Dirt and camouflage paint hid his face, but his eyes were recognizable. When the film refocused her father was playing cards on the ground with a few other men. They were all in camo face paint, but there was no mistaking which one was her dad.

Right before Jim stopped the video it showed dozens of bodies in various states of decay.

"I'm sorry. I tried to stop it before that part." Jim wound the film back onto the the reel. "That's all the film I have until I was back stateside."

"Thank you for sharing that with me," Matilda said, trying to process all she had seen. "I guess I need to load Morag back into my car and head to Santa Monica. Unless there is anything else you can tell me about my parents before I go."

"Stay and have dinner. It will be too dark to drive safe. You can sleep in Hala's room." Jessa said.

"There is a store downtown that converts old film to VHS tapes," Jim said. "Would you like me to get this copied, so you can take it back to Mississippi?"

"That's all right. I've already imposed too much." Matilda halfheartedly turned them down.

"Nonsense. You will stay. I will make pork chops," Jessa said.

"And I'll run these films downtown right now," Jim said.

Matilda nodded. "Thank you," she said. "I'm going to go out to check on Morag." What she really meant was *I need space.*

She was hyper aware of herself as she went to her car. Matilda considered leaving. She could back out of the parking space and just forget she'd ever come to Mesquite, Nevada.

Her eyes were closed, and her hand was on Ophelia's handle. She could be home by this time tomorrow.

"We're walking to the store. Wanna come along?" LJ asked from behind her.

"Sure," she said releasing the car door. "I need a Dr. Pepper. Do you want me to drive?"

"It's only a few blocks. By the way, this is Mike and Danny." He gestured to the drummer and guitarist respectively. "Do you go by Matilda, or something else?"

"Tildy," she said.

The boys walked eastward along First Street. As soon as the house was out of sight, Mike produced a pack of cigarettes. "Want one?" he asked after passing the pack to Danny.

"Yes, please. I haven't had one in days." She took the generic smoke, and held it as LJ lit it. Matilda held his eye contact until the cherry glowed. The first draw was harsh. Whether it was the brand or the fact she hadn't smoked in a while, she wasn't sure. Tildy didn't let on though.

It was obvious that Danny wasn't really a smoker. When he took a drag he held it in his mouth for a while before exhaling it. That had been what Matilda did when she was a beginner.

"So, what's the name of your band?" she asked.

"We had a lot of names, but none of them stuck," Mike said.

"Might steal your dog's name." LJ said.

"Go for it. Morag would approve," Matilda said, watching the cigarette clasped between her fingers burn down. She wasn't a smoker anymore.

The store they stopped at was connected to a laundromat. Matilda bought a soda and sat on a folding table to drink it.

"That's fucked up about your parents," LJ said as his friends bought their junk food.

"Yeah."

"How old were you when your mother left?" he asked.

"Not even a year. I don't remember her at all, and my dad died before I was born."

"I was born right before my father left for Vietnam, and don't remember anything about it. My mother's parents came to America from the Philippines during World War II. While he was in Vietnam they kept pushing her to marry a Filipino guy."

"Yikes. That had to suck." Matilda said.

"Yeah. Well, his parents are Havasupai Indians, and they wanted me raised on the reservation, and they pushed for my mom to surrender me to my aunt. That's why we live in Nevada. She applied for a job, and she and I relocated with nothing that wouldn't fit in a Dodge Coronet."

"That's brave," she said.

"Maybe your mom was trying to be brave too. Maybe she wasn't running away, but trying to rebuild her life." LJ was trying to comfort her. "Maybe that's what you're doing too."

"I like my life. No matter what happens here," she held his eye contact again, "or when I get to Santa Monica. I'm going home to play in the marching band, sleep through AP history, and to tell my best friends to either stop having sex or admit they're in a relationship."

"It sounds like you have a lot going on right now." LJ laughed.

"Too damn much, to be honest," Tildy said.

Danny and Mike came back to the laundromat side of the building. They were seeing who could shove more Twinkies in his mouth without choking while saying the alphabet.

"Fierce competition," LJ said.

The walk back to the house was filled with Danny and Mike trying to see who could sound more like Glenn Danzig while also gargling Mountain Dew. These dorks were so similar to the kids Matilda had always hung out with, but her friends had better taste in music.

With all the toxicity and horror she had been involved in within the past week, it was nice to laugh.

"You'll have to forgive my friends. They haven't matured much since fifth grade," LJ said.

"It's cool," Tildy said. "Being a grownup sucks. It's one shitty scenario after another."

"Bake sales, band camps, and bullshit; adulthood is an alliterative nightmare of epic proportions," LJ snapped his fingers like a beatnik poet.

"Sounds like you've just written your first gold record," Tildy said. "So, what's it like living this close to Vegas?"

"It's probably the same as living in Missouri; school, work, and hanging with your friends," Danny said.

"And dating girls," Mike added.

LJ looked embarrassed. "Yeah, lots of dating. As long as by dating you mean playing bass and going to the arcade to play Donkey Kong."

"You dated Lisa Ersery last year," Mike said.

"They didn't date. They just made out," Danny volunteered.

"Wow." Matilda laughed. "They are just throwing you under the bus."

"Well, what do you do in Missouri?" LJ asked, changing the subject.

"Marching band, school, and church takes up most of my life." There was no way that she was going to tell three complete strangers about her dating history. There hadn't been any dating, technically. She'd hooked up with a trumpet player in her marching band at the old graffiti bridge a few times. Jason from church camp taught her how to make out in a canoe without flipping it over. There had been a few other guys that didn't warrant a rerun in her memory. She always thought they would be fun, or special, or that they would make her feel different — they didn't.

"Hello?" LJ said.

"What? I was somewhere else. Sorry."

"What instrument did you say that you play in marching band?" he repeated.

"I play second chair clarinet in a class of two clarinetists." She smiled.

"No shit? I played clarinet too." Danny said. "Mike played the drums in band too."

"What about you, LJ?"

"Didn't play in the band. My parents tortured us with soccer instead. I was also in ROTC, but that didn't pan out."

"Why didn't it pan out?" Matilda asked as they arrived back at the house.

"I'm just not cut out to go into the Army. I'm a free spirit --" LJ was cut off by Morag's high pitched barking.

Hala was still sitting in the grass with Morag, who was dragging her back legs around in the yard, and barking like a maniac.

"She's so funny," Hala said.

"Yeah, she's a riot," Matilda said as Jim came out of the house.

"They will have that VHS tape ready tomorrow afternoon. Jessa has made dinner. You should come eat." Jim said.

"You boys staying for dinner?" Jessa called out the screen door.

"Not tonight. Our mom made tamales," Mike yelled back. "It was cool to meet you, Tildy. If you're ever back this way, you'll have to come watch us jam."

"It was nice meeting you," Matilda said.

Jessa has made pork chops, mashed potatoes, green beans, and fruit salad for dinner. Her Betty Crocker cookbook was still open to a picture of brightly colored fruit salad in gelatin.

Dinner was delicious. LJ sat next to her. She accidentally ran her fingers along the edge of his leg when everyone was distracted talking. There was no doubt that they had an effect on each other.

After dinner Jessa insisted on cleaning up alone. Hala made up the couch, and put a cushion down for Morag to sleep on. LJ showed Matilda where the bathroom he shared with his sister was and loaned her a Buzzcocks shirt and sweatpants to sleep in.

They watched MTV in the living room. Hala was stretched out on the couch in her Strawberry Shortcake pajamas, leaving Matilda and LJ the loveseat.

They sat as far apart as possible, watching all the pop music that aired during the prime time hours.

"What do you think of punk music?" LJ asked her.

She turned herself towards him and crossed her legs, tucking her feet in. Her knees rested against his thigh.

"Honestly, it's very loud and aggressive, and often I have no idea what the hell it's about."

"So, you into pop like Madonna and The Cars?"

"No. It's all ok, but I'm a metalhead. I'll take Motley Crue or Quiet Riot any day." Matilda said. "What do like about punk?"

"I like it all. The fact that they don't give a shit about being corporate shills. Their music is visceral. If you don't know what's happening you need to listen with your gut instead of your brain."

She and LJ sat up talking about music until after midnight. The heavier music had come on the TV, but they were too engrossed in their conversation to notice.

Sometime in the night Matilda had fallen asleep. LJ covered her with an Afghan and went to bed himself.

When Matilda woke in the morning, people were reluctantly getting ready for school and work.

Jessa and Jim both wore white button up shirts and black slacks. Each wore an identification badge for an area casino. Hala wore a cute dress and jelly shoes. Even though Matilda hated jellies, they were cute on Hala. LJ looked exactly as he had the night before; jeans and a punk t-shirt, but his glorious hair was braided down his back.

"I hope you like Captain Crunch cereal. It's on the counter. Milk is in the fridge. Make yourself at home. We will be home at three." Jessa said, shooing her children toward the door.

Morag whined as Hala left.

"Traitor," Matilda said. "Now you don't get Cap'n Crunch for breakfast." She stretched as she stood. Laying in the awkward position all night left her with a sore neck.

Matilda turned the television to MTV and ate a bowl of the sugariest thing she'd ever consumed. It was awesome.

She washed her bowl while listening to someone that sounded like Billy Idol singing in the other room. Matilda set the dish in the drainer and went back toward the living room when the music suddenly cut off.

She wasn't surprised to find LJ sitting on the loveseat with the remote control.

"That shit will rot your brain," he said. "You are going to love punk by the time my parents get off work."

She smiled. "Are you truant, Mr. Siyuga?"

"Don't give me lip, Miss Runaway," he said, turning off the television. "I'm grabbing my tapes. Prepare to be swayed." LJ disappeared for a few moments, returning with a large case of cassettes.

He opened the case onto the table, and pulled out a mixtape labeled with only a large black exclamation point. LJ removed the liner, and handed it to Matilda as he went to the glassed-in stereo system.

"The first song is a little harder, but once you catch onto the hook it will win you over."

"Sounds like you're going to try to sell me crack. Nancy Reagan would not approve."

"This is more addictive than crack … I assume. There's no real way to tell unless we get some crack and do a comparison contrast."

"For science?" Matilda laughed.

"Yes, science." He started the tape, "This is *Mommy's Little Monster* by Social Distortion."

The music was frantic, and she quickly lost track of the lyrics. It was fun to watch LJ play air guitar along with the band. He jumped around the living room when another song came on, giving Morag a fright.

"This is The Buzzcocks, *Ever Fallen in Love*." He pulled Matilda onto her feet to dance to the song, and sang every word.

I can't see much of a future
Unless we find out what's to blame, what a shame
And we won't be together much longer
Unless we realize that we are the same
Ever fallen in love with someone

> *Ever fallen in love, in love with someone*
> *Ever fallen in love, in love with someone*
> *You shouldn't have fallen in love with*

LJ was singing every word, and Matilda felt the lyrics.

"That's a pretty powerful message. The music is terrible, but the lyrics are amazing," she said.

LJ leaned forward to kiss her.

"Whoa," she said, pushing him back, but not releasing his shirt. "Didn't you hear that I'm leaving tonight?"

"Sorry," he said, but he didn't seem apologetic, just intense. "You are just the most honest person I've ever met."

Matilda pulled him back to her, and kissed him. She parted her lips, and scraped her tongue along his bottom lip. "You need to know that I gave up smoking three days ago on accident, and that I haven't shaved since I left Missouri."

"You rebel," he said, biting her bottom lip.

Matilda had the feeling she would never need to lie to this man.

"I'm not interested in a relationship," she said against his cheek.

His eyes were saucers. "Of course not. We've just met."

She leaned her head against his chest, and they slow danced to a song she never wanted to hear again. She didn't want to rush things with him. Also, there was no way that she was heading into senior year knocked up.

LJ held her tight against him. He kissed her on top of the head, He didn't try to get fresh, he just held her.

LJ reclined against the arm of the couch, and Matilda stretched herself atop the length of him. She was comfortable, and sleep would feel so good. Instead she kissed him, gently at first, leading to a solid make-out session.

"I can come with you," he said, stroking her hair.

"That would be crazy. You graduate in a month and a half. I'm not going to let you throw your life away on me." Matilda took off the Buzzcocks shirt, and lay on him in her bra and jeans..

"You're trying to distract me."

"Is it working?" Matilda asked.

"I love you," he said.

"No, not yet, you don't." She kissed his cheek. "If you ever find your way to Missouri then we can talk about love. For now let's just be in awe of each other."

"I am in awe of you, and I'm going to hold you to that Missouri thing." LJ squeezed her tight.

"You better." She smiled. "Because I could do this all day."

By the time Hala's bus arrived, Matilda was strung tighter than LJ's bass. Jim and Jessa arrived a short while later.

"I have your VHS tape," Jim said, laying the tape on the kitchen table.

"Thank you, sir. I can pay you for it," Matilda said.

"It's the least we could do," Jessa said.

That night after dinner Matilda watched Morag -- the band -- practice. She had a new understanding of their terrible music. Tildy let Morag the dog play with Hala in the backyard. If she had her camera she would have snapped pictures of both events. There was no doubt that she'd see these people again.

When the house was silent, Matilda sneaked into LJ's room. They snuggled and talked about their separate dreams for the future.

Matilda woke up in Hala's room as she was getting ready for school. She waited in bed until after Jessa left to take the kids to school to get up. There was a note and a cassette on the pillow.

Tildy,

I want you to keep my Buzzcocks shirt. It's my favorite, so I have a good excuse to go to Missouri to get it. After you fell asleep I made you this mixtape. It's mostly the songs I played for you already, but there are a few foundational pieces that you should hear before passing judgement on an entire musical genre. I hope you find what you're looking for in California.

I'm writing my phone number and mailing address on the bottom, so we can keep in contact. You don't believe me, but I do love you. After I graduate I'll have time to prove it to you.

Love, Little Jim Siyuga

She held the letter to her chest. He made her feel loved even if it was too soon to be real.

Matilda was glad that he'd given her permission to keep his shirt, because she'd already decided that she was keeping it. She got dressed, gathered Morag, and got on the road to Santa Monica.

Chapter 13

She crossed into California as the clouds thinned, and an air of calm fell on the car. She planned her next move. When she researched the Vietnam War for her AP History class she'd gone to her local library. The librarian had shown her how to use the microfilm reader to look up local newspaper articles. In truth, she'd done a day by day search for her father's name in the obituaries.

The obituaries is where she would find her mother's name. She knew that now. Crystal Huggins must have killed Annette to try to save her marriage.

Matilda was growing anxious. The sky was bluer than she thought was possible. The warm dog on her stomach made her feel at peace.

When Morag began to sniff and bark Matilda decided to pull off at a rest stop.

She and Morag walked all over the rest stop as drivers were waking up. There had been a ton of cars when she stopped that morning, but now the place was almost empty.

Morag consumed her dog food one piece at a time, and Matilda counted enough change to buy a cup of terrible coffee from the vending machine. At least it was entertaining to watch the machine brew the beverage.

A couple of teenagers passed nearby. Morag growled and barked ferociously, the way only an elderly blind chihuahua can.

"I'm sorry. She thinks she's a Doberman," Matilda said.

"She's cute," the girl lied. "Are you heading to California for Spring Break too?"

"Sort of. Going to Santa Monica." Matilda didn't want to go into the details.

"Nice. We're heading to Malibu," the guy said. "It's going to be crazy." He looked like a surfer. His hair was a blonde messy mop, and his skin was tan. He was the polar opposite of LJ.

In a different world that could have been her. No cares other than fun in the sun. Instead she was an anxiety ridden seventeen year old straddling the fence of being a good little girl and a cynical old maid. She didn't often pine for "what could have been," but that is exactly what she was doing now.

Matilda envied the version of herself that would argue with her parents about the silly teen rebellions that she'd long ago abandoned; makeup, boys, school, and dreams. She envied dreams that weren't riddled with dead parents and a loss so ancient that she could only remember having the scar, but not receiving it.

Matilda waved goodbye to the pair as she loaded Morag into her box. Morag's tongue was flopped out of her mouth again. She was such a weird little dog, but she was growing on Tildy.

Now that she and Morag were fed and watered, they headed further into the Mohave.

Driving around Los Angeles was a nightmare. She white-knuckled the steering wheel as vehicles honked and sped past her. It was hard to watch the road signs with so much traffic, but eventually she made it to Santa Monica. The ocean was vast and glorious in front of her.

"Wow," she said to Morag, who was now on her shoulder sniffing the air.

She parked Ophelia and carried Morag to the pier that marked the end of Route 66. It made her nervous to walk onto the pier. Matilda touched the sign and said goodbye to her father. Goodbye to the little boy that his parents remembered, goodbye to the teenager that had married her mother, and goodbye to the dark-eyed man that died a world away from his family.

"This is where she would have sprinkled the last of him," a familiar voice said behind her. Matilda let loose a squeal as she turned to see Aunt Caroline.

"How did you know I'd be here?" Matilda cried.

"I've been here a couple days. Started thinking that you wouldn't come," Caroline said.

Matilda threw her arms around her aunt, trying not to smash Morag. "There is so much I have to tell you. Here. Hold Morag."

"What in God's name is this, and why does it smell like that?" Caroline took Morag as the creature growled and snapped the air around her.

Matilda pulled pictures from her purse, and swapped them for her dog.

Caroline thumbed through the pictures. "Did you find her?" Her voice cracked, and she looked almost afraid.

"Almost," Tildy answered. She didn't want to say she thought her mother was dead. There would be time for that once she had the proof.

Caroline hugged her again as they walked back towards the parking lot. "Let's go call Grandma and Granddad."

In the parking Caroline stopped and gaped at Ophelia. "Holy shit! How did you find your dad's car?" Caroline ran her hand down Ophelia's trim.

"It was a little detective work and a lot of luck; most of it bad. She was in hiding in Tucumcari. How did you get here?" Matilda looked around for Caroline's truck or Grandma's car.

"I searched that town," Caroline said. Tears filled Caroline's eyes again. "My God! I wasted so much of my life trying to find her, and I don't want that for you."

The two women hugged again, squishing the annoyed dog between them.

"How did you get here?" Matilda repeated.

"Jonah loaned me enough money for a plane ticket," Caroline said, wiping away the tears that had fallen on Morag.

Matilda nodded. "I need to go to the library. This pier is the last place I have proof that she was."

"No. Let's just stop. There is nothing you could find that would make it better. She's dead or she doesn't care about us," Caroline said.

"I haven't come this far to give up," Matilda said. "If you don't care, then leave, but I'm not going anywhere until I have what I came for -- answers." Matilda reached for her door handle.

Caroline held her hands up in surrender. "I'm sorry. I'm sorry. Please, whatever you need. Just don't run away again. What do you need? Let me help."

"I just need to get something to eat, and then find the local library."

"There is a cafe at my hotel. It's not far from here."

Matilda reached into her car and moved Morag's box into the tiny backseat.

Caroline climbed into passenger's seat, and navigated Matilda to her hotel. Her eyes were on Matilda the whole way.

They ate on the patio so Morag could sit in her box nearby. Matilda ordered all-you-can-eat pancakes and bacon. Morag gummed lots of bacon. After breakfast, Matilda used the phone book in Caroline's room to locate the library.

"You watch Morag. I'll be right back." It took a lot of convincing to get Aunt Caroline to stay behind.

Chapter 14

Matilda yawned as she moved the microfiche around on the machine. She had started on November 30, because that was the postmark on the last letter her mother had sent. Matilda read any articles about murder; dreading the moment she would find her mother's name. Each cell of the fiche only held half of a newspaper page, and with each newspaper having at least a dozen pages; she was almost asleep by the time she switched to the December 1 fiche.

She was on the December 3 cell when her stomach dropped out. Her hand was shaking as she focused the microform machine and enlarged the cell.

***

Annette Sterling Banks stood as far west as she could go and upended the small canvas sack that contained what was left of her husband's ashes.

The brisk, shifting winds whipped the ashes into a small cloud, spiraling and rising, then seeming to dip toward her for an instant before flying out to disappear over the cold, churning waters.

He's gone, she thought.

Nettie sat down at the edge of the Santa Monica Pier and cried. Mark, scooting his desk closer to hers in English class so Mr. Ingram wouldn't see they were holding hands. Mark, face flushed and jubilant after catching a touchdown pass in the Camdenton game, yanking off his helmet and finding her in the crowd even as his teammates pummeled him. Mark, putting the doughball on the hook for her at Bennett Spring. Mark, sitting in the glider on his parents' front porch, bright eyed, holding her hand and talking to her about all the worlds they would conquer together.

Mark, Mark, Mark.

Sending electric joy through her with just a look. Making love for the first time. Holding her so tight and promising this was forever.

Nettie drew her knees up to her and wrapped her arms around them. She had cried -- often -- since receiving the telegram, but not like this. Her sobs racked her, and she felt like she was coming apart. She couldn't stop, and she knew she probably needed to. Gales of grief lashed her again and again, and the memories would not stop.

Most of all was the memory of Mark, kissing her goodbye, hoisting his duffel over his shoulder and walking through the gate at the airport. Turning back for one little wave, smiling for her, then gone.

Gone, she thought again. And again.

Nettie had not realized how angry she was. At the government for taking him away and at Mark for not coming back. At her parents for not understanding and at little Mattie -- even her baby -- for having those same beautiful blue eyes. At her whole life, a life that failed to prepare her for the destruction of all her hopes and the realization of all her fears.

It seemed impossible that things had gone on. Even now, behind her on the pier, children were laughing as they rode the fake, worn horses on the old carousel. Others were whooping in the arcade, in victory or chagrin, depending on how well their games were going. Behind all that was the country, where people were smoking weed and making love, where other people were struggling to pay their bills, where some people were coming home from war and others were preparing to go. People were cooking and eating meals and going to their jobs and learning in schools and colleges as well as in streets and fields.

Life goes on, she thought. *It shouldn't be able to, but it does for no good reason.*

Little by little she got control of herself. She used her sleeve to scrub at the tears in her eyes and their streaks on her face. She sniffed and wished she had a tissue or a whole box of them. She concentrated on breathing deeply, calming down. Nettie looked at the ocean, at the thousands of tiny sparks of reflected sunlight, there and gone in an instant. *That's us, all of us.*

She didn't feel better exactly, but she felt lighter. Annette didn't know how long she had been sitting on the pier, but her legs protested as she slowly stood up. For a moment she didn't turn around. Turning around and taking that first step toward home would mean that this was really over.

I guess I could stand here until they build a couple thousand miles onto the end of this thing, she thought. *Who knew Route 66 was so short? It didn't mention that in the book.*

She had to go. Crystal was waiting in the coffee shop on the beach. Annette turned around and took a step, then others, and the small empty canvas bag fluttered unnoticed from her unclenched hand.

A few men, mostly old, were fishing from the pier near where she had sat for so long. None made eye contact as she passed them, for which she was grateful. *They probably think I'm a lunatic.* Farther on, a few people hustled in and out of the remaining amusements on the pier, which had definitely seen better days.

The day was warm enough, mid-60s probably, and fair. Nettie would miss the California December weather when she got home. She hurried along the weathered wooden planks until she was just part of the crowd again, then stepped off the pier onto the sand. The coffee shop was across the street, but Annette didn't see Crystal's Fairlane parked out front as it had been.

A little bell jangled over the door as she entered. It was probably mid afternoon -- Nettie's sense of time was a little muddled -- and the few tables in the place were unoccupied. A couple of lone coffee drinkers were at the counter, but Crystal was nowhere to be seen.

That's odd. She said she would wait here until I was done. Maybe Crystal had gone to gas up the car and get snacks for the trip back. Annette took a seat at the counter, and a minute later a waitress came over. The woman was about Nettie's age, her dark hair pulled back in a ponytail and wearing bright pink lipstick and probably a little too much eye makeup.

"Hi," Nettie said. "I'm looking for my friend. She was going to wait here for me. She's blond, kind of short, and has on a tie-dyed shirt and blue jeans."

The waitress nodded. "Yeah, she was here. She had the ham sandwich. She left me 50 cents."

"Did she say if she was coming back or if I should wait here?"

"No, she didn't say anything," the waitress said. "Just ordered her food. And a Coke," the woman added as if that information might be helpful.

Annette nodded. "Thanks, um, Dana," she said, reading the nametag. "I guess I'll just wait for her then. Can I get a cup of coffee?"

"Sure honey," Dana said. She went down to the end of the counter and got a pot from a warmer, then returned. Nettie flipped her cup on its saucer and the waitress poured, then produced a small metal decanter of cream from under the counter.

"Hey, would you have anything I can write on? And a pen?" Annette asked. Dana looked thoughtful, then snapped her fingers.

"If it's still here ..." she said, and went to the other end of the counter. She reached beneath the cash register and produced a notebook. "Some kid left this in here," she said, returning and handing it to Annette. "You're welcome to it."

Nettie thanked her and took the pen Dana offered her. *How do I write this?* She put the pen to the corner of the page and drew an oval standing on its end, then a wavy line coming off that and a little circle for a nose. A small line served as the cartoon dog's closed eye. Tada, Snoopy.

"Dear Mattie," she wrote.

***

Annette finished her letter, tore the pages from the notebook and carefully folded them before putting them in her back pocket. She began to face the idea that Crystal wasn't coming back. Dana had refilled her coffee twice now. It was getting on toward the dinner hour, and the coffee shop was beginning to get busier.

Almost all of Annette's money was in her purse, which was under the front passenger seat of the Fairlane. She had the change in her pocket from breaking a fifty to get gas and supplies at the beginning of their trip yesterday.

She couldn't believe Crystal would run out on her like this, but in a way it made sense. The woman had been eager to drive her to California. Nettie had suspected Crystal wasn't as cavalier about Annette's relationship with Lorne as she had pretended. She knew Crystal was going to be happy to have her gone, but Crystal had agreed to bring her back to Holbrook and then see her on a bus back to Tucumcari, where Annette would pick up her car and go home. That was the plan.

I might have enough cash for a bus ticket back to Ophelia. Damn it, Crystal!

The Church of the Blue Oracle had been about pot, love and taking care of each other. Annette hadn't taken it very seriously as a viable lifestyle, but she had appreciated that some of the members did. Apparently not Crystal.

Nettie was getting angrier by the minute as she continued to wait in the coffee shop. Finally she decided it was no use and got up, digging in her jeans pocket for a few coins to pay for the coffee.

"Giving up?" Dana asked, coming over with her ticket.

"Might as well," Nettie said. "I think I've been abandoned."

"Well, I hope it turns out okay," Dana said. "Maybe your friend got sick or something."

"Maybe," Annette said, and left.

She stepped out of the shop onto the sidewalk and looked west where the sky was beginning to glow orange as the sun hovered closer to the ocean. It would have been nice to wait and watch it, but Nettie didn't want to be hitchhiking in the dark.

For now she would ride her thumb as far as she could, maybe all the way back to Tucumcari. What she needed was a truck driver who wasn't a creep going a long way on Route 66.

An hour later, she was no closer to getting out of the Santa Monica warren of confusing streets. Annette hadn't seen a sign for Route 66 in a while and feared she had left it behind for good. Her feet were starting to hurt. She hadn't tried hitching yet because she didn't know where she was and she might be getting into a car headed away from the direction she wanted to go.

It was starting to get dark, and she was starting to get scared. Even if she could find a hotel, it would seriously deplete her cash to stay in town overnight. But she didn't want to spend the night wandering lost around a strange city either.

Damn you, Crystal! she thought again.

She had been looking for a gas station for a while now. Gas station attendants were usually good at giving directions, right? But she didn't seem to be in that sort of business district. The street she was on seemed to be all shuttered shops and office buildings, places that locked up at five on the dot.

Finally, about a block ahead of her, she saw a small panel truck idling in front of a store that still had its lights on. As she got closer, Annette saw it was a bookstore and felt relief. Nobody who worked at a bookstore could be a bad guy.

She went along the side of the truck nearer the store and almost ran into a middle-aged man carrying a carton.

"Ooph! Oh my, I'm sorry, Miss. I didn't see you there," the man said. "Wasn't trying to run you over. Hey, could you open the back door on the truck? My hands are full and I didn't think ahead. It's my failing, my wife says."

Annette nodded and retreated to the rear of the truck, turning the chrome handle to open the double rear doors. She stood back so the man could muscle the carton into place among a dozen others.

He stepped back and sighed. "Books! Don't go into books, Miss. It's a good business when you're young, but burdensome to carry around when you get a little older. Burdensome! Was that a double entendre or simply the way the word was meant to be used when it was first invented? I should write that down.

"Now, what may I do for you, Miss? You seem as if you have something on your mind. Not that any young people truly have anything on their minds these days. I suspect you're a duly sworn officer of the court disguised as a flower child here to deliver a subpoena? Crafty of you, but you'll find I'm no easy prey!"

Annette was overcome by the torrent of words, but amused. The man's smile showed he was joking about dodging her court papers, and she wished she had some just to see the look on his face.

He reminded her a little of Dad. He was stocky, dressed in corduroy pants and a button-down flannel shirt with the sleeves half rolled up. Despite his complaints about his work, the forearms she could see looked well able to carry much heavier loads. But he was perspiring and obviously winded by his efforts.

I guess it's been a long day for both of us, she thought. "No subpoenas today, I'm afraid," she said when he stopped talking to draw a breath. "I was hoping I could ask you for directions out of this crazy town. I've been walking around in circles for an hour."

"Directions? Ha!" The man raised an authoritative finger. "Young lady, you have stumbled into the right venue for such a query. Directions! If only more people sought my guidance, this country would be in far sadder shape. I mean much less sadder shape. Well, you know what I mean.

"But of course in order to know where you're going, you must be acquainted with where you have been. Oftentimes that's the issue, you see. You may also find that a stitch in time may save as many as nine, but usually it only saves four or five, hardly worth the effort."

The man closed one of the rear doors and perched on the edge of the truck's bumper. He pulled a handkerchief from a shirt pocket and wiped his face, then folded it and replaced it in the pocket. Next he dug out a wrinkled pack of cigarettes and a book of matches. He offered her the pack first, and she took one, noticing that the smokes were Pall Malls.

The man waited until after he had lit both their cigarettes before resuming his monologue. "Francis Walsh," he said, introducing himself. "You will note that the store in front of you is named Walsh Books. That's not a coincidence. I own the place. Well, to be truthful, a large share is owned by my fellow investors, banks which believed themselves to be lending instead of contributing at the beginning of our relationship.

"But this will never be First National Books!" he proclaimed dramatically, waving his cigarette for emphasis. "I would swear it on my mother's name if I knew it."

Annette laughed, and Francis Walsh appeared pleased. She closed the other rear door so she could half-sit on the bumper beside him.

"I'm Annette. Call me Annie," she said. "I'm trying to get to --"

"Sad, that," Francis interrupted. "Back in my day, surnames were free to everyone, but these days they are prohibitively expensive. Have you considered investing in one of the cheaper ones, say Smith or Jones? A young lady of your wit and charm should have a full name that reflects her stature."

Annette was a little embarrassed, but she didn't want to share very much information with a stranger, even one as friendly and harmless as Francis seemed to be. "It is sad," she agreed, joining his game. "I once bid on the name Kerbumperfeld at an auction, but I lost to a guy named Horace."

Francis turned to look at her, delighted. "You could have put such a name to much better use," he judged. "Wit and charm. Now, as I have only a finite number of years remaining to me in this dark and cruel world, I must get back to loading this truck. Did you say something about needing directions?"

Annette nodded. "I'm going east to Kansas. I was going to hitchhike, but I've lost the highway somehow."

"Ah," Francis said. He stood and flicked the remainder of his cigarette, a bare stub, into the gutter. "I suppose I should lecture you about your hobo lifestyle now. Instead I will tell you that if you had kept walking past my truck, you would have come to signs pointing toward the on-ramp to Interstate 10 in a few more minutes."

"I did see a couple signs for that," Annette said. "But I think I-10 goes a lot farther south than I need to. I was trying to get back on Route 66."

"A traditionalist! Bless your heart, child. I think what you need is a road atlas. You might get one at a bookstore if you could find one open at this hour."

"Actually, that would really help," Annette said. Despite only knowing this man for ten minutes, it was obvious he was offering her the book. "Thank you."

Francis nodded and led the way into the store. It smelled like dust and wisdom and old sweat, and the lights were dim. The shelves she saw looked half empty, which wasn't surprising considering the number of books he had loaded in the truck. Francis went behind the counter and riffled through what appeared to be a disorganized mound of magazines. She was surprised when he pulled out a paperbound atlas that was only a couple years old.

"Walsh's First National Books," Francis said grandly, holding it up. "We rarely have what you want, but we sometimes have what you need. Now that's a slogan to sell books. I must go and make a television commercial at once."

"How much is it?" Annette asked. "I only have twenty four --"

Francis interrupted her again. "You need to save your money to invest in a last name. If you only have twenty four thousand dollars, as you were about to say, I'm sure, you're going to have to be frugal in order to outbid the next Kerflufflebumper or whatever it was."

Annette smiled and took the book, then realized she had nowhere to put it. It had been a long time since she hadn't carried a purse or bag of some sort. Francis saw her dilemma and came to the rescue with a cloth sack that she could sling over her shoulder.

"Well if you won't let me pay you, I can work for it," she said. "Do you have more books to load?"

It turned out he did. Within a few minutes, four more cartons were squeezed into the back of the truck. Annette had carried three of them after seeing Francis stagger against the truck carrying the first. She began to wonder if he was well. He was perspiring again and out of breath by the time she slammed the rear doors closed on the truck for the last time.

"Thank you, Miss Annie," Francis said. "I suppose I should bid you adieu and be on my way. I have to have these books arranged at the Barstow shop at 9 a.m. tomorrow, so I must put the pedal to the meadow and make like a drum and leave."

"Goodbye, Mr. Walsh," Annette said. "And thank you so much for the book."

"It's what I do," he said simply, then fluttered his hand in a shooing motion at her, crossing in front of the truck to get in the driver's side.

Annette turned and went down the sidewalk a couple steps, then turned back. She went to the truck and tapped on the driver's side window. Francis rolled it down.

"Did you say you were going to Barstow?" she asked. Francis nodded.

"I could probably get on I-40 in Barstow," Annette said. "After I help you unload these books."

Francis smiled. "Well, you're lazy and arrogant, but I suppose I could employ you for a few more hours. Hop in."

Annette did.

A few minutes later she wondered if it might be faster to get out and walk despite her aching feet. Traffic was unlike anything she had ever seen. Francis was uncharacteristically quiet, his hands kneading the glossy wooden steering wheel as he balefully regarded the sea of brake lights between them and the Santa Monica Freeway.

"I'm going to swing over and take Pico up to Euclid," Francis decided. "I think it's going to be easier to get on the freeway there."

Annette had no choice but to trust his judgment. She was really starting to worry about him, however. Only illuminated by the green of his dash lights and the red of the taillights in front of him, Francis looked ghastly. And he didn't seem to notice how much he was absently removing a hand from the steering wheel to rub his chest.

"Are you feeling all right?" she asked him. "You don't look like you feel very good."

Francis flicked her a glance, then smiled. "Oh, it will take more than a bit of traffic to take down this old warhorse. You're not from here, but it's almost always like this, sometimes worse. I have sat in traffic long enough to grow corn and sell it to my fellow drivers. I've been in traffic jams that can be seen by the Apollo astronauts as they wander around up there. That's why so few of them decide to come back. That's something your newspapers won't tell you. Most of them stay up there to avoid the traffic."

Annette could almost believe it. They inched forward in random jerks until finally Francis was able to dart down a side street to a relatively clearer area. He made a series of turns, seemingly at random, and Annette laughed out loud when she saw the Santa Monica Pier sign in front of them.

"See? We made it!" Francis said with mock pride.

Annette doubled over in her seat, laughing uncontrollably. *I am having a really bad day,* she said to herself, and that was even funnier. She felt tears streaming down her cheeks and realized Francis was laughing as well, though not as manically.

"Well," he said at length. "You get three tries to get on the highway here. It's in the city code. I think it's a little impatient of you to expect that we would be halfway to Barstow by now."

"Yeah, that wasn't fair of me," Annette said with as straight a face as she could manage. "I guess we could try again, but I think the third time we'll be starting from Hawaii."

Francis tried to look hurt, but she could see he was enjoying himself. He put the truck in gear and rumbled down yet another sidestreet.

A couple minutes later they were on Pico Boulevard, heading away from the ocean, as well as Annette could determine. Francis was still rubbing his chest occasionally, and his color didn't look any better. She was really starting to worry about him.

They were approaching the intersection at Main Street near a huge, modern looking auditorium when Francis let go of the steering wheel and wrapped his arms around his chest. "Oh, the elephant," he gasped.

The truck veered to the left, straight at an oncoming car. Annette grabbed the wheel and yanked it back. The truck careened to the right and over the curb, crashing into a light pole. Annette felt her forehead hit something and rocked back in her seat. The truck was stopped. The engine was stalled. She heard a scream.

The car.

She leaned forward so she could see Francis' face. He was panting, unconscious, his features contorted in pain. There was nothing she could do for him. She had to get help.

Annette's shaking hand found her door handle and twisted it upward. She spilled out of the truck, barely keeping her feet. She tottered to the rear of the vehicle, dazed from slamming her head, and only now realizing there was something wrong with her neck. It didn't want to hold up her head, and any movement to either side resulted in agony.

I'm hurt, she thought. *I got hurt in a car wreck.*

The screaming happened again.

Annette cleared the rear of the truck and saw the car. It rested on its passenger side in the middle of a sea of broken glass and chrome. Its front was mangled, crushed against a low stone wall. Between Annette and the car was a woman, sitting on the street with her arms braced at her sides, her legs bent unnaturally in front of her. The woman screamed again.

"My baby! Oh God my SON! Please somebody ..."

Annette wanted to go to her, and she wanted to go back to Francis, and she wanted to walk away eastward as far as she could go and leave this nightmare behind her.

But she knew she was no longer living the life she wanted to live, and there was someone else crying, a baby, an innocent, scared baby who was trapped inside a car that now had flames licking up the sideways hood. Something had ruptured and something else had sparked and you didn't need to watch a lot of movies to know there was going to be an explosion soon.

And there was a baby crying that sounded so much like Mattie.

***

Police Seek Tips on 'Angel'

SANTA MONICA (Dec. 3) -- Police are requesting information from the public about an unknown woman who saved a child's life after a car crash Friday evening but died at the scene.

The woman is Caucusian, between 16 and 24 years old, with curly brunette hair and hazel eyes, and wore a simple gold wedding band. She apparently had given birth within the past year, according to police.

The family of the child who was saved is offering a $50,000 reward for anyone who aids in identifying "the angel," according to a press release from the family's attorneys.

The accident occurred at about 7:04 p.m. when a 1958 GMC panel truck being driven by Mr. Francis Walsh, 51, of Santa Monica crossed the centerline on Pico Boulevard near the junction with Main Street. A 1965 Lincoln Continental being driven by Mrs. Pia Araya, 23, of Los Angeles, swerved to avoid the collision and crashed into a retaining wall.

Mrs. Araya was thrown clear of her vehicle but suffered fractures in both legs as well as a concussion, cuts and bruises. Mr. Walsh was not injured in the accident, but police believe he had suffered a heart attack, which had caused the truck to swerve into the path of the Lincoln.

Both Mr. Walsh and Mrs. Araya are recovering at Santa Monica Hospital.

Mrs. Araya's written statement to police described the way her son, Vincent Araya, 23 months old, was saved by the unknown woman.

"The car was sitting on its side and ready to fall over, and it was on fire," Mrs. Araya wrote in her statement. "The woman came out of nowhere and started climbing up over the roof. She got on top and tried to open the doors but they were too heavy, so she busted the glass out and climbed in. Next thing I know I saw my baby flying through the air and landing in the grass in front of the civic center. Then I saw the woman was trying to climb back out, but the car fell over on top of her."

The young woman was extricated from the wreckage and transported to Santa Monica Hospital where she was pronounced dead on arrival.

The police report indicated the child suffered only minor scrapes and bruises.

The unidentified woman was a passenger in the panel truck. Mr. Walsh told police he had hired "Annie" to help him move some merchandise from one of his bookstores, but he didn't know her last name.

Anyone with information about the identity of the young woman may call the Santa Monica Police Department at 555-8491.

Matilda stared at the screen for a long time. She felt like someone had dumped ice water over her, and she felt like she was going to vomit. The sketch, as crude as it was, was her mother, she had no doubt.

My mom is dead. She's really gone.

All her life, Tildy had known there were two possible reasons her mom never came back. Either she wouldn't or she couldn't. Now she had her answer, and she wasn't sure whether she would have rather had it the other way. *Let Mom be alive somewhere, living a good life, happy, maybe with a good husband and a bunch of other kids.* Let her still be there to maybe someday come back and explain things to her firstborn.

But the news article left no room for other possibilities. Her mom hadn't returned because she was dead.

Matilda fell off her chair in front of the microfiche machine, weeping. She curled into a ball and let her sadness have its way. Her mom was still a stranger to her despite all she had learned in the past two weeks, but her lack of a mother had been a constant, a scar that she now knew would always be with her.

I'm crying for myself, and I know how selfish that is, but I can't help it.

She must have been making some noise, because after a few minutes she sensed someone else was in the microfiche room with her. A gentle hand touched her shoulder.

"Honey? Are you all right?"

Matilda couldn't answer the librarian. She tried, but just ended up crying harder. She freed a hand from covering her face and waved vaguely at the machine, offering the only explanation she could. The touch on her shoulder became a pat, and the librarian's voice was much closer as she began to make soothing noises. She must have been kneeling on the floor beside Matilda.

Matilda wanted to just shut everything out and cry. She did, for long minutes, but the librarian's presence demanded she offer some kind of explanation. "It's my mom," she choked finally. "That story is about my mom."

The gentle patting ceased, and after a few seconds she heard a gasp. "Oh my," the woman said.

Matilda uncurled herself and sat up, rubbing the heels of her palms against her eyes. She drew a shuddering breath, then another, then looked up. The librarian was looking as if she might cry too as she extended her hand to help Tildy to her feet.

Matilda faced the machine and almost lost it again at the sight of the police sketch of her mom's face, but she held it together this time. She prepared the cell to print, and her hand shook as she pressed the print button.

"I'm so sorry," the librarian said. She reminded Tildy a little of old Witchman, but kind.

"It's … " Matilda swallowed. "It will be all right. I guess I need to get to the police station and tell somebody."

The librarian nodded. "Come get your pages from the printer," she said. "I can send one of the volunteers with you if you'd like."

Matilda noticed a mousy, bespectacled girl behind the librarian, eyes wide. She didn't think the child would be much help for her. "That's okay. If you could just point me in the right direction …"

"Four blocks down on the corner," the librarian said, pointing the way.

Matilda didn't get back into Ophelia. Instead she walked to the station, reading the article twice more on the way.

She entered the small station and laid the article on the counter. "This is my mother."

The officer looked at the article, and then back at Matilda. "I'll get a detective for you to speak with." The officer gestured to some folding chairs by the door. "Just have a seat."

Matilda traced the lines of her mother's face on the paper with her finger until a detective came to speak with her.

"I'm Lieutenant Garner," he said. The man was tall, dressed in a brown suit, with deep lines on his face and silver showing through his black hair.

He extended a nicotine yellowed hand to her, and she shook it. "Can you show me the article?" he asked.

Matilda handed it over and watched as he quickly skimmed it. "So, you think this mystery lady is your mother?" he said. He sounded skeptical.

"It *is* my mother," Matilda insisted. Garner searched her face for a moment, then grunted.

"I'll have an intern run to the basement to find the evidence packet for this case. You do look a lot like the drawing," he said.

Matilda nodded. "A lot of people say I look like her," she said.

The detective grunted again. "Come on back," he said, and led Matilda through the swinging half-door to the area behind the desk, then through a door marked DO NOT ENTER. Down a short hallway was a large room with five unoccupied desks holding typewriters and overflowing baskets of paperwork. Against the far wall was a computer terminal with a glowing amber screen.

Garner waved her to a folding chair beside one of the desks. "Name?" he asked.

"Matilda Banks," she answered. "My mother left her home in Missouri in 1967 to sprinkle my father's ashes along Route 66, and the last correspondence from her was mailed on November 30th. This is my mother."

"Do you have any identification, ma'am?" he asked, beginning to scribble notes on a coffee stained legal pad.

"No, I was pickpocketed on the bus in New Mexico on my trip out here."

"Where did you come from?"

"Landover, Missouri."

"Is there someone there that can confirm your identity?"

"My aunt has a room in a hotel here, but I don't remember its name. You can call my grandparents." Matilda gave him her grandparents' phone number, and he dialed it.

"Hello, ma'am, this is Lieutenant Garner from the Santa Monica Police Department," he said. He listened for a moment, his chin close to his chest. "No, it's okay, everything is all right." The detective's eyes widened, and for the first time he looked a little amused. "No, ma'am, she is fine. She is sitting right in front of me. Would you like to speak to her?" He handed Matilda the phone.

The sound of her grandma's voice wilted her.

"Matilda? Oh my word. Are you all right?" Grandma was speaking too fast to make out everything she said.

"Grandma. Grandma, I am fine. I am so sorry for running away." She took a deep breath. This was going to be so hard on them. But when there's nothing you can do, do nothing.

"Grandma, I found Mom. She didn't disappear. She died saving a little boy's life. She was a hero," Matilda said. Her eyes threatened fresh tears, but she forestalled them by biting her lip.

Grandma was quiet for a long time. "Well," she said at length. "Well. I guess I half expected it. Not the part about the little boy. I just knew she wouldn't leave and not ..." Her voice trailed off.

Now Matilda did start crying again, not caring what the detective thought.

"Well," Grandma said again. "You get home, child. There will be plenty of time to tell us all about it, but right now I want you home."

"I'm sorry that I scared you when I left," Matilda said. "I'm heading home in the morning. Caroline's here, so you don't have to worry. I will be home in a few days."

There was silence on the other end of the phone, and then a small voice returned. "Be safe. We love you."

"You didn't tell me that you were a runaway," Garner said, taking the phone receiver from her. "I'll need to contact your local police department to let them know you are here and that you are safe."

Matilda nodded. "Please tell them about my mother's case as well."

Within an hour Matilda was sitting in front of a police captain's desk with the detective.

"Miss Banks, your local police department is glad that you are safe, and they'd like you to stop in as soon as you return home," the captain said. "You aren't in trouble. They just want to make sure you are safe and sound."

He placed a manila envelope in front of her. "These are the items that were found to be in your mother's possession by the coroner's office." He removed two cellophane bags. "A gold wedding band, $23, and a letter. The letter has some blood stains on it, so if you don't want to see it, I understand."

"Of course I want to see it," she said. She held her shaking hand out for the letter.

The two men waited in silence as she unfolded the old paper and began to read. The brown spots on the pages didn't interfere with the message.

Dear Mattie,

I know that you won't remember these few months that I've been away, but I want you to know why I was gone. When I lost your father I lost myself too. While I was gone I said goodbye to him at most of the spots we had planned to visit on our honeymoon.

Saying goodbye to him was the hardest thing I've ever done, but as I sprinkled the last of his ashes into the Pacific Ocean at the Santa Monica pier, I finally felt like I was ready to come home to you and be the mommy you deserve, not some used up shell.

You, whose eyes are the exact same as his, are the product of true love. When you would cry I would feel him around your crib. I don't know why it took me so long to say goodbye, when as long as I have you, he won't be very far away.

WIthin a day or two, I'll be home, and I cannot wait to hold you in my arms again. I hope you haven't completely grown up in these past few months, but I'll spend the rest of my life making up for my absence.

Love, Mom

Chapter 15

Matilda waited in the lobby of the police station for Caroline to arrive. Everything was surreal. She was an orphan. Her parents had both been heroes. If she thought about all this too much, she was overwhelmed, but she couldn't stop.

The outside door of the station opened, breaking her train of thought. Matilda stood up, expecting her aunt.

"Are you her?" A large woman rushed to Tildy, gathering her into her arms. "You are her!"

Matilda tried to back away, but it was no use. This hug might last an hour. "I'm Matilda. Are you Mrs. Araya?" she said against the woman's shoulder.

The woman's grip loosened a little so she could face Matilda. Tears were running in constant streams down Mrs. Araya's cheeks. "Yes. Your mother saved my baby," she said.

"Mom, let her go," a male voice said. For the first time Tildy was aware there was a young man behind Mrs. Araya. He looked embarrassed. "I'm so sorry. Mom! Let. Her. Go!"

The woman released her, and Matilda rocked on her heels. The guy reached out and steadied his mom, who had mascara stained cheeks.

"Thank you for contacting us," he said to Matilda. "I'm Vinny. I'm told that your mother saved my life."

Tildy shook his hand awkwardly. She didn't know what to say.

His mother began weeping again.

"You look just like she did when she was laying there in the ..." Mrs. Araya started crying, and her words came in hiccups. "in the hospital."

Now Matilda was crying too.

"We gave her a proper burial, but had no name to put on the headstone," Mrs. Araya said.

"Thank you," Matilda said. This time she initiated the hug. "Thank you for taking care of my mother after her death."

Caroline entered the police station almost at a run, looking haggard. The police had tracked her down at her hotel, and Matilda had told her the news over the phone. It had been worse than the call to Grandma.

Matilda gave a little wave. "This is my aunt," she said to Mrs. Araya.

The women began a fresh round of hugging and crying as Vinny sighed nearby.

Caroline and Matilda sat in the grass at Annette's grave. The stone read, Guardian Angel December 1, 1967.

Mrs. Araya promised that her family would pay to have the stone updated with Annette's information. She also insisted they accept the reward money her family had offered for the information leading to the identification of their guardian angel.

Now the Arayas stood back at the gravel pathway through the cemetery, giving Caroline and Matilda privacy.

"This is the closest I've ever been to her," Matilda said, running her hands through the freshly cut grass.

"You lived inside her for nine months. You've been closer to her," Caroline disagreed. "She doesn't live in this grave. She lives in your heart, in Ophelia, and everyone that remembers her."

Caroline reached over absently and brushed Matilda's hair out of her eyes. It was a gesture she'd performed thousands of times before and probably would perform thousands of times in the future. Matilda liked thinking that.

"Do you forgive me for taking off?" Tildy asked, patting Morag on the back as the creature dragged her hind legs around in the grass.

"No," Caroline said. "But I love you. Don't ever do it again though, or I'll kick your ass. And you better not start

314

thinking you're not in trouble, because Dad's been wandering the place around looking for the perfect stick to beat you with for two weeks. I'm sure he's found just the one by now, and I'm going to be right there when his arm gets tired."

Matilda turned her head to hide her smile. Her aunt was all bark, no bite, and Granddad wouldn't smack a bug if it bit him first.

"Now, let's go home." Caroline stood, pulling Matilda to her feet.

Matilda did not want to walk away from her mother's grave, but more than anything she wanted to be in her home with her family. Her family loved her despite her shortcomings and weirdness, and she loved them more than she ever knew was possible.

Chapter 16

Matilda sat on the porch with Granddad as he smoked. It was warm for this early in April. She was glad that it was because there were too many people inside the house.

Everyone was here for an Ozark potluck. Friends, family, and well wishers offered support for the Sterling and Banks families. With Annette buried in California seventeen years ago, this would stand as her wake.

The Sterlings were not frequent entertainers. Grandma had been fretting for a week about what to serve, while Caroline was in favor of serving nothing and just eating the guests' food. Grandma had won that one by pointing out that there wasn't a cook in the county that could come close to her potato salad, and nobody could argue that. Matilda knew the secret was that you had to let it set a while.

Grandma also had begun frying chicken at first light yesterday, and the house smelled so good Tildy's mouth even watered in her sleep.

In the weeks since Matilda had returned to Landover she'd repeated the tale of her journey no fewer than ten floppity jillion times. She hoped that after today everyone would have their fill.

The pictures of her parents that Matilda wanted to share covered the coffee table in the living room. Brandon and the AV club had carefully edited the video of Mark in Vietnam. It played on repeat on the console television with the aid of a VCR on loan from the video store.

A few times today, Matilda had shared the story of her mother's journey, her father's death, and her own personal experiences in solving the mystery surrounding her mother's disappearance. She had come to terms with most of her trek across the country, but she didn't share the parts that still clawed at her when she tried to sleep. Knowing those details would only hurt or worry her family more.

Missy and Brandon were arguing about something petty as they sat on the porch step eating fruit salad. Things had been tense when Tildy first got home. They hadn't been happy she had taken off on an adventure without telling them, and Missy had spent a few uncomfortable hours being grilled about what she knew, first at home, then at church, then by just about everyone at school.

Bruised feelings were eventually put aside, however. Matilda felt like she had a little more patience for the couple's hidden relationship and petty squabbles. They were just a quirk that she feared they'd never outgrow.

In contrast, the Sunday nights when she got to call LJ were full of deep conversations and what felt like evolution. By the middle of the week when she craved his voice and his vibe she'd receive an envelope full to bursting with daily letters, sketches, song lyrics from terrible bands like the Sex Pistols and Minor Threat, and dreams for their future. In return she mailed him song lyrics from good bands like Anthrax and Black Sabbath, love notes she wrote in chem class, updates on Morag -- who she referred to as his step-dogger -- and complicated plans for their journeys together down the Mother Road.

Granddad smiled as Caroline and Jonah pulled up. "How long do you think it will be until they get hitched?" he asked Tildy.

"Can't they just live in sin? It's the hot new thing. Everybody's doing it," Matilda joked.

"Not my Caroline. She deserves her white gown moment, and her gimpy old dad is going to walk her down the aisle." Granddad got misty eyed as Jonah ran around the car to open the door for Caroline who was waiting awkwardly for the sweet gesture. "Someday, a long time in the future, I hope I'm still here to walk you down the aisle too."

She leaned against Granddad's shoulder. Matilda wasn't sure he was going to forgive her for running away, but he'd finally stopped threatening to send her to a convent. He wept when Matilda told him what she had gleaned about Annette's last few months of life.

Matilda hadn't told them about Lorne or her own battles in Tucumcari. Her mother deserved to keep some of her secrets, and Matilda wasn't ready to share all of her own.

Telling her other grandparents about Mark's death wasn't as dramatic. They always assumed he'd died a hero, but there was relief that they now knew for sure. Grandma Banks cried into her hands as Matilda shared the pictures and unedited video she'd gathered on her trip. The video of Mark waving in AIT had been the one that hit Grandpa Banks the hardest. They were planning a trip out west to meet the Siyugas in the fall.

Grandma carried out a snack tray and greeted Caroline and Jonah. Grandma, with her hair freshly permed and pink apron, looked like a sitcom housewife. Her new cookbook, Microwave Hors D'oeuvres, had been well read and practiced -- and improved upon -- in the past few weeks. Jonah took the tray from Grandma so Caroline could hug her.

Caroline wore a Willie Nelson t-shirt and jeans, but with her auburn hair loose and dark eyes glittering she looked softer, younger than Matilda could remember. A few days before, Caroline had shared with her that she and Jonah had talked about building a house by her trailer that would be big enough that they could start a family. They had connected because Matilda had run away, and Tildy made sure to bring that up anytime things were getting too sad or serious.

"So is everybody here?" Caroline asked. "I'm ready to eat. The rest of you can do what you want."

"Just about ready," Granddad said. "I think we might have one more coming."

Matilda counted in her head the people who were already here, and she couldn't think of anyone missing. Maybe one of his friends from the VFW?

It didn't take long for her to satisfy her curiosity. Before long there was another crunch of tires on the gravel drive, and a large red Cadillac pulled into the yard next to Caroline's truck.

"Now we're all here," Granddad said. Something in his tone made her look. His eyes glittered. He grabbed his hickory cane and stood up, flicking his cigarette into the yard as Russell Claxton emerged.

Claxton was easily the largest man in Laclede County. He towered over everyone, nearly seven feet tall, and was built like a refrigerator. Today he wore a white suit without a tie and a red shirt. His boots were white too, gleaming and polished, and his oversized belt buckle shone like gold from beneath a fold of fat.

That hat, Tildy thought.

Claxton had worn the same straw Panama hat since he quit the sheriff's department thirty years ago to start his own private detective agency-slash-bail bonds office. Now he took it off, regarding the small crowd on Granddad's porch, and wiped the sweat off his forehead with the back of his sleeve. He replaced the hat and pushed up the front of the brim with a forefinger.

"Sterling," he said. "You having some kind of party here? I thought you wanted to talk about that four thousand dollars you still owe me. All the rest of you folks can just go on in the house."

Matilda looked around. It looked like everyone had come out on the porch to see who the new arrival was. The faces weren't friendly, and nobody budged.

Granddad hawked and spat. "I do want to talk about that, Claxton. And some other things."

Claxton hooked his thumbs into his belt. "Well, I'm standing here. I guess I could go for a glass of that lemonade, ma'am," he said to Grandma Banks, who was holding the pitcher. Matilda was surprised when her father's mother only returned a cold stare.

Granddad waved to Claxton in a beckoning motion with his bad hand. "Come on up if you want to talk business, boy," he said.

Claxton's face was flushing red. Matilda suspected he wasn't used to being in a place where people didn't cater to him.

Claxton walked toward the porch in an arrogant saunter and put one white boot on the first step. When Granddad didn't move out of the way, he stopped, looking confused. Granddad smiled, but not like Tildy had ever seen him smile before. He scared her a little.

"That's far enough, Claxton. Now, I'm going to tell you what we're going to do about that four thousand dollars. Not a goddamn thing," he said.

"Language," Grandma said from behind him. Tildy gaped at her and saw she looked embarrassed for having spoken.

Claxton's face flushed redder. "I've got a note that you signed, Sterling. And there ain't a judge in this county wouldn't attach this property as soon as I say the word. You know it and I know it. You better be thinking about what you're doing."

Granddad stood as straight as Matilda had ever seen him. "What I'm thinking about, Claxton, is that a little girl ran halfway across the country and did the job I paid you to do when I was flat on my back and couldn't do it myself.

"That little girl grew up thinking her mama had run off and abandoned her because you didn't do your fucking job," Granddad's voice was … intense. He wasn't shouting, but he lashed Claxton with every word. Matilda couldn't tear her eyes away. Grandma didn't comment on the F-word, and when Tildy sneaked a glance, Grandma's face matched Granddad's voice perfectly.

Claxton went up another step toward Granddad. Now he was looking down at the older man, but Granddad was not backing down.

"Everywhere Tildy went," Granddad said, and now *he* took a step forward and the men were almost nose to nose. "Everywhere she went, people talked about how you came around and asked a couple questions and then got bored and took off. Meanwhile you've got all our savings and my best forty acres of pasture. It must have been pretty funny to you.

"And this child," Granddad said, thrusting his right arm straight at Matilda without looking, "This child found out more in two weeks than you did in four months."

Claxton looked enraged and embarrassed at the same time. He snatched off his hat and leaned toward Granddad. Matilda sensed movement behind her grandfather and saw that Grandpa Banks and Jonah Wilkes had moved to stand at Granddad's shoulders.

"So no, Claxton, you're not getting that four thousand dollars. The only thing you're getting from me is that I'm going to make it my mission to make sure everybody in this county knows what a lying, stealing dog you *are*."

And with that final word Granddad's hickory cane heel jabbed right in the center of Claxton's chest. Rage turned to shock on Claxton's face as he staggered backwards. He might have regained his balance except that his right boot encountered a blind chihuahua, and he fell backwards off the step, landing flat on his back in the dirt of the yard.

Morag squealed and ran under the house.

Matilda and the rest of the onlookers were stunned. And then Brandon said, "You know, the bigger they are ..."

And the tension was released in gales of laughter. Claxton's hat was crushed beneath him, his white suit was ruined, and worst of all, a small disabled man had knocked him down in front of a crowd. Matilda didn't think she would ever see anything funnier than the look on the blowhard's face at that moment.

Granddad leaned on his cane, staring down at his enemy. "Now you can get the hell off my property," he said, and nobody was surprised when Claxton did just that, his tires spitting angry gravel as he made his escape.

Matilda hugged Granddad, and he leaned against her. "Wasn't really sure how that was going to go," he admitted, and chuckled. She hugged him tighter.

"Might be a good time to go in," she suggested.

Granddad nodded. "Yeah, a man can work up an appetite knocking down assholes."

"Language," Grandma said, but when Tildy looked at her, she was beaming.

This was her family; past, present, and future. Matilda would do anything in her power to protect them, love them, and support them. She wondered if today would be a good time to tell them she, Morag, and LJ planned to spend the summer photographing all of Route 66?

Phyllis York is an author, blogger, and unapologetic fangirl. She lives in the Ozarks, but loves traveling - especially on Route 66. York is a four time winner of NaNoWriMo, and the author of many novels, articles, and Yelp reviews.

<u>Social Media Links</u>

PhyllisYork.com
Twitter.com/Phyllie417
Instagram.com/Phyllie417
Facebook.com/PhyllisYorkAuthor.